CAROL MARGARET TETLOW

Best Served Cold

First published by Editions Dedicaces in 2018

Copyright © Carol Margaret Tetlow, 2018

ISBN: 978-1-77076-700-3

This book was professionally typeset on Reedsy.
Find out more at reedsy.com

Contents

How it all began

At precisely the same time as her grandfather clock struck one, Mrs Emily Hardcastle, aged seventy-two, of 6, Hornbeam Crescent, was pronounced dead.

It was a hot and sticky Thursday, the temperature uncharacteristically high for May and Dr Grace Dunstable, a twenty-eight-year-old doctor in the final stages of her training to become a general practitioner, having finished her morning surgery, was out doing her house calls, hoping to rattle them off quickly so that she could spend a lengthy lunchtime sunbathing in the garden of her local pub while she enjoyed a drink with her boyfriend, Mark. Finally, after an insipid spring, which had never amounted to much, the weather had exploded into gloriousness and Grace was determined to make the most of it. So much so that she had deliberately chosen two of the easiest looking visits – an elderly man with a chesty cough and a child with a fever and then she had rung Mark to say that she wouldn't be above an hour.

Grace's day had not got off to the best of starts. Sleeping in was not to be recommended as it led to a frantic scurrying around, grabbing clothes with little thought, pulling them on to a body still damp from the shower and smudging her mascara. She arrived at the surgery just in time but all the parking spaces under the trees had been taken which meant that by the time she set off again the temperature of the front seats was hot enough to fry an egg. The traffic, though, was forgiving and she was pleased to find that the visits met with her expectations and were straightforward. A prescription for antibiotics for the rheumy old man with eyelids drooping like a bloodhound and lots of reassurance for the apologetic mother who had to fetch the previously feverish child in from the garden where she was busily making a den.

A glance at her watch told Grace that she was ahead of schedule and she wondered whether it was worth stopping off at home to change into some fresh clothes. Mulling over this option, she was interrupted by her mobile phone squawking. Muttering under her breath, she answered it – number withheld which meant that the likely caller was the surgery. Sure enough, the voice she heard was that of Margaret, matriarch of the receptionists, greeting her far too cheerfully and handing over details of another visit in tones that defied anything other than acceptance. Of course the visit was on the opposite side of town, they were never just around the corner. A Mrs Hardcastle with bad indigestion.

Shaking her head, Grace silently wrote down the details. She remembered the patient. She'd seen her only last week when she had been into the surgery with a similar complaint. On that occasion Mrs Hardcastle had looked the picture of health and her loquacity had made Grace run late.

'Can't she come to the surgery?' Grace asked, not holding out much hope.

'No, I've asked but she's sorry, she really doesn't feel well enough in this heat and there's no one to bring her down.' Margaret's voice had an air of finality to it.

'Oh, for goodness sake...'

But Margaret had rung off, safe in the knowledge that she had passed the message on and thus her job was done. She had worked at the surgery for many years, from the days when she had worn a white coat and written appointments down in a huge ledger that was balanced on the front desk. In those days, doctors didn't answer back. They simply did what she told them to, as did the patients. She was not entirely in agreement with these modern ways and young doctors who thought they knew better than she did.

Still grumbling to herself, Grace realised begrudgingly that there was in fact still time to do this visit and not be too late to meet Mark. He would understand. In the few months they had been together, he had quickly learned that Grace's profession did not lend itself to punctuality and to date had been understanding.

Hornbeam Crescent was an arc of desirable residences, each one boasting an eponymous tree and surrounded by well-established and equally well-tended gardens. Number six was no exception and once she had tackled the rather tricky latch on the front gate, Grace ambled up the path noting the dry, cracked soil in the flower beds and a forlorn goldfinch pecking at an empty concrete birdbath.

Incongruously, the bay trees on either side of the front door were lush and dark leaved. Closer inspection as Grace waited for the doorbell to be answered revealed them to be artificial. A forgotten Christmas bauble peeped out from beneath the leaves. With no answer forthcoming, she tried the handle and the door slid open. She called out as she stepped into the rather dark hallway and followed the shrill reply, which led her into a lounge of enormous proportions. The green decor was refreshingly cool but smelled musty, with a hint of damp.

Lying on the sofa, dressed in a full-length nightgown of palest mauve, was Mrs Hardcastle. Her shingled hair and the long loop of pearls which dangled around her neck and disappeared into her cleavage hinted of a time long past but fitted perfectly with the furnishings and colouring of the room. She reached out one hand to Grace.

'I'm so glad you've come,' she whispered. 'I feel so ill. It must be the heat. I've been like this all morning.'

'Tell me about it,' suggested Grace, wiping wisps of hair back from her face and perching on the edge of a jade velvet-covered chaise longue. She felt too untidy for this lovely room.

Mrs Hardcastle swallowed with apparent difficulty. She fanned her face with a copy of that day's newspaper, folded to expose the crossword. A handful of clues had been filled in.

'My mouth, it's so dry,' she explained. 'This damned indigestion just won't go away. It's had me up all night too and I've been a little sick. I couldn't eat breakfast – couldn't face a thing, not even a cup of tea and all this burping – well, it's making me feel quite breathless. I know it sounds stupid. I've been taking those tablets you gave me, exactly as it says on the box, but I'm sorry, they don't seem to have made any difference.'

Thoughtfully, she rubbed her left shoulder, a puzzled look coming over her face. Before Grace could ask for any more details, the newspaper slithered to the floor and Mrs Hardcastle's hand moved to her left breast. Trying to sit up, she leaned forward towards Grace, a look of horror and fear in her eyes and then she slumped back against the cushions, uttering a guttural groan.

'Mrs Hardcastle!' Grace tapped her arm. 'Emily!' She shook her, at first gently, then more vigorously, willing her to open her eyes and start to laugh.

But of course she didn't and, for a split second, all Grace's training deserted her and she was unable to recall for the life of her what to do next.

By now, Mrs Hardcastle had assumed the same colour as her nightgown, not a good look, and a frothing noise was emanating from her throat. Grace knew she had to do something. Every six months since qualifying, she had attended the obligatory resuscitation course and immediately afterwards was brimming with confidence. Opportunities to use her skills were rare and so her self- belief trickled away with the passage of each day. Since qualifying her only experiences of collapse had been on well-staffed hospital wards, where people responded immediately to a call for help and someone else took charge and barked out all the decisions.

'ABC,' shrieked Grace, triumphantly. 'Airway, breathing, circulation!' That was it, but get help first. She called out to the empty house but the only reply was the monotonous tick tock of the grandfather clock, admonishing her for taking so long. Every second counts...

Ambulance summoned, Grace turned her attention to Mrs Hardcastle, now blue around the nose and mouth, a little trickle of tenacious saliva seeping from the corner of her mouth. There was no sign of breathing, or of a pulse. With a strength she didn't really expect, Grace shoved the coffee table across the room with some force, ignoring the falling vase scattering anemones and water all over an expensive emerald rug. A large photograph of a young man at his graduation ceremony did a somersault and the glass cracked as she dragged her patient on to the floor. She set about cardiac compressions, adding in a few rescue breaths for good measure, all the while singing the tune to 'Nelly the Elephant' to ensure that she achieved the correct rate.

It was far more exhausting than she imagined and Grace

found she had to stop and get her own breath back, listening optimistically for the sound of a fast- approaching ambulance and feeling less optimistically for a pulse.

She had to keep going for as long as she could. Surely help wasn't far away now?

Sweat poured from her and dropped on to Mrs Hardcastle, not that she was in any position to object. As further precious seconds passed, Grace's efforts became more frenetic and less organised as she desperately tried to do her best but realised the futility of her every move.

The paramedics took over, albeit briefly. The flat line on the electrocardiogram trace and Mrs Hardcastle's fixed and widely dilated pupils told no lies and the three of them sat back on their heels and looked at each other. Grace nodded slowly after one final glance at the large body lying before her and all efforts to revive Mrs Hardcastle ceased at precisely thirteen hundred hours.

The events of that morning were to return and haunt Grace, years later when she least expected it.

Chapter One

Five Years Later

Grace backed her brand-new car efficiently into a rather narrow space between two black 4x4s. She was fortunate to have found anywhere to park at all. Usually she had to make several circuits of the hospital car park, prowling at a slow pace, waiting to accelerate as soon as she spotted someone leaving, like a lion pouncing on its prey. Breathing in, she wriggled out of the door and then readjusted her skirt and blouse before setting off for the main entrance with a quick glance back at her gleaming prized possession. She was looking forward to the lunchtime meeting which promised not just free food but also a talk by one of the new consultants, a neurologist, Dr Gideon Barlow.

Often, she was too tied up with work at the surgery, where she had been a partner now for nearly five years, to make it to the meetings but today it was the turn of Andrew Maddison, the senior partner, to cover emergencies and her own morning had uncharacteristically run to time. She snaked her way down the main corridor through a melee of obstacles. Cheery porters pushing wheelchairs or trolleys, chatting away non-stop to their passengers, patients bewildered by the complexity of the

hospital, unsure whether to be guided by sign posts on the wall
or coloured lines on the floor and huddled groups of worried-
looking relatives, deep in conversation; all of these had to be
negotiated before Grace reached the postgraduate centre and
made her way to the lecture theatre. It was already half full and,
much as she'd hoped, tables arranged down one side of the room
groaned under the weight of a generous spread of sandwiches,
snacks and pastries to say nothing of some delicious-looking
creamy puddings, many well drenched with chocolate sauce.
She spotted her other two partners, Harry Stevens and Janey
McBride, sitting with the current registrar, Amber O'Malley and
after filling her plate and hoping that she did not look too greedy,
Grace made her way over to join them.

'Hi,' she greeted them, 'how's everyone's morning been? Isn't
this lunch fabulous?'

'Fine,' Janey replied, wiping her mouth briefly before opening
it for another forkful.

Far from setting an example of good health, Janey, who would
never have made any mention of the fact, probably weighed
in excess of twice her ideal weight. When Grace first met her,
she had been somewhat taken aback by her largeness but had
warmed to her largesse. Undeterred by thighs that chafed and
arms that could barely meet over her belly, Janey rejoiced in
her size, made a statement of this fact by dressing in loud,
bright colours and squeezed her feet into vertiginously high
heels, which somehow she managed to wear all day without
complaining. Her character was as large as her body mass
index, while her etiolated husband perpetually looked as if he
might blow over in a gentle breeze. Together they laughed their
way through life, enjoying a relationship of such closeness that
Grace yearned for similar one day and their five children (Janey

had studiously ignored all her obstetrician's advice about the risks of more pregnancies) were a fusion of energy, athleticism and intelligence with flawless manners. Janey had been at the practice for over ten years, but chose to live a few miles away in a large but rather ramshackle house which provided plenty of accommodation for the human members of the family, one dog, one cat, four goats, three ponies and more guinea pigs than Grace had ever been able to count, thanks to their proclivity for reproducing.

Harry, mouth full and chewing, nodded his welcome. Amber, picking half-heartedly at a bowl of fruit salad with no cream, said nothing and merely smiled wanly. Having only started at the practice a couple of weeks ago, she was still shy and hesitant, taking advantage of her long blond hair which turned into a convenient curtain to hide behind. She kept glancing over to the other side of the room where a group of other registrars, all friends of hers, were all in a huddle together, gesticulating to her to come over and she was wondering how she could escape politely from present company and go to join them. Without realising, Grace scuppered whatever plans she might have been hatching by sitting in the seat next to her and effectively blocking off her escape route.

'Don't let me eat too much,' Grace warned them, deftly catching a samosa wobbling on the end of her plate, 'or I'll fall asleep this afternoon! Have you got enough there, Amber? Don't be afraid to have plenty.'

There was just time for them to devour what was on their plates, send Harry back for similarly decadent portions of fruit pavlova and profiteroles before Dr Barlow was introduced to his audience and a polite and expectant hush fell in the room.

Tradition dictated that newly employed consultants were

invited to speak at one of the meetings and Grace, plus or minus her partners, liked to come along as often as she could, to put a face to a name. Gideon Barlow did not disappoint. His presentation was inspiring. Gifted as a speaker, he commanded and held everyone's attention from his first sentence. Not overly tall, there was no doubting his slightly atypical good looks, dark hair and eyes, the suggestion of a shadow of stubble on his chin. He was smartly dressed in a dark blue suit, the jacket of which he removed and hung over the back of his chair to reveal a white shirt, open at the neck, sleeves rolled up to his elbows.

After clearing his throat and then coughing, he addressed his audience. His curriculum vita was impressive. Having qualified, with honours, in Cambridge, he had then moved to London and Edinburgh before studying for his doctorate in New Zealand. This was his first consultant post and he had big ideas for the department.

He went on to summarise the latest news about various neurological conditions, including hopeful new drugs for multiple sclerosis and Parkinson's disease, his two main interests. To finish, he presented a few individual case histories that he had come across in the brief time in his new job.

If he hadn't already won over the general practitioners in the room by that juncture, when he professed that he was delighted to liaise with them at all times, to discuss patients, or to give advice and that a simple telephone call to his secretary would secure some of his time, then that sealed the deal. The well-deserved round of enthusiastic applause at the conclusion of his talk went on for a couple of minutes, far in excess of that received by most of his peers.

'He seems great, doesn't he?' Harry turned to Janey and Grace.

'Just what we need. His predecessor would barely acknowledge our existence,' Grace agreed, watching Gideon nodding and smiling around at everyone before gathering up his papers and taking a sip from his coffee cup.

'I think I'll give him a ring about Mrs Parker, the lady with ataxia and see what he thinks,' Harry decided.

'Go and speak to him now,' Janey urged him. 'Look, he's only tidying up his notes and he said he was happy to take questions. And while you're doing that, ask if he'd like to come and talk to us all at the practice one day – you know the sort of thing, how we can help each other, what sort of referrals he likes. We could take him out for supper afterwards. All the good relations bit.'

'OK, leave it to me.'

With one bounce, Harry sprung out of his chair and ran down the few steps to the speaker's podium. The others watched him go. As usual none of his clothes quite matched. Blue shirt, brown jacket, grey trousers and black, scruffy shoes. Each day he wore a different tie decorated with animals. That day's was maroon and covered with black Labradors in a variety of cute poses. If he was aware that the receptionists carried out a daily bet on what species he would be supporting, then he was diplomatic enough to say nothing as to do so would spoil their harmless fun. His blond hair was woolly and wild, confluent around the perimeter of his face with his beard, producing a leonine effect but his kindly face was the sort that patients felt safe with from the moment they saw him. Gideon greeted him with a large smile and shook his hand warmly. After an exchange of some sentences that involved a considerable amount of laughter, Harry turned, pointed out his colleagues and beckoned for them to come down. Glancing at each other, Janey and Grace followed in his footsteps, sandwiching as they did so an embarrassed Amber who would have preferred to take this opportunity to slink out, find her friends or, at the very least, go back to work.

'Let me introduce you,' Harry started, holding out his arm to welcome them. 'Gideon, let me present my partners, Janey McBride and Grace Dunstable. Not forgetting our new registrar, Amber O'Malley.'

'A pleasure to meet you all. Grace – is it all right for me to call you Grace? I think I've already seen some of your patients. Didn't one of you refer in that chap with transverse myelitis – the one who'd been on holiday in Cyprus and had to be flown home?'

'Oh,' agreed Grace. 'Yes, that was me. How is he?'

'So, so. Early days yet. I'm sure it's a viral aetiology. With any luck he'll be fine in the long run. He told me how grateful he was to you for arranging everything so quickly for him.'

Grace blushed a little, uttering a nervous giggle. 'That's kind.'

'I'm sure he meant every word.' Gideon's reply was genuine. He held her glance for a moment before turning to them all as a group, making sure he had a few words with each of them, asking about the whereabouts of their surgery and some practice statistics, and reassuring Amber that he had already been booked to do an afternoon's teaching with all the registrars. Yes, he would be honoured to come and speak at one of the evening meetings at the practice and his efficient secretary, Hattie, was the one to contact, as usual.

'Look,' he suggested, after a quick glance at his watch, 'I've a few minutes before clinic. Let's have a cup of coffee together. I don't know a lot of people in the area and it would be lovely to have a chat.'

'Great idea,' agreed Harry.

'Wonderful. Right, Harry and I will go and get the drinks and the ladies can go and sit down. What's everyone having? Sugar?

Milk?'

Grace and Jane returned to their seats, finally giving Amber the opportunity to sidle off and see her friends. Harry returned promptly with his and Janey's coffees.

'Gideon's bringing yours, Grace – he just had to wait for some more hot water.'

'Sorry, sorry, here we are! Tea for you, wasn't it, Grace? No sugar, just a drop of milk.' Gideon carefully passed her the cup and saucer.

'Perfect,' Grace thanked him and took a sip. She wrinkled her nose. 'Isn't it odd how tea and coffee taste weird after fresh fruit?'

For ten minutes they talked medicine, as all doctors do when they get together, relaxed in the security of the subject that required no personal revelations. Inevitably they had some friends in common and by the time they left, largely to make Gideon feel more at home, they swapped telephone numbers and promised to get in touch with him about a night out, with or without an educational meeting first.

Grace's afternoon was not her best. To start with, she rattled through her list of patients with customary efficiency but then began to flag. Despite the stuffy atmosphere in her room, she felt shivery and noticed goose pimples up her arms. A dull headache ensued, making concentration difficult and she allowed herself a five-minute break for a glass of water and two painkillers. They stayed in her stomach for only a matter of seconds before she had to rush out to the nearest toilet and be sick. Rather than improve matters, violent colicky stomach pains set in, the forerunner of explosive diarrhoea, more vomiting and profuse sweating. Unfit for work, she rang Harry who nobly offered to see the rest of her patients.

'It must have been something you had at lunch,' he suggested.

Agreeing with the obvious explanation, she carefully drove home and crawled, half dressed, thankfully, into bed.

'I'll never eat buffet food again,' she muttered, making her way to the bathroom for the umpteenth time, a little later on. 'I wonder how many other people have come down with this food poisoning as well.'

Chapter Two

G race was relieved and pleased that she had been fortunate enough to join a partnership in Harrogate not far from where her parents lived. While others might have chastised her for being unadventurous and not seeking her fortune in a more exotic location, she had never had any particular desire to travel, other than on holiday and, say what they might, nobody could deny that the leafy spa town and surrounding area were anything other than delightful. Douglas and Sylvia Dunstable had made the decision to retire there, having visited while on a coach tour of the Yorkshire Dales and fallen in love with the place.

Both in their seventies, they believed that their enduring good physical health was due to the weekly pilgrimage they made to take the sulphuric waters followed by prolonged relaxation in the Turkish baths. Douglas had once been an orthopaedic surgeon, but on his retirement had announced that all matters medical were a thing of the past and that he would now be transferring his passion to genealogy, gardening and getting a dog. Like Grace, he had light brown, wispy hair, blue eyes and a slim, fit physique. He filled his days from dawn to dusk, unable to relax and sit idly, a relic of his career.

Sylvia had also been a doctor. She had trained in psychiatry but her own mental health issues had forced her to take many absences while she battled with the relentless demons of mania and depression that infiltrated nearly every day of her adult life. The diagnosis of bipolar illness was no surprise but devastating. Unexpectedly, in her early forties, she was staggered to find out that she was pregnant. Years of trying to conceive unsuccessfully had convinced her that she was infertile and they had agreed that maybe it was a good thing, in view of all the medication she had consumed to help her function in an approximation of normality. Douglas was elated, found the idea of becoming a father at forty-five hilarious and coaxed her gently through each stage of a pregnancy beset with problems, including high blood pressure, gestational diabetes and breech presentation.

Grace was born by Caesarean section, late one Monday afternoon and even though the doctors were anticipating it, nobody could have predicted the catastrophic slide into post-natal depression that Sylvia suffered. Antidepressants failed to help, tranquillisers merely oversedated her. When she was found wandering in the hospital car park, clad only in slippers which did not match, with no clue of where or who she was and worst of all with someone else's baby in her arms, she had to be detained under the Mental Health Act. As a last resort, ECT was employed and thankfully, gradually, a cautious improvement began.

For as long as Grace could remember, Sylvia had been fragile and volatile. Totally reliant on Douglas and more often than not reliant on medication, Sylvia had found motherhood yet another of life's insurmountable challenges. Whilst there was no disputing the complete and utter love she felt for her daughter, even the simplest of decisions proved to be difficult and Grace's childhood was sporadically interrupted by her mother's disappearance back into the psychiatric ward, sometimes for weeks on end. Consequently she was brought up mostly by her father; she looked to him for advice and help but as soon as she was old enough to realise the gravity of her mother's condition, she became his major source of support. Together they had helped Sylvia maintain as much independence as possible. Determined not to interrupt their way of life, when Grace decided to follow in her parents' footsteps and pursue a career in medicine, she insisted on enrolling at the nearest medical school so that she was still able to live at home and be there as much as she could.

Douglas had tried again and again to persuade her to move out, protesting that he would manage. He'd been looking after his wife for years, he had argued, and it was important that Grace developed a life of her own. She should be out having fun with people her own age, not staying in with the 'oldies' as he referred to himself and Sylvia. Grace though was adamant. Aware that her father was physically nowhere near as agile has he once was, she dug her heels in and refused to go, only acquiescing when a little semi-detached house opposite theirs came on the market and Douglas suggested he bought it for her as an investment.

Grace was half lying in an armchair in her parents' living room. Sylvia was knitting something large, colourful and totally unidentifiable. Whatever it might be already spread over her knees and rippled down to the floor. Douglas was reading and Charnley, the Border terrier, was upside down asleep on the hearthrug, paws twitching as he dreamed of rabbits, rats and countryside walks. She felt as weak as a half-rung-out dishcloth, even though the intestinal distress had thankfully worn off. She looked around her, viewing yet again the panorama of her life. Hundreds of photographs, arranged in ornate silver frames, mapped out every milestone, starting to the left of the brick fireplace with baby snaps and then moving onwards, in a strictly clockwise direction, around to the collection on top of the television cabinet, which had been taken when Grace qualified as a general practitioner. No flat space was unoccupied. Their order was sacrosanct. Sylvia forbade any rearrangement. Instinctively she knew if one was out of place. Only she was allowed to touch them and this she did daily, with monotonous precision, dusting each one fastidiously and then polishing the silver frames on Saturdays and Sundays.

Other rooms were similar testaments to Sylvia's obsessional tidiness. The kitchen resembled that from a show house; the empty work tops were wiped down repeatedly, whether necessary or not, the taps and sink shone from persistent polishing and the floor was swept and mopped at least three times daily. In the cupboards, foods were filed alphabetically. Upstairs the bedrooms defied the tiniest dust mote to enter, ivory bed linen was wrinkle-free, the cushions plumped and placed with the same meticulousness of the photographs. No items of clothing were left out for later or to be washed. Behind the closed wardrobes and drawers, all garments were colour coded and folded or hung in order, approximating the spectrum as closely as possible. The preponderance of black served as a chilling reminder of Sylvia's depressive days.

Quite how Charnley had been allowed to have his bed at the foot of her parents', Grace often marvelled but seemingly he was the only exception to Sylvia's rigidity. Even so, his bed was swept and washed, his blankets ironed, his toys placed in a neat pile, which he took great delight in destroying.

'Can I get you anything, darling?' Sylvia's concern for her daughter was palpable. 'You do look pale, still. Don't you be going back to work until you're properly better. She's got to look after herself, hasn't she, Doug?'

Grace smiled at her mother. 'A cup of tea would be lovely, Mum, but let me make you one. You've been running round after me all day. Sit down for a bit. It's time I made an effort to do something.'

'Rubbish, that's what mums are for.' Sylvia admonished her with a wagging finger. 'I'm going to bring you a dry biscuit as well. Something to line that tummy of yours would be good.'

Before Grace could rise from her chair, Sylvia let her knitting fall to the floor, not bothering to finish the row, and was bustling out of the room, mind set on having a task to do. Grace sat up, preparing to follow.

'Leave her to it,' Douglas said, without looking up. 'She's in her element looking after you.'

'She looks so frail, though, Dad,' Grace voiced her worries.

Douglas balanced his book over the arm of the chair. 'You think so? I find it hard to tell, living with her. I don't usually miss the subtle changes. And when she's fairly well, as she is at the moment, I'm so relieved that I let myself stop worrying for a bit.'

'Oh, Dad, I'm so sorry. I should never have moved out.'

'Of course you should. You need your independence, as we all do. Anyway, you're still in to see us every day and we know that if we want you, virtually all we have to do is wave out of the window or raise our voices slightly. If it wasn't for the crossing the road, I'd have trained Charnley to come and get you.'

Grace laughed. The arrival of the dog had given her father a vibrant new interest in life. Named after a type of hip replacement that Douglas had performed many times, Charnley had arrived as a small, mischievous, scrunched-up-faced puppy, but had subsequently grown into a handsome dog and a devoted companion to his master.

A curious sensation made Grace wonder briefly if her intestinal unrest was returning to haunt her but she realised with relief that her mobile phone was vibrating in the back pocket of her jeans. Wriggling to get hold of it, she did not recognise the number and tentatively said hello.

'Grace? Is that you, Grace?'

'Yes... Who's that?' The voice was not one she recognised.

'Grace, it's Gideon, Gideon Barlow – remember we met the other day. I rang the surgery and they told me you were off sick. Harry was kind enough to let me have your mobile number as I'd lost it. I meant to ring sooner but I've been ill as well. Dreadful D&V. Is that what you've had?'

'Yes. I think it must have been something at the buffet lunch. Something I ate, as none of my partners have been unwell. Janey said she felt a bit sick but nothing more.'

'You poor, poor thing. If you've felt anywhere near as bad as I have then my heart goes out to you. How are you now?'

'Improving thanks. Starting to get my appetite back and feeling a bit stronger. I'll have to let the hospital know, in case they need to tell public health.'

'Somebody has already done that. I checked. I'm so glad you're on the mend. I've come back to work today but, on reflection, it perhaps wasn't one of my wisest decisions.'

'It's kind of you to ring,' Grace added.

'I was worried,' he replied. 'Look, I know this might sound like the last thing you want to think about at the moment, but, I was wondering if you'd like to come out for dinner with me. Perhaps one evening next week? That should give us both time to recover fully.'

Grace was taken aback but flattered. This was the last thing she had been expecting. She glanced up at Douglas, who was back immersed in his book, rubbing Charnley's tummy with his toes.

'I'd love to, thank you.'

'Great. Shall we say Friday? That's a week from today. I'll have a hunt around and see where it would be nice to go...unless you've any favourite spots you can recommend.'

'No, I mean, well, I do know some places, but you choose. I'm afraid I'm not very keen on Indian food though.' Her guts performed a small somersault at the mention of spicy food.

'What a coincidence. Nor am I. Right, leave it to me and I'll ring you Tuesday. Is that all right?'

'That's lovely. I'll look forward to it.' Grace found that she could not stop smiling.

'Likewise. Now you take care and I'll speak to you soon.'

'You too,' Grace started but he had rung off.

Douglas peered at her over the top of his reading glasses. 'Not that I was listening of course but that sounded suspiciously like a date being arranged.'

Laughing, Grace got up to clear a space for the tray that Sylvia had arrived with.

'A date?' Sylvia was quick to pick up. 'You never told us you had a boyfriend.'

'It's just dinner with a new friend. Nothing serious, Mum.'

'Who is he? Will you bring him to meet us? I'd like to see him and say hello. Is he as good looking as your father?'

Douglas guffawed, breaking up a biscuit and feeding it to Charnley who had woken at the sound of a potential snack.

'Of course and don't worry. He seems very pleasant. He's a neurologist. Just moved here.'

'Oh, he does sound very suitable,' Sylvia decided. 'Let me know when you're coming with him and I can make a cake.'

In the past, Grace had brought a handful of boyfriends home to meet her parents. None of these events were happy memories. If Sylvia had been in a trough of despair then she had just sat, silently, and in a secret world of her own, oblivious to any visitors and probably just as unaware of Grace and Douglas. On the other hand, if she had been high in mood the occasions had been no more pleasurable. Hyperactive, Sylvia's constant motion, in, out of the room, into the garden, on the telephone to check if there were any messages, going upstairs to get changed and coming back again only to decide that the new outfit was no more suitable than its predecessor quickly wore any potential suitors out and many and various reasons were cited as to why they suddenly had to leave. Few, in fact none, ever returned. Possibly the main reason for their inability to cope was that none of them had ever encountered anything quite like this in any way, shape or form and while the prospect of introducing Gideon still filled her with a certain amount of dread, there was some hope, Grace decided, that he might just understand and be more accepting. Anyway, she told herself that was a long way off. Dinner might turn out to be a disaster. In some ways that would solve a lot of angst in the future but, secretly, she really did want it to go well.

Most of her contemporaries were married with families. They had young children already starting school, toddlers and babies on the way, chaotic homes full of fun and laughter. Grace, anxious that she was being left behind, had the house and badly wanted the other ingredients to make up her dream of the happy family. Her last long-term relationship – if you can call a whole eight months long term – had been with Mark. He had seemed ideal, or so she thought. With hindsight, she was seeing what she wanted to see, willing him to be what she wanted but of course he had not been and it quickly became clear that the initial chemistry she felt was more in her imagination than in reality.

'Never think a man is going to change for you,' Sylvia had consoled her in one of her rare moments of clarity, as Grace cried on her shoulder after the final telephone call from Mark, announcing that he did not want to see her again, 'because they won't. Don't try to make someone like you. It should be natural, no effort. Just you wait and see. It'll happen, I promise.'

There was something indefinable about Gideon that was an instant attraction. A different feeling to any she had experienced before. So despite the fact she had no idea whether he was married or attached to someone, as she laid in bed feeling dreadful, she concocted a variety of plans to help her find out more about him.

His phone call had saved her a lot of trouble and filled her with anticipation and excitement. The very best tonic she needed to promote a speedy recovery. Plus a week would give her time to have her hair cut and highlighted and perhaps look for some new clothes – nothing too obvious though as there was nothing worse than trying too hard. She felt certain that he would not be impressed by such naive behaviour.

Feeling better than she had done for days, she washed and dried the few dishes they had used, ignoring her mother who was fussing behind her, itching to wipe down the worktops and fold the tea towel into a perfect rectangle.

Chapter Three

'**W**ell?' quizzed Janey, 'where's he taking you?'
They were in the meeting room at the practice, pausing to catch up and have coffee before afternoon surgery began.

Grace tried the nonchalant look. 'Nowhere special. The Red Kite at East Whitteringham,' she replied, shrugging her shoulders.

'That's got rave reviews. There's a new chef apparently who's turned the whole place around and put it on the map. I wonder if he'll talk about neurology all evening?'

Laughing, Grace sat down and picked up one of the homemade cupcakes that Janey had brought in for them, feeling that they needed a reward for getting half way through another busy week. A typical gesture. She was invariably able to come up with some sort of excuse to bring in cake. Not just birthdays, but gloomy Mondays, mediocre Tuesdays, middle of the week Wednesdays, it's nearly the weekend Thursdays and happy Fridays – there was a good reason every day to indulge as far as Janey was concerned.

'Mmm, this is good.' Grace licked the toffee icing off her top lip. 'I'm so glad to feel hungry again. Did you make these?'

'No she didn't. They're from that new bakery behind the

community centre,' Harry revealed. He was seated in the corner, busy at one of the computers. There was a dollop of chocolate ganache resting in his beard.

'They're delicious, wherever they're from. Thank you, Janey. And no, I don't think he'll talk about the cerebellum and extra-pyramidal tracts all the time. If he does, I won't know what to say back as neuro-anatomy baffled me from the first lecture at medical school and so the conversation will be very one sided and the evening very short!'

Janey chuckled and reached out for a very large double chocolate and raspberry cupcake.

'Are you nervous? I mean when did you last go on a proper date?'

'I've just about forgotten and yes, I am. Though being asked came as such a shock that it hasn't really sunk in properly yet.'

'Just be yourself. It'll be fine. I think you make a lovely couple!'

Grace pulled a face at her. Neither of them heard Harry burp morosely.

It wasn't fine. It was fabulous.

Gideon picked her up from her house and as he escorted her down the short path to his car, Grace could see Sylvia watching from the bedroom window, making no attempt to conceal her presence. She had actually been there since the middle of the afternoon, pretending to polish the glass, determined not to miss the moment. Pointing her mother out, Grace waved and to her delight Gideon waved too. Joyously, Sylvia disappeared from the window and bravely appeared at the door, keen to get a closer view and possibly an introduction but by then Gideon had opened the passenger door for Grace, climbed in and started up the engine.

Grace had dressed with care. After careful consideration, she had gone ahead and had her hair cut and highlighted, having rationalised that it needed doing anyway but had eschewed the new clothes, instead choosing a vintage-style dusky pink dress with a boat neck and full skirt, which she had had for some time but rarely wore as there never seemed to be a reason to do so. To complete her outfit she had some pink flats on, not wanting to risk wobbling about on heels, which she wasn't used to, or being taller than Gideon, which would definitely make her feel very awkward. The final result, she scored nine out of ten as she contemplated her reflection from all angles and added a waft of a light, summery perfume.

She greeted him at the front door. He handed her a small but carefully arranged posy of flowers.

'You look very lovely,' was Gideon's verdict, as he navigated down the road, carefully avoiding the cars parked on either side.

'Thank you,' Grace said, wondering if she should comment on his appearance but not wanting to sound too trite. He did look attractive, there was no denying. She liked his cream casual trousers and dark blue jacket. Not brave enough to comment, she opted for the safe option. 'Do you need me to direct you? It's not the easiest place to find.'

Glancing right and left at the junction, he shook his head. 'No, I had a practice run last night.'

'Really?' Grace was incredulous.

'Yes, I didn't want to show myself up and look daft when you were with me!' He blushed.

Grace warmed to him following this admission of vulnerability.

'And I did sample the beer when I got there…it was very good indeed.'

'That's nice. You've gone to a lot of effort.' Grace wanted to kick herself for muttering and sounding so pathetic. She must try to be more interesting. She racked her brains. Definitely not the weather, not politics either. Sport? Not an area she had much confidence in. What about books, films? She ought to find out more about him – hadn't she read somewhere that people always like talking about themselves? But what to ask...?

There was one of those hideous awkward pauses before...

'How's work?' They asked each other simultaneously and burst out laughing.

'If all else fails, ask about work!' Gideon cried, slapping the steering wheel. 'Tell you what, let's NOT talk about work. Tell me about your family. Your mum looks nice.'

Grace took a deep breath. She had been hoping that it might be possible to avoid the subject of Sylvia that night and save it for a future meeting, were she lucky enough to secure one. But he had asked and she had to be honest.

'Let's wait until we're sitting down,' she suggested, playing for a little more time to weigh up what she was going to say. 'There's quite a lot to tell you.'

With half a glass of chilled white wine in front of her (the other half creating a comforting warmth in her stomach) Grace felt a tad more relaxed. Hesitantly, she began to tell Gideon about her parents. He sat attentively, barely interrupting her save for seeking one or two clarifying points. Thanks to his professional listening skills, finely honed from years of experience, Grace discovered that she was telling him far more than she had originally intended but felt a huge wave of relief that he knew, for now the rest was up to him. She had put her cards on the table, warts and all and now she simply had to wait and steel herself for his reaction. He got up, went to the bar, unwittingly prolonging her agony and returned with more drinks and two menus.

'I cannot begin to imagine how terrible all that has been for you or for your father. It can't have been easy for you to tell me all that, either.'

He took her hand in his and looked into her eyes. Grace saw compassion, caring and trust.

'Thank you for listening,' she whispered as he raised her hand and softly kissed it.

'You know, I can't wait to meet your mum and dad. They sound like remarkable people. But now, let's have a look at what there is to eat. I've heard the food here is incredible and I'm starving.'

The food was good – traditional pub dishes but cooked with flare and precision. After their enforced starvation, both relished the rich gravy that came with the steaks, the crisp golden twice-fried chips and then rhubarb crumble and ice cream for dessert.

Conversation flowed easily and mutual interests became apparent. They valued their time away from medicine, aware that their vocations easily became all consuming. Neither was particularly sporty but agreed that a reasonably long walk in the country had the potential to be very pleasant, especially if punctuated by a stop for lunch or tea at a local pub or cafe. Both professed to enjoy the theatre, good films including musicals and detective novels. Gideon enthralled Grace with stories of his travelling and told her briefly of his family – he was an only child. His father had died when he was small and his mother some years later. By the end of the evening, she felt that she had known him for ever, plus they had so many common interests that it was verging on the uncanny.

Waiting at the window for their return was Sylvia. It was dark but Grace was able to make out her outline, ghostlike in a white nightdress. She suspected, correctly, that her mother had taken up her position as soon as they left. With some difficulty, as certain instincts were telling her otherwise, she said goodbye to Gideon in the car, rather than invite him in. It never looked good to seem too keen on the first date and her mother's anxiety would hurtle off the scale if she did. He kissed her gently on one cheek and then on her lips, with a softness and tenderness that shook her to the core in a delightful way.

Chapter Four

*H*arry was worried. Not even his green tie with grey walruses cheered him up. Sitting at his desk, paperwork in front of him, his mind was miles away from the subjects of writing referral letters and reviewing test results. For once, he didn't care about Mrs Schofield's anaemia, sending Mr Tyrwhitt to rheumatology or arranging podiatry for Mr and Mrs Midson who were no longer able to reach their own feet or each other's; at that moment all he cared about was Grace.

On the day she came to interview for the partnership, Harry fell in love with her. Whether it was her natural prettiness, her smile that made his heart melt or the transparency of her caring soul he did not know, even though he had cogitated on the subject more times than he cared to admit, in evenings on his own at home, glass of red wine in one hand, television remote control in the other.

Typically he had never plucked up the courage to do anything about his feelings. They simply grew in magnitude on a daily basis as he worshipped her from afar. Some fifteen years older than Grace, he had no doubt in his own mind that she would not be interested in the likes of him. She could, he was convinced, have any man that she chose to set her sights at and it was a mystery to him (and nothing short of miraculous) that she had not been snapped up by someone.

Of course he knew about Sylvia, as both she and Douglas were his patients. They had discussed the pros and cons of her relatives being registered at the practice where she worked and he had tried to advise her against it but she was adamant. She stipulated emphatically that she would not interfere with any aspect of their care but needed to know their doctor was someone she had complete trust in. He was honoured that Grace thought so highly of him that she wanted him to care for her parents. His own father had had problems with depression, nowhere near as bad, thank goodness, but necessitating life-long medication and this he felt bestowed upon him some insight into Grace's problems and an additional bond between them.

Harry's ex-wife had repeatedly chastised him for his penchant to prevaricate. This, she had taken delight in informing him, was one of the main reasons she had divorced him – that along with his myopia regarding her financial requirements, his long-standing mistress, also known as work, and the fact that he was unable to satisfy her needs, physically and emotionally. Harry had cringed as he read the character assassination in the letter that arrived from her solicitor, barely recognising himself. Surely he hadn't been that bad?

They had met when he was a houseman, just qualified, bouncing about like a puppy, eager to please and she was an impressionable junior nurse with her sights set on marrying a doctor. Her securing him was seen as a bit of a coup amongst her friends, who had so far failed to net suitable partners. Wrongly she had imagined that the future would be one of wealth and everything she wanted but Harry's income, whilst plenty for a delightfully comfortable existence, did not come close to the amount needed to accommodate all her desires.

Erroneously, he had thought that they were jogging along nicely enough, perhaps not in the realms that warranted the adjective exciting but then how many couples were after a few years together? Everyone calmed down and settled into a sedate way of life and Harry knew that he had done his best professionally and was rightly proud of what he had achieved. No matter what he did, it was never enough for her and he had ended up branded as a 'useless example of manhood', to quote the solicitor's letter.

Anyway, weren't there two sides to every story? By no stretch of the imagination was she perfect. What about her profligate lifestyle? All she had wanted to do was eat out in expensive restaurants, even on week nights, when he returned home weary and longing to put on his slippers and have a cool beer and a ham sandwich. She constantly yearned for holidays in luxury hotels, seeking a species she referred to as celebrity and as for those god-awful clothes she flapped around in, were they really exclusive designer labels? He had thought them hideous and had made the mistake of saying so.

He had quickly come to terms with their parting, the knee-jerk feeling of loss replaced by a considerable degree of relief. The whole thing had been a tragic mistake and never should have taken place. He had contentedly slipped back into the bachelor lifestyle, buying a small cottage, acquiring a cat, Thadeus, and trying his hand at growing vegetables. Most evenings he was at the local pub, only the one pint, half an hour before closing time, but a chance to enjoy some conviviality with a few male friends. How much simpler had his life become, no one to please or report to, master of all he surveyed – even if it wasn't very much – and able to indulge in habits that had hitherto been frowned up, such as eating in front of the television ('it'll leave a horrid smell in the lounge,'), eating breakfast in bed ('I can't sleep here, all these crumbs, I'm going in the spare room on my own…') and leaving his shirt not tucked in ('for God's sake, smarten yourself up, I can't be seen with you looking like that').

Not the slightest pang of desire for another woman coursed through his circulation until that day when he saw Grace, neat and tidy in her interview suit, the belt accentuating her waspish waist, her tiny ankles, shapely legs and adorably fragile features, pallid with nerves, which cried out to be loved.

He had been rendered totally speechless and the questions he had planned to ask all the candidates flew from his mind, replaced by fluttering butterflies and romantic fanfares of trumpets. Thank goodness Andrew had been chairing the interviews. He and Janey had taken over until he, Harry, had recovered some semblance of control and managed to splutter out some query about her views on abortion and whether she was interested in teaching. Luckily for him, Grace had stood out for all of them and when she accepted their offer of partnership, Harry had been over the moon. Nobody, to this day, knew that he had crossed each day off the calendar on his desk to her arrival.

Now, five years later he had never taken their relationship any further than that of very good friend. Someone she could always come and talk to for advice about professional or personal issues. Someone who would happily go for a drink after work or even share a bowl of pasta for two or a pizza at the local Italian restaurant after a particularly gruelling day. Naturally, he had asked Grace if she might be able to look after Thadeus while he was away on holiday and she had accepted with alacrity, an arrangement often repeated since that first time.

Harry was able to live with the situation as long as Grace was unattached. That way, he still had in his heart a tiny fleck of hope that there might be a chance for him, or rather, for them. Many times, he wanted so badly to take their relationship a step further, to hold her hand or put his arm around her, a way of letting her know that he was more than just a good friend. Courage constantly deserted him and although he did manage to pat her forearm one day and envelop her in an avuncular hug on another, Grace had had no reason to read anything more passionate into either of these two gestures.

Now, though, there was Gideon. The trouble was he seemed like a good bloke. Hard working, a good laugh, friendly. He was clearly brilliant at his job and was taking the neurology department by the scruff of its neck and giving it a much-needed shake up. And all that was fine and highly commendable. What was definitely not fine was his developing liaison with Grace. Harry was aware that they had been out several times now. It was impossible not to know as Grace and Janey talked of little else at work. For dinner mostly and now Grace was talking about having him around for supper and also to meet her parents. As a couple, Grace and Gideon, quaintly alliterative as their names may be, were not a good match. Harry, ignoring the fact that his own track record was hardly one to boast about, knew that Grace was entitled to better, in other words, Harry himself.

What to do about it? It was one thing to know a situation was wrong; doing something about it was an entirely different matter.

He ran his fingers through his thick blond hair and rubbed his hairy cheeks, trying to summon up a solution. Infuriated, he contemplated the irony of how he was able to sort out his patients' problems without a moment's hesitation but when it came to himself he was nothing short of hopeless. Now it was time to change and quickly, before it was too late. How on earth was he going to tell Grace of his real feelings?

Chapter Five

*Sylvia got up in the early hours to get ready for her visitors that afternoon. Truth be told, sleep had not been forthcoming. Her mind, a restless ocean of plans with heaving waves of worries, had relentlessly troubled her throughout the entire night, preventing any rest. She so wanted everything to be perfect. It wasn't often that Grace brought suitable young men to the house and it was clear to see that this doctor, Gideon, had had a major impact on her daughter in a short space of time.

Mother's intuition.

Sylvia knew this was something special. Douglas had laughed off her comments, correctly pointing out that Grace and Gideon had barely started to see each other. But no, Sylvia knew. There was a unique connection, she reminded her husband, between mother and daughter that was both indescribable and infallible. Those other whippersnappers that she and Douglas had met over the years were cold fish, superficial in emotion and devoid of personality. Less than a glance had told her none of them was worthy of their wonderful daughter Grace. So, having already happily placed Gideon in the category of potential son-in-law, she couldn't wait to meet him.

Leaving Douglas and Charnley, who were snoring more or less in unison, Sylvia crept downstairs in her candlewick dressing gown and put the kettle on. Time for a quick cuppa and her tablets before she got started on her preparations. But the panic was starting to build up inside. Her heart was racing and her guts writhing and wringing like an escapologist struggling to get free from a sack.

So much to do and so little time. Housework, tidying, baking and then more tidying, just to be on the safe side.

It was imperative that she made a good impression. She wanted to be a mother-in-law that was loved, not one that was the subject of jokes. Clutching her mug in her shaky hands, she turned to the worktop where her notebook and pen lay. So far the to-do list filled four pages and that didn't include the cooking. The generously sized, well-rounded letters with copious doodles around the page edges did not make for easy reading.

Sylvia's mood was apparent from her handwriting. The variation from tiny indecipherable italics to looping, curling flamboyancy provided Douglas with a convenient early warning system of how she was and which direction her mood was heading. When the sentences stopped making sense he knew it was time to ask for help. Had he seen her list, warning bells would be starting to ring.

Bound by the rigid schedule that she had compiled, she checked the clock, tutted a little in annoyance and poured all her tea down the sink for there was no time for such luxuries. She washed the mug, polished it dry and put it back in the cupboard. No time for her tablets either. She needed all her energy today and the medication often made her drowsy and slowed her down.

Armed with a basketful of cleaning products, she set to work, starting as ever with the photographs of Grace in the lounge.

No lingering over each one today, reliving memories, just extra elbow grease to get the frames shining.

When Douglas was woken up, by the sound of vigorous vacuuming, it was not the aroma of grilling bacon or newly toasted bread that reached his nostrils. Instead he was assailed by the eye-watering smells of bleach, spray cleaner, air freshener and more types of polish than he could identify – brass, silver, floor, wood to name but a few. He rubbed his eyes and reached for Charnley who, sensing his master was awake, had jumped up beside him sneezing for all he was worth.

'Oh dear, Charnley, old pal,' he whispered into the dog's ear, cuddling him close. 'It's going to be a difficult day.'

He dressed casually, as always – cord trousers, baggy round the knees and round his bottom, checked shirt and crew-necked pullover with leather patches on the elbows. Gathering his strength, he called Charnley and the two of them ventured downstairs.

'There's no time for breakfast!' cried Sylvia, seeing him in the kitchen doorway and waving her arms to repel him as though he were a noxious odour. 'And don't let that dog make a mess anywhere.'

She was almost invisible in a fog of flour, beating up some ingredients in a large bowl that was usually reserved for the Christmas cake (made regularly on 9th September without fail).

'Take it easy, dear,' he tried to reassure her. 'It's not gone eight o'clock yet and they're not coming until late this afternoon. We've plenty of time and now I'm up, I can help. Now what exactly are you doing?'

'Making a cake, can't you see? But I don't know what flavour to do. Chocolate? Lemon? Should I do both?'

'Stick to plain old Victoria sponge, with a nice jam and

buttercream filling. Everyone likes that.'

'You mean that you do. He might not. Oh no, what if he's diabetic? I hadn't thought of that. Oh my goodness! Where's my recipe book?'

'If he was diabetic, then Grace would have told us. Calm down. I'm going to have coffee and toast and I think you need to do the same. I'm guessing you've been up for hours and haven't had anything.'

'Well, there's no time,' she repeated.

Erratically, she spooned the gloopy mixture into a tin and shoved it in the oven.

'That's that done. Do you think I should make my own bread? The smell of newly baked bread is supposed to be very welcoming, isn't it?'

'Yes,' agreed Douglas, 'but that's when you're trying to sell your house, which we're not. We'll get a loaf at the supermarket this morning. Nice and fresh and you can make a few ham sandwiches. Everyone likes those too.'

'What if he's Jewish?'

Douglas rolled his eyes. There was no talking to her. He opened a tin of dog food for Charnley, added some biscuits and then let him out into the garden. He buttered thick slices of brown toast and spread marmalade generously onto them. Pouring two mugs of freshly brewed coffee, he put his hands on Sylvia's shoulders and gently but firmly steered her to the little table in the corner of the kitchen and sat her down into a chair. Breakfast was placed in front of her and he sat down to join her.

'Now eat and drink. Have you taken your tablets? No, I suspected as much. I'll get them for you now.'

Sylvia eyes flickered around the room as she took brisk bites of toast. Still so much to be done. Mentally she ticked off what she had achieved, which was good but now she was having toast and that was making a new mess, one that she had not reckoned for, which had to be cleaned up.

Douglas took her hand. Years of marriage made him believe that he was able to read her mind. Most of the time this was true but she still managed to surprise him frequently with a bizarre sequence of thoughts that amazed and baffled him.

'I must wash these things up.'

'Sylvia, this has got to stop. Calm down, please. Let's get some fresh air and take Charnley to the woods. You know he loves that and it's a beautiful morning. You'll feel the benefit for it. When we get back, we'll sit down together and plan the rest of the day.'

'I can't.' Sylvia shook her head emphatically. 'I've a taxi coming in ten minutes to take me to the shops. There are still some things I need to buy.'

She jumped up and grabbed her handbag.

Douglas sighed. 'Why have you done that? You know I'd have taken you in the car.'

'Because I need to get on. How much plainer can I make it? I know you don't like shopping and anyway, Charnley wants his walk. I'll be fine. I'll get the stuff I need, get back home and finish off. Oh, I do hope he'll like us. I wonder what he's thinking at this very moment. Do you think he feels as nervous as I do?'

'I hope not,' answered Douglas with feeling. 'Mind you, if you carry on in this state, he will end up feeling awkward and so will Grace and I.'

Sylvia deflated somewhat. 'I'm sorry, Doug. I don't want to put him off. So sorry. I really think this is THE ONE!'

'I know. You just want it all to be perfect. And it will be. But don't get your hopes up and don't be pushy. Grace is a sensible girl and she'll choose the right chap in the end. Now, if that taxi's due you'd better go and put some proper clothes on and leave the washing up to me.'

She glanced down, shocked to find that she was still in her night attire. 'Ooops, silly me,' she giggled and ran out of the room tearing off her dressing gown as she went.

Grace and Gideon arrived on time, for which Douglas was eternally grateful. It meant he was spared Sylvia's catastrophising about road accidents and other natural disasters such as hurricanes and earthquakes that might have delayed them. Sylvia was dressed in a bright purple dress, white shoes and an orange-fringed shawl. Douglas tried to dissuade her from the tiara but she was adamant. This was a special occasion. At least he had successfully managed to veto the bow round Charnley's neck. He noticed that she was visibly trembling from head to foot as the front door opened. She suddenly looked exhausted, the lines of fatigue in her face showing through the thick layer of foundation and rather clownish make up she had put on. She was so child like. His heart went out to her and he muttered a prayer that the next few hours passed uneventfully.

'Mum, Dad, this is Gideon Barlow,' announced Grace.

Sylvia looked as though she might burst when Gideon held out his hand.

'How lovely to meet you, Mrs Dunstable,' he began, politely.

She ignored him, embracing him wildly and clutching him to her breasts.

'Sylvia, please. And it is perfectly perfect to meet you. Come in, come in. Don't stand in the hall. This is the lounge. Of course it is, you can see that, can't you! Let me show you some photos of Grace when she was a baby. They're so beautiful.'

Grace looked at her father, who shrugged apologetically. 'You knew this would happen. She's been on the go since goodness knows when,' he told her.

'Is she OK? She looks a bit wild...'

Douglas nodded. 'She is rather but I'm hoping she'll calm down a bit now that you're actually here.'

Gideon appeared from the lounge. 'I forgot the flowers I bought for your mum. Back in a mo!'

Grace and her father went to join Sylvia, whose face bore a look of rapture.

'Isn't he wonderful? So good looking. Like what's his name on the TV. He's got me flowers! And chocolates, he says! I'll pop and put the kettle on, while I think of it.'

She rushed off, Grace following in her wake, eager to help and relieve some of the pressure if possible.

'I hope you haven't gone to a lot of trouble, Mum. He's only come for a cup of tea.'

'No, no, of course I haven't. I've made a cake or two and some sandwiches. Your dad suggested it, really.'

'I'm sure it'll be lovely. Oh, listen, that's Gideon back. Why don't I mash the tea and you go and get to know him better.'

Sylvia looked doubtful. 'I should really see to this, Grace. I am the hostess after all.'

'All I'm doing is making a pot of tea, Mum...'

Reluctantly Sylvia acquiesced and returned to the lounge. Grace, while waiting for the water to boil, heard rapid questions being fired at Gideon about every subject under the sun. What were the chances of him coming out of this ordeal unscathed? And more to the point, what about their embryonic relationship?

Grace carried the tray of tea into the lounge. Sylvia leapt to her feet, hands holding the tiara in place.

'No, no, no. Not in here. I've set the table in the dining room.

Come with me, Gideon. I hope you're hungry.'

Sylvia wafted out of the room, a blur of contrasting colours, and opened the door to the dining room.

Grace, her father and Gideon gasped audibly and simultaneously. Never before had they seen so much food in one place. Almost bending under the weight, the table was piled high with plates of sandwiches, pastries, buns, cakes, scones and biscuits.

'Ta dah!' Sylvia announced proudly. 'Here, take a plate, Gideon, and help yourself. Have plenty. I'm sure there's something you'll like. I wasn't sure what sort of food you enjoyed, so from the left there's ordinary bread, then gluten free, vegetarian fillings, vegan fillings, fat-free sponges, scones for diabetics and chocolate cake with chocolate filling and icing for greedy chocoholics – that's me! Then there's a trifle, some Bakewell tarts, Swiss Roll and flapjacks. Oh, and a coffee and toffee cake – I've not tried that one before but I invented it. I like the way the names rhyme. And that one there's a Battenberg but it's all yellow as I didn't have any pink colouring. It possibly shouldn't slant to the left like that but I know it will taste delicious.'

She stopped to draw breath, panting.

'Goodness!' exploded Gideon, finding his voice. 'What a spread you've put on. How very kind you are. You've gone to an enormous amount of trouble.'

'No trouble at all!' Sylvia loaded his plate up with a variety of sandwiches as he was not helping himself quickly enough.

Grace stared at the veritable monument of food, feeling sick. 'What's this, Mum?' She pointed to a dish in which some pale yellow battery substance lay.

'Oh, that's the cake I made this morning. But I forgot to put the oven on! But waste not, want not. People love cake mix. You did when you were a little girl. You used to beg me not to scrape the mixing bowl out. You'd end up with it all over your face. Don't you remember? We can eat it with spoons! Just like you used to!'

Sylvia busied herself, dishing out plates, encouraging everyone to take more and then sit on one of the chairs that she had arranged around the perimeter of the room, rather in the manner of a day room in an old people's home. With no table nearby, Grace and Gideon found that they had a plate in one hand and a cup and saucer in the other, thus effectively prohibiting either eating or drinking. Whilst Grace was simply too overwhelmed to eat, Gideon rose to the occasion, balanced his cup on the windowsill and tucked in with gusto to Sylvia's delight.

'It's hard to say which of these delicacies is the best. You certainly know how to bake, Mrs Dunstable,' he praised her.

'Oh please call me Sylvia. So much easier don't you think? Mind you, I must confess, I haven't baked all these things.' Her voice dropped to a stage whisper. 'Some I bought from the shops this morning.'

'I would never have known,' was the gallant reply, which sent Sylvia into fits of giggles.

'How is your job going? Are you enjoying it?'

Gideon finished another mouthful. 'Very much, thank you. I'm delighted to have been appointed a consultant in such a delightful town as Harrogate and of course there is the added bonus of having met your lovely daughter.'

He looked warmly at Grace, who lowered her eyes, both embarrassed and pleased.

Sylvia clapped her hands together with glee. 'So you're looking to settle down? Do you like children? I've always thought that Grace was maternal plus she has very good child-bearing hips...'

'Enough, Mum, please...' Grace pleaded, then mouthed an

apology to Gideon.

Sylvia pulled a face and went to slice the chocolate cake.

'I really don't think I can eat another thing,' confessed Gideon as a ridiculously large wedge of this was dumped on his plate with some force.

'Nonsense. Have a little rest and then start again. I'm sure you'll find a teeny corner for some of my speciality cake.'

Grace was relieved when she felt that she and Gideon were able to make an escape. Within the hour, an exhausted Sylvia was prostrate on the sofa, snoring loudly. Douglas saw them to the door, waving away Grace's offers to help clear up the remains of the afternoon.

'Whatever will you do with all that food, Dad?' she asked.

He sighed. 'Whatever I can. Freeze some, give some to the neighbours, take some to whomever I can think of. You're welcome to take as much as you want. Take it to work. I'm so sorry about this, Gideon. I had no idea what she was up to. I took Charnley out this morning and admittedly we were quite a long time but when I got back, the kitchen was spotless and she was singing at the top of her voice in the bath. It never occurred to me to look in the dining room as we use it so rarely. Oh my goodness, I hope she settles now it's all over. I can't bear the thought of her having to go into hospital again.'

Grace hugged him tightly. 'Let her have a good night's sleep. Then I'll come round first thing before work and we'll see how she is.'

Douglas nodded wearily. He too looked worn out.

'Thank you for everything, Mr Dunstable.' Gideon shook his hand. 'If there's anything I can do to help, please – I'm more than happy to.'

'Thank you, you're very kind.'

Gideon took Grace's hand and led her across the road, up her drive to the front door.

'I don't know what to say,' she began.

He swept her up in his arms and kissed her on the lips. 'You don't have to say anything. I'm here for you now.'

Burying her head in his shoulder, Grace was on the verge of tears at his kindness. She felt him run his fingers through her hair, loving every moment. Wiping away the tears from her eyes, she stepped back and attempted a laugh.

'I suppose it's too much to expect that you'd like to come in for supper!'

He nodded. 'I'm rather full up and think I might not eat for a couple of days. You look as done in as your dad, so get some rest and I'll ring you tomorrow to see how things are. Maybe we'll go out for a drink in the evening?'

'That would be so nice, Gideon. Thank you again for this afternoon, for your understanding…'

He stopped her mid-sentence with another kiss, longer and more passionate than the first, leaving her wanting more.

'We'll speak tomorrow. Take care.'

She waved him off, watching his car disappearing down the road and wishing that he would turn around and come back. With some regret but acknowledging the truth that she needed a hot shower and some time alone, she closed the door and went inside.

Chapter Six

❧

*D*ouglas had already summoned Harry before Grace arrived.

'It's no good, your mum only slept for a couple of hours after you left and since then she's been up all night, dancing, playing wedding music and trying on all her hats. She says that she's invented a cube with seven sides that she wants to be the centrepiece on the tables at your reception. I rang Harry at home as soon as it was light and he's on his way.'

'Oh, Dad, that's too bad.' Grace was horrified.

'We've seen it all before, more times than I care to remember and there's no other option. Each time I hope it'll be different but it never is. I wonder if she's been taking her tablets regularly. Probably not. I do supervise them but, sometimes, she's too clever for me and pretends to take them when all the while they're slipped into her pocket or under a cushion. If you want to get off to work, I'll phone you later. Harry's visit is just a formality. She'll never agree to go in so she'll have to be sectioned again. What a bloody mess all this is.'

'Yoo hoo!' cried Sylvia from the first floor. 'Is that my beautiful bride to be?'

'Hello, Mum,' Grace called back. 'How are you today?'

'Fine and dandy, thanks!' She wafted down the stairs, humming the Wedding March, clad in the dress she had worn for her own nuptials years ago. Unable to fasten it up, as time and much medication had not been kind to her figure, she had improvised with ribbons and scarves to stop it from falling off. Net curtains draped from her head, held in place by a bowler hat, and clutched in her hand was the bouquet of flowers that Gideon had brought. Charnley, on this occasion, had not escaped so lightly and had a feather boa tied to his collar, which he was fighting with to be rid of.

'How do I look?' She twirled on one foot, nearly losing her balance and Douglas reached out to save her.

'Lovely, Mum. Let's go and sit down for a bit.'

'Sit down? Whatever for? I've so much to do. Now I think it would be nice if you were to wear this dress for your wedding. History repeating itself and all that. A good clean and it'll look new as a bobbin. How'd that be?'

'Whatever you say.' Grace knew better that to contradict her mother when she was like this. Doing so only resulted in anger and vitriol towards Douglas, who inevitably turned into the scapegoat.

The doorbell rang.

'Whoever can that be?' Sylvia suddenly alert, looked fearful. 'It's far too early for callers.'

Douglas entered the room with Harry.

Amazingly, amidst the chaos of her brain, a clutch of brain cells recognised what was happening.

'No, oh no!' shrieked Sylvia. 'You're not doing this to me again. Get away from me, Harry! I've a wedding to plan.'

She tried to rush from the room, only to be prevented by Douglas who brought her, protesting, back to the sofa.

'Sit down and have a chat with Harry. You know very well that all he wants to do is look after you and make sure that you get the very best care. You need to have one of your rests. You can make the wedding plans while you have it.'

'Please don't send me to hospital. I won't go! I won't.'

She ran into a corner and crouched in a small ball, her dress cascading around her as she hid her face in her hands. Her wailing was pathetic and traumatic to hear, like an abandoned dog baying for food. Douglas indicated for Grace to leave and sat down next to his wife, trying to pull her close, hoping it would help.

The outcome was inevitable, Grace knew but it did not stop her from crying all the way to the surgery. Harry caught up with her on his return, spotting her from his consulting room as she scuttled across the waiting area and followed her, closing the door behind them.

'Grace, what is it? Can I help?'

She was touched by the concern in his voice.

'I'm OK, thanks, Harry. It's just Mum. Did you have to section her?'

He nodded. 'I'm afraid so. She refused voluntary admission. Such a shame as she's been doing so well recently. What a blow for you and your dad.'

He passed her the tissues she reserved for upset patients and wondered if he dared give her a hug. A good friend would do. Cowardice prevailed and he decided best not to and was left looking at her, impotently trying to think of something to do and say. He fiddled with his tie, golden meerkats on a magenta background. Resorting to the usual tactics, he rang reception and asked them to bring in a cup of tea for Grace.

'And I'll see her first few patients,' he added. 'That'll give you time to sort yourself out,' he turned to Grace, who nodded, numbly.

'Thanks, Harry,' she murmured.

'What are friends for?' he responded.

'I don't know why I'm so upset. It's happened before and I dare say it'll happen again. She'll be in hospital for a couple of weeks, maybe three, hopefully not more and then home again almost as if nothing had happened. But she'll be that little bit more fragile. Each admission saps her of a tiny bit of her. The saving grace is that she never remembers how bad she was, what she did and said. She'd be mortified if she did.'

'That's the nature of the beast she lives with, isn't it?' Harry said. 'It's incomprehensibly evil.'

'You're right. You know, Dad and I always hoped that as she got older, the disease might burn out but there's no sign of that whatsoever.'

'You cope wonderfully and you know that all of us here will cover for you and support you however we can.'

Grace managed a watery smile. 'You're a good friend, Harry.'

Harry glowed inwardly; her comment had made his day.

'Always there for you, chum.'

He punched her gently on the shoulder, taken aback by his sudden audacity. Better still, she didn't seem to mind. On the verge of reaching out for her, he was interrupted by a knock on the door and the arrival of the cup of tea. He cursed the receptionist's timing. Still, he had taken a teeny step in the right direction and felt that a preliminary threshold had been crossed.

'Here you are. Now, you stay here and take your time over this. I'll crack on and make a start seeing patients. They'll be muttering because of the delay but I'll explain that you've been held up by an emergency. No need to say any more than that.

Send me a pop-up on the screen when you're ready to start but there's no rush. OK? I mean it….'

'You're fabulous, Harry. I can never repay you.'

She blew him a kiss as he got to the door. His day was getting better and better until she said, 'Gideon's been so wonderful too. I don't know what I'd do without him.'

Harry returned to his room, cursing Gideon who had effortlessly blocked the route to Grace. I wish I had more self confidence, thought Harry, slamming his door shut and luckily unable to see the shocked faces of his waiting patients. How can I get Grace to realise that I want to be more than a friend?

His consultation skills had been better. Not exactly in receipt of short shrift, both his patients and a couple of Grace's realised that all was not well with their usually accommodating, bonhomous doctor and out of kindness they kept their agendas to a minimum, planning a return visit in the near future to try again. Anger and frustration were still festering within when the last one had gone, clutching a handful of repeat prescriptions, a specimen bottle and shaking her head from side to side at the substandard service.

They met up for a coffee with Janey and Andrew. Janey was sharing a box of chocolates that she had received from a grateful patient. The top layer had already been consumed. Grace rang Douglas who was busy with the consultant psychiatrist but quickly confirmed that Sylvia was to be admitted that afternoon.

'It has to be,' Grace said, resignedly, hanging up. 'There's no alternative. Poor Mum. I'll go and see her this evening.'

'Aren't you seeing Gideon?' asked Janey, much to Harry's annoyance. Did this man's name have to crop up continuously?

'That was the plan. We were going for a drink, that's all. I expect we can just meet later than we'd planned. No way can I ask him to come with me.'

'I could come,' spluttered Harry, spotting an opportunity, then gulping for fear he was looking too keen. 'I mean, I could wait for you outside the ward while you visit. She'll still be really angry with me for setting the section in motion, so maybe it's best if I don't see her.'

Grace thanked him. 'Don't worry, I'll meet up with my dad. It's probably best that she only has family visiting to start with, while she's so muddled.'

'No problem. My offer's open any time.'

'Thank you all of you. I'm lucky to have such wonderful partners.'. She rallied. 'Any way – the day must go on and there are house calls to make. I'll do those ones at Stoneleigh nursing home as that's just around the corner from Mr Bagshaw with the swollen ankles who I promised to go back and review.'

She packed her bag and made her way to the car park, Harry was in hot pursuit, shirt tail hanging out under his jacket, leather Gladstone bag half open in his rush. His stethoscope fell out on to the ground and he scrambled to pick it up.

'Meet you back here for lunch?' he suggested hopefully.

'That'd be great. I'll bring the sandwiches as you've got more visits than me. You can make the coffee.'

'You're on. See you in a ... Hang on, Grace – what's that?'

'What's what?' Grace spun round to see Harry pointing at the far side of her car where, to her horror, a line of deep scratches, like an erratic stave of music, had been gouged from one end to the other of the passenger door. 'Oh God! My lovely new car. Look at that! How on earth did that happen?'

Harry ran his fingers along the damage and whistled. 'It looks deliberate. What a mess!'

'Deliberate?' echoed Grace. 'Why would someone do that?

And more to the point, who would do something like that?'

'Search me. A patient?'

Grace thought quickly. 'I can't think of any of them who dislike me that much. That's a pretty violent act, you know.'

'When do you think it happened?' Harry patrolled the vehicle looking for but not finding other signs of damage.

'This morning maybe? Who knows? I didn't look. I was in a rush after seeing Mum and jumped into the car to come here. Why would I have checked? The car was in the drive, as always, and I'm sure I'd have noticed, so that means it must have been done here.'

'Maybe it was mindless vandalism. Someone spotted it was a new car and decided to target it, having no idea who it belonged to.'

Grace nodded. 'I think that's right. I can't believe it though. It'll cost a fortune to have repaired.' She sighed. 'What a day this is turning out to be. I can't wait to tell Gideon all about it. He'll be horrified.'

Harry rolled his eyes and silently gnashed his teeth. There had to be a way to entice Grace into his arms but he was oblivious as to what it might be.

Chapter Seven

∽◌♡◌∽

'I'm glad I've had the opportunity to have a chat with the two of you.'

Dr Phillip Richardson did not fit the archetypal mould of consultant psychiatrist. His short grey hair was immaculately trimmed, as was his moustache. His white shirt was creaseless, his leather jacket adventurous and his black jeans reassuringly casual. Sitting with Douglas and Grace in his scrupulously tidy office, he was possessed of an entrepreneurial air, as opposed to that of a doctor. He had been in charge of Sylvia's care for years now and was close to Douglas as a friend and ally.

'How is she? Has she settled in?' Douglas was anxious.

'She's doing OK. She's very confused and disorientated, as you'll find when you go to see her. Any ideas to what's sparked this off?'

'Maybe she's been hiding her medication again,' proffered Douglas. 'I do my utmost to make sure she takes it but you know how it is, she feels better so she thinks she doesn't need it.'

'It might be that. It's a common enough cause. She's been increasingly volatile when I've seen her in the clinic lately but I had hoped we might avoid this. Don't worry, Douglas, I'm not blaming you. I know that you do your best all the time, against

48

all odds. I have to be honest with you though and say that she's almost the worst I've ever seen her. I'm afraid it's going to take some time to get her back on the rails.'

Douglas cradled his head in his hands, rocking slightly. Despite Phillip's reassurances, he still felt guilty. Grace spotted a tear splash onto his trousers and pulled her chair close by to protect him. Putting an arm around him, she was saddened to feel how bony and fragile his body seemed. It was as though he had deflated to a mere shadow of his former self.

'I'm so tired of all this,' Douglas admitted suddenly, looking up into Phillip's eyes, imploring him to help. 'I've lost count of the number of times you and I have been sitting opposite each other, like this, having this conversation. I love Sylvia more than life itself but she exhausts me, physically and emotionally. When she's high, I worry about how I can reel her in; when she's low, I spend every moment of the day trying ways to drag her back up. Even when she's as well as she ever is, I can't enjoy it. I don't relax because I'm constantly worrying about how long it's going to last, which direction her mood's going to go next. Each time I think I've cracked it and can foresee what's going to happen, she does something completely unpredictable and bamboozles me. It's a bloody nightmare and I'm not sure if I can do it for much longer!'

Grace was appalled at his admission. As a child she had believed that her father would always cope, be constant in his support and faithful in his role of carer. Since adulthood, even since her medical training, she found it so hard to be dispassionate about the situation, preferring to shun reality and resort to her lifelong hopes.

'Dad! Why didn't you say something? Look, you're just worn out, Dad.' She turned to Phillip. 'The last couple of days have been dreadful for us,' she explained, 'Dad's had no sleep to speak of.'

Phillip nodded sympathetically. He leant forward on this desk and dovetailed his fingers.

'Douglas, I can understand how you're feeling and I am very relieved and glad that you've come out and admitted it. Lesser mortals would have cracked under the strain many moons ago because they were too afraid to say anything. As I say, she's going to be on the ward for a good while, so you must take this opportunity to put yourself first, get plenty of rest, eat well, enjoy that dog of yours. You can rest peacefully knowing that Sylvia's in good hands and being looked after. Visit whenever you want but to start with, not more than once a day and don't stay more than a few minutes. At the moment, she's too ill to appreciate it. How about you, Grace? Are you coping?'

'Yes, thanks. I think so. I've got work to go to which helps take my mind off Mum and some good friends. It's invariably harder for Dad as he's with her all the time. I'll make sure that he does as you suggest, I promise. I'm just as concerned about him as I am about Mum.'

'For sure,' acknowledged Phillip. 'Now I need to talk to you about Sylvia's treatment plan. I'd like to make some substantial changes.'

He outlined what he was intending to do, how her drugs were going to be changed in the initial phase and if this was rapidly successful, then long-term use might be an option to consider and discuss, though the side effects were potentially more bothersome. Douglas, listening with one ear only had nothing to add but Grace asked some pertinent questions, fearful for the future when Sylvia went home.

'We'll set up a care package, naturally,' Phillip promised.

'I don't need any help,' growled Douglas. 'I don't want the house full of do-gooders. I'm the only one who knows her well enough to look after her.' He scraped his chair back and stood up, terminating the conversation.

'Where is she? I need to see her. I can't sit here any longer listening to this. I've heard enough for one day. I must think about all your proposals. No offence, Phil, you know that.'

'Of course. She's down the corridor, to the left and the first room on the right. Shall I take you?'

'No, no. We know the way, sadly. You've plenty to be doing. We'll pop in to say our goodbyes before we go. Come on, Grace.'

He was out of the room in a flash. Grace shrugged, looking helplessly at Phillip and then rushed after her father. She caught him up just as he was at the door to Sylvia's room. Tentatively, he pushed it open and crept in, Grace following. Sitting cross-legged in the far corner was Sylvia, naked to the waist, hugging a pillow to her chest and singing softly. The room was stark. White walls, uncarpeted floor, a solitary bed and one chair. The faint whiff of disinfectant hung in the air.

Hardly an ambience to encourage recovery.

They both knew that while her mood remained so capricious, it was vital that she was nursed on her own and where there was no risk of her self-harming. Sylvia glanced up at the arrivals. Rather than recognition, indignation flared in her eyes at the interruption. Before Douglas or Grace was able to speak, she shouted at them.

'Get out. Can't you see I'm feeding my baby? She needs peace and quiet or she won't suckle. She's called Grace and if she doesn't eat, she won't put on weight and then I won't be able to take her home and my husband Douglas is waiting for me.' She turned her attention to the pillow. 'Shhhh now. I won't let anyone hurt you.'

'Hello, Mum,' ventured Grace.

'Mum? What are you talking about? This is my baby, not you! Go away.'

Grace and Douglas exchanged glances.

'You try, Dad,' whispered Grace, knowing full well that success was unlikely.

He shook his head, dejectedly. 'There's no point. Your Mum's got no idea what's going on. Let's leave her and come back tomorrow.'

Sylvia was on her feet, her tights wrinkled around her ankles, her skirt pointing the wrong way.

'Who are you, anyway? Get me my husband, now! He'll be very cross if he knows you're here without permission. Now scoot before I have to shout for help.'

Turning his back on her, Douglas retreated to the corridor without so much as a farewell. Grace feeling that this was very harsh, advanced a couple of paces and started to say goodbye but this only resulted in Sylvia squeezing the pillow even harder and glowering, retreating to the perceived safety of her corner.

Chapter Eight

A few days later, Grace was sitting in the hospital restaurant waiting for Gideon. It was cluttered and noisy with hungry doctors and nurses wanting to refuel before the afternoon work began. Nobody wanted salad but there was a queue, snaking back out of the door and down the corridor, waiting for good rib-sticking fodder such as steak pie, lasagne, chips and coffee sponge pudding with coffee sauce. The latter was clearly labelled owing to the fact that since it had first appeared on the menu, far too many customers had mistaken it for gravy and poured it on their main course.

Grace had appropriated a table by the window, not that the view was very inspiring as the glass was steamed up by the hot atmosphere. She resisted the temptation to draw a smiley face with her finger. Life was looking up. Sylvia, still a long way from coming home, had improved. The fact that she now recognised Douglas and Grace came as a great consolation to them, especially Douglas who religiously visited on a daily basis to sit with her and, if allowed, hold her hand. She was back on the main part of the ward and Grace was thankful that the pillow had been returned to its rightful place on the bed and that her mother was now fully dressed, albeit in a choice of clothing that would raise eyebrows.

Gideon had been a godsend. Though his job was desperately demanding, he still managed to find the time to be in touch constantly. They had seen each other every day and he never seemed to mind if Douglas came along to make up a threesome. Never before had Grace had such a thoughtful and diligent boyfriend. Rarely did he arrive without a gift. It might be flowers (she had more or less run out of vases now), chocolates (she'd need to keep an eye on her weight if this carried on) or books – serious, funny, literary and easy reading. She was thrilled when he brought her a milk jug that matched her plate and cups – the ones with the little hens on, as this personal touch revealed his powers of observation and consideration.

The physical side of their relationship had been slow to get off the ground but this was hardly surprising, decided Grace, considering all that they had had thrust upon them since the first date. Not many men would have withstood this trial by fire and emerged unscathed and wanting to keep on seeing her. Understandingly, Gideon had announced that he did not want to pressurise her into a deeper commitment until she was ready. I mean, she had said to Janey, just how many men behave like that? Unfortunately, Harry had been in the room when this discussion had taken place, his face becoming blacker and blacker as the main topic of their conversation was this apparent paragon, yet again. Wasn't there anything that man who was rapidly becoming his nemesis did wrong? Surely nobody was that perfect.

That day, Grace was pushing cold ham and salad, plain and simple, around her plate. No coleslaw, no bread bun and butter but lots of tomato and lettuce. Very healthy, very boring and for a very good reason. She was planning to ask Gideon to supper at her house. Douglas had been asked round to a neighbour and, much to her surprise, had accepted. He appeared to be much calmer and well rested, back more to his normal cheery and optimistic self. So for once the opportunity to be alone together was being handed to Gideon and Grace on a plate. She was busy planning to serve some of her favourites for him, which hopefully might become his favourites too. They had continued to find more and more that they had in common. A light starter of scallops and chorizo was to be followed by a simple pasta dish with chicken and then the perennial favourite, chocolate mousse given a fresh slant by a slug of Cointreau. Some good wine to drink, maybe prosecco to add an air of fun and frivolity and then if all went well, she was going to ask him to stay over. What she glossed over was the fact that everything was bought ready prepared and needed heating up. Cooking had never been a big part of her life. Eating, possibly, but feeding one solitary person did not, to her, equate to a good enough reason to start from basics, especially nowadays when it was possible to purchase such a fabulous range of good quality ready meals. On the days when she wasn't alone in her house, invariably she was at her parents and Sylvia insistent that Grace, as their visitor, did not lift a finger to help.

Today was not the day to attempt heights of cookery that she had never before even considered, let alone achieved. Another occasion, maybe, but tonight had to be perfect. Gideon loved to eat, another mutual interest and she was sure that the food he was to be given would be well received. Unlike some people she might name, it did not occur to Grace to try to pass the food off as her own. She planned to be, as usual, scrupulously honest with Gideon. He'd dealt with enough skeletons popping out of her cupboards to date to be put off by her inability to cook.

She couldn't wait. In hot anticipation, the sheets on her bed had been changed to the lovely dark blue ones and the house tidied to such a degree that an intelligent onlooker might have ventured to suggest that she had inherited some of her mother's tendencies. The very thought of what lay ahead had her stomach full of butterflies. Little wonder that she did not want to eat. Then her heart lurched in her chest at the sight of him wending his way around the tables to where she was sitting.

He bent down to kiss her and she had to stop from squirming with ecstasy. Such complete abandon and public show of affection, especially in his workplace, was tantamount to an announcement that they were officially together. Grace had a sneaky look around the room convinced that all eyes were upon them but was disappointed to find that nobody seemed to be aware of what had taken place seconds previously. All were too intent on their food or deep in conversations about patients, drugs, disasters and problems.

'Hi, you look beautiful,' were his opening words. He paused to gaze deeply into her eyes, as though to emphasise his words.

'Hi, yourself!'

He put his tray down on the table. Pie and a double helping of chips and a mug of tea.

'How's your morning been?' asked Grace.

'Good. Fascinating clinic, which overran a little, hence my being late for you. I saw a case of hemiballismus.'

Grace racked her brain to remember what this was and failed. 'Oh, really,' she nodded, hoping she sounded convincing.

'Anyway, I'm here with you now, so work can wait for half an hour.' He splattered a generous amount of brown sauce over his lunch.

He chose to use a fork only, so he could hold Grace's hand at the same time as he ate. She coyly invited him for supper, stroking his thumb, wondering if he had the ability to read between the lines and grasp the subliminal message but it appeared not as, while accepting gratefully, he continued to shovel as much food into his mouth as quickly as possible. Obviously the prospect of what lay ahead had not had quite the same impact on his appetite as Grace had experienced. Never mind, he was a man who had worked tirelessly all morning and there was time for all that later.

He arrived promptly on the dot of seven, freshly showered and smelling adorably of an exclusive cologne. Short-sleeved beige linen shirt and dark brown chinos, brown loafers. In essence, Grace was unable to fault his appearance. Wrapping her in a warm hug, he felt Grace melt into his arms. She led him into her lounge and passed him the bottle of prosecco to open. On cue he admired her champagne flutes, elegantly tall and slim and studded with tiny gold beads. She had fallen for them some years ago when browsing in one of those shops that looks uninteresting from the outside but is awash with fabulously fantastic and unusual objects once its depths are plumbed. Since purchasing them, they had rarely been out of the kitchen cupboard, as she had no cause to share their beauty with someone special.

If he was put off by the repeated ping of the microwave then he concealed it well. He ate heartily, showing no signs of still being full from lunch and asked for seconds. Grace discovered that she was now starving. Her nerves had gone as soon as he arrived and he commented on how he liked to see a woman enjoying her food rather than worrying about its calorific content.

They toasted each other over dessert, Grace daringly offering Gideon a spoonful of her own mousse. Their eyes locked, he licked at it lasciviously until a blob fell on his chin, breaking the moment and creating fits of laughter.

'I'm sorry I'm such a hopeless cook,' apologised Grace, still giggling.

'No problem,' Gideon assured her. 'It's been great. I often do exactly the same myself but I do like to cook from basics as well. I'll teach you. Here, let's raise our glasses to the supermarket!'

Their glasses touched and they drank.

'Lovely stuff, this,' Gideon successfully aborted a burp.

'Shall we take our glasses into the lounge?' Grace suggested. 'I'll make coffee, too.'

'Let me help you wash up first. It's only fair after you spending so much time preparing this meal.'

Playfully, Grace thumped him before he was able to dodge out of the way.

'OK, you wash and I'll dry.' She threw him the pan scourer.

Together, they slotted into a scene of domestic harmony. Standing side by side, Grace wondered if all this was too good to be true. Moments like this she had only ever dreamed of and now it was actually happening. She tingled all over each time he passed her a plate or piece of cutlery. Whoever knew that washing up could be so erotically charged?

In the end, after more wine and no coffee, it turned out that there was no need for Grace to offer a formal invitation to her guest. As frequently happens, one thing led to another, culminating in her audaciously taking his hand and guiding him up the stairs to her room, a trail of clothing following in their wake. A creature of habit, even when considerably drunk, Grace made an excuse so that she could go and clean her teeth only to find on her return that Gideon was naked under her lovely blue duvet, rolled on his side and snoring loudly. Love may be blind but at that moment it was also deaf as the strident chords that were emanating from his throat sounded like music to her ears and happily she crawled in beside him, put her arm over his sleeping form and lay contentedly listening to his breathing and trying to synchronise her own.

Chapter Nine

*D*on't you think it's a bit early for that?' demanded Douglas, impatiently looking right and left at a junction, drumming his fingers impatiently on the steering wheel. 'You've not known him that long.' He swung the car out into the main road in a jerky fashion, causing Charnley to ricochet across the back seat. The teatime traffic was predictably dire and the journey looked as if it was going to be stop, start, stop all the way.

'No,' responded Grace truculently, for she had been anticipating this reaction. 'I simply know it's the right thing to do.'

'It seems very premature,' Douglas continued, genuinely concerned.

'Well, it's not. I knew you'd say that.'

Grace had announced that Gideon was moving in with her. He had asked her in a sublime post-coital moment, her defences at a low, and she had jumped at the idea and then he had jumped on her. Her cheeks felt hot as she remembered. She had found it quite hard to break the news to her father and after several failed attempts had managed to blurt it out while they were driving to the hospital to visit Sylvia.

'I don't want you to get hurt, that's all,' Douglas went on. 'You've had more than your share of difficulties and you deserve some happiness.'

'I am happy,' Grace insisted. 'Gideon is caring, thoughtful, kind. He puts me first above everything else all the time.'

Douglas remained unconvinced. 'I'm sure he is a nice chap. He seems to be from what I've seen but why the haste? I don't know what your mother will have to say,' he grumbled. 'Though knowing her, she'll be ecstatic, rush around making wedding arrangements and spend a vast amount of money on a hat big enough to accommodate a siege of herons and a couple of homeless cats.'

Grace smiled at the vision. ' Well, then, let's not tell her yet. Let's wait until the new medication has had more of a chance to kick in. Though she already seems very much calmer.'

Douglas snorted. 'We have to tell her. It's only fair. It's better we tell her as soon as possible so that if, and I'm only saying if, there is any fall out then she's in hospital when it happens. They're looking to discharge her next week, if the upcoming weekend home visit is as successful as the last one and I really don't want any shocks waiting for her that might knock her sideways. This has been the longest admission she's had for a decade or more.'

Grace knew better than to argue for her father was, as always, right. Her most distant memories were of his unfailing ability to read a situation and analyse it correctly, a skill deployed both professionally and personally. His advice had always been sound and dependable and she had relied on his wisdom on more occasions than she could recall.

Genius he may be, but absolutely nothing was going to stop this. The last couple of weeks had been nothing short of a whirlwind. So much had taken place, decisions taken, foundations of plans laid. Following the unscheduled ending to the supper evening, Gideon had proved that he was a gifted and original (Grace preferred not to think how he had acquired these skills) lover. Unbeknown to Douglas, he had all but moved in anyway, returning each night after work with more clothes and personal possessions, thrilled to be able to get away from the hospital accommodation that he was renting while he searched for a property to buy.

He had no trouble in feeling at home. In a matter of days, he started to put his stamp on Grace's home. Little by little, she noticed happily how his books were snuggled up to hers, his toiletries littered the bathroom and his coats, scarves and hats were hung up on the row of hooks in the hall. All these created an air of permanence about his presence, which she loved. Even his medical bag was placed symmetrically beside Grace's own, another touching sign of unity.

For Grace, however, the transition was proving to be harder. Completely used to her own space and her belongings, it was weird to see the osmosis of someone else's things into hers and starting to look as though they might take over.

Accidents had happened too in the process of amalgamation. Some of her plates had been broken, along with the bone china horse and foal that her parents had given her for her twelfth birthday as the mare closely resembled her best pony at the riding school she attended on a weekly basis, more often if allowed. Gideon had been profuse with his apologies and sworn that with a bit of glue here and there he could fix it and it would be like new but one look at the myriad of fragments was enough to diagnose that such a promise was unable to be fulfilled. With a sad sigh, Grace had swept up all the pieces and placed them in the rubbish bin.

As for the plates, replacing them was easy for they were a well-known brand, but wait a minute, Gideon had his and they were a particularly charming and discrete pattern and needed to be used, so why bother?

The much-beloved champagne flutes, however, were irreplaceable and Grace was gutted when she heard the crash after Gideon had disappeared into the kitchen with them one evening. More than slightly tipsy, he had been pretending to be a waiter and had flamboyantly balanced the tray on his outstretched hand. He promised to find her better ones, but that wasn't the point, she thought. Still, accidents do happen and it was not only her possessions that had suffered. Gideon told her he had lost some cufflinks and that one of his paintings had been slightly damaged.

The little grey clouds were quickly dispersed by the sunshine and joy of being a couple, of sharing each day – and night, eating together, talking and laughing together. It was fun to get up in the morning, scuttle around and shower, dress and eat toast simultaneously, kiss while they stood in the drive before heading off in their respective directions. Even more so it was wonderful to get home at night, either to find him already home or revel in the anticipation of his arrival.

In the short time that they had been cohabiting, Gideon had wasted no time in persuading Grace to spurn the aisles in the supermarket where the ready meals were temptingly arranged and spend more time with the fresh produce so that she was able to take her first tentative steps into the world of cookery. Eager to please him, rather than eager to learn, she had obliged. He promised to teach her and like all the things they did as a couple, there was no doubting it was fun. To date, disasters were rather in excess of successes, the former of which Gideon always seemed to be able to salvage and turn into something worth eating and the latter which he heaped with praise. It quickly became apparent that Gideon, who very much enjoyed his food, particularly liked rich, indulgent food and ingredients hitherto never seen in the fridge started to make an appearance – butter, cream and lots of alcohol.

On the evenings they were both finished late, they tended to meet in town and eat out, often expensively but deliciously and if Grace suggested that a snack such as beans on toast with cheese would be enough or a humble pizza accompanied by a glass or two of wine, then Gideon insisted that they needed to keep their strength up, eat properly as he called it and what better way to sit, dissect the events of the day and begin to unwind for the night.

Evenings at home were spent companionably in the house, usually in the same room, perhaps watching television but sometimes separately, working, studying, catching up but even these times Grace found blissful as the mere awareness of his presence in the house made her feel complete and secure.

Not surprisingly, Grace found her father's attitude disappointing. She had so hoped that he would be elated for her; no, for them. Under the impression that Gideon had charmed her father over the recent weeks, which indeed seemed to be the case, Douglas's comments left her feeling a little let down and rather annoyed. She tried to put herself into his place and decided that with all the uncertainty about Sylvia, no wonder he was unsettled and concerned. Maybe when she was home, life might resort to as normal as it ever got. There was a distinct chance that the addition of Gideon to the family circle might create a new dimension that would be beneficial for Sylvia. Just supposing, that Gideon did propose (and the thought of that left Grace breathless with longing) then it would definitely be good for

Sylvia to have something to concentrate on and organise with, of course, Grace's help and guidance to make sure she stayed on the right track.

She was having a wool day. Red wool skirt, pink twin set, matching thick tights, a scarf of the finest cerise wool and a black wool beret from under which her hair sprouted randomly. She seemed oblivious of the warmth of the ward and the fact that the first thing Grace and Douglas had done on arrival was to take their coats off.

Hugs were distributed all round.

'How are you, Mum?'

'Fine, thanks. I can't wait to come home.' She turned to Douglas. 'Is it this weekend?'

'It's very soon,' he promised. 'Just got to sort out your tablets and then you'll be given your marching orders.'

'Promise?'

'Of course, my darling. Now, Grace has something to tell you….'

Sylvia twisted around, her expression curious.

'Gideon's moving in with me.' Instantly Grace wished she had not been quite so matter of fact with her announcement. More tact had definitely been needed.

Grace expected her mother to clap her hands together with glee, rather in the manner of a baby who has just learned this manoeuvre but she didn't. If anything she looked sad and concerned.

'Are you sure about this?'

Grace nodded enthusiastically. 'Yes, he's a wonderful man, Mum.'

'I hope you're making the right decision. Don't rush into anything.' She grabbed her arm and squeezed. 'I had hoped that he'd come and see me. He hasn't been once.'

'He's busy, Mum. And he thinks visiting time is for families. Now, he's on a conference and not back until tomorrow. But I know this is the right thing to do.'

Sylvia looked deeply into her daughter's eyes, as if probing into her soul. 'Well, if that's the case, then I'm happy for you. You are our only child and what's most important is that you don't get hurt. Nobody is allowed to hurt my precious Grace.'

Douglas got up and paced around the room. He was longing to say how he felt but knew there was no way he could do so. Sylvia had taken the news in her stride and nothing must upset that. Her reaction had been quite natural, full of concern but no hyperbole and this must surely be a good omen. All he wanted was Sylvia back home with him, well. He was glad they had decided to swap her medication during this admission, even though this was one of the reasons her stay had been so protracted. He'd been wondering whether her previous drugs, unaltered for many years, were starting to be less effective at holding her moods steady. Now she seemed settled on the new regime, he was aware there were differences. Looking at the situation positively, which he had a remarkable capacity for doing, her mood seemed controlled and she was quiet and unstressed. Others reviewing her would make a different assessment and conclude that she was subdued, slowed down and her normal personality punctured beyond repair. Phillip had been careful to warn Douglas that there was a degree of trial and error with this swap but so far, all in all the signs were encouraging. The main objective was to prevent any episodes of mania or depression. The real test of course was still to come, when she got home and back into the real world as opposed to the very artificial ambience of the ward.

Douglas watched his wife like a hawk throughout their visit. Her reaction to Grace's revelation had taken him aback but he was pleased. It seemed a normal mother's reaction. Sylvia's concern was appropriate and contained, there was no rushing off at tangents, no delusional ideas and, amazingly, not even the mention of the word wedding. She even, off her own bat, brought up other subjects she wanted to know about, like home, Charnley and had her favourite magazine arrived yet. No doubt about it, her improvement was promising and sustained. Thank goodness for that. He took a risk, relaxed and began to enjoy what was left of visiting time.

'So you think she's ready to come home?' asked Grace as she and her father made their way back to the car park.

'Definitely. She needs to be home. Back to all her things, her usual routine.'

'I don't know, she's ...'Grace struggled for the right words, 'She's not Mum. I mean she is, of course, but it's like someone's taken out her batteries and forgotten to replace them.'

'Rubbish,' barked Douglas. 'She's weary, that's all. It must be hard to sleep on that ward. It's way too hot and noisy.' He fell silent for a second. 'You know, Grace, I really think that this time it's going to be different.'

'I do hope so,' Grace was careful to concur for she so wanted this to be the case. 'She didn't seem very happy about Gideon moving in.'

Douglas put his arm around his daughter and hugged her close. 'I expect it came as a shock. Let it sink in a bit. You wait and see, she'll be full of it next time we see her.'

It was growing dark as they headed for the car. Vehicles were reversing and turning in all directions as visitors began to wend homewards, leaving their loved ones for another night. They heard Charnley barking from the car, overjoyed to have heard their approaching voices. Douglas dropped Grace off at outside her house, before turning into his driveway.

'Come in for supper, Dad,' she offered, knowing full well that he would happily munch his way through the pre-prepared spaghetti bolognaise or cannelloni that she had bought in earlier.

'Thanks, but I'm bushed. I'm going to take Charnley out for a quick constitutional around the block then pull up the drawbridge and have two poached eggs on toast with a very large glass of whisky.'

'If you're sure...'

He smiled affectionately at his only child. 'I'm certain. I'm so excited by how well our visit went that I want to make the most of it. I'll sleep like a top once I've caught up with my favourite programme and watched the late-night news. You take care and I'll see you tomorrow. Oh, and Grace? I hope it works out for you and Gideon. But take your time, OK?'

He blew her a kiss as she climbed out and ran to her door, waving as she did so, pleased by his final words. It seemed odd, even after such a short time of co-habiting, to go into a dark house and know that she was to be on her own. Gideon would ring later, he had promised, and until then she too felt like celebrating, in her case with a hot bath, glass of chilled white wine and hot pasta, steaming from the microwave. Her culinary skills and interest needed to develop considerably before she was at a stage where she would bother to start from scratch just for herself. Dessert was mint choc chip ice cream and she ate curled up in the big armchair, catching up with the soaps that Gideon didn't exactly frown on but made it quite clear that he had no time for.

When the telephone did ring, there was no one there. Grace

dialled call back but it was a withheld number. Obviously a mistake on someone's part and all the more infuriating when it happened again and then a third time, half an hour later. She tried ringing Gideon on his mobile but it was switched off. He had warned her that there was an evening lecture session and a buffet supper afterwards, so it was better if he called her rather than vice versa.

It was getting late though now and Grace's thoughts were turning to bed and sleep. A full day's work lay ahead of her the next day, two long surgeries and doubtless half a dozen house calls. Wondering why he hadn't rung, fretting, she went upstairs with both the house phone and her mobile, ready for whichever way he chose to contact her. The house phone rang again and she answered it eagerly, knowing that this time it would be him.

'Hi, Gideon?'

Nobody there. Was that breathing she could hear or a bad line?

'Hello? Is anyone there? Gideon, is that you? I can't hear you.'

The line went dead. Reaching for the novel on her bedside table, she snuggled down under the duvet, missing Gideon and trying to find the scent of his aftershave on the pillowcase. She began to read, soon immersed in the storyline.

She jumped out of her skin when a stone hit the window and then the doorbell rang – a repeated ding-dong with a sense of urgency about it. Heart thumping, her first thought was that it must be her father and something was wrong. Was he ill? Had he heard bad news from the hospital? Not stopping to think that his most likely action would have been to telephone, she threw off the covers, ran back downstairs and pulled back the locks. A blast of cold air claimed her breath as she pulled open the door. She stood, shivering in her thin pyjamas, teeth chattering uncontrollably.

There was no one there.

Across the road her parents' house was in darkness, incontrovertible evidence that Douglas was sound asleep and likely snoring loudly after his hypnotic of best single malt. The street was noiseless and still. Only a few of the streetlights were alight, one of the new cutbacks from the local council. A tabby cat trotted silently across the next-door lawn, eyes momentarily green in the glow from Grace's hall. Now she was afraid and her eyes darted this way and that, trying to make sense of what they saw in the semi-darkness, trying to interpret shadows and subtle movements of leaves on bushes and trees as she took in all around her.

Nobody.

Flustered, Grace pushed the door shut and carefully fastened all the locks and double checked them.

Children, it had to be kids playing a joke. Or someone who mistook her house for another and was too embarrassed to own up to it. Perhaps they'd been drunk and had staggered up the wrong drive before realising their mistake. That made sense, it had to.

A sudden panic hit her and Grace ran through to the back door and double checked those locks as well. Goodness, she felt so unnerved. A warm drink was the answer to soothe her frazzled nerves, so she heated some milk and concocted a rich, thick hot chocolate. Reluctant to go back to bed, she stayed in the lounge, all the lights on, the television turned up loudly, giving out as many signs of life as possible to ward off strangers in the night.

Gideon finally rang just after midnight. Whatever had been on the menu to eat at the buffet supper had evidently been complemented by a generous supply of wine.

'I love you, Grace and I'm missing you desperately,' he declared in a slurred voice punctuated by hiccups. Her spirits soared.

He had never before actually told Grace that he loved her and ideally she would have preferred that the first time the three magic words were uttered were not under the influence of alcohol. But, the fact that he had said them was more than enough to make her feel wonderful. Her plans to tell him of her experiences that night seemed unimportant and silly now, so she kept quiet, preferring to bask in his adoring words.

He loved her and that was all that mattered.

Chapter Ten

'What a miserable day!' Janey, Harry and Grace were having coffee and dividing up the house calls. Outside the rain had teemed down relentlessly since they had awoken and even though it was only mid-morning, it was clear that it was going to be one of those soupy grey days that fail to get light properly. The gloominess of the weather had transferred to the patients and demand to be seen was unprecedented. Moods were low, spirits flagging and that was just the doctors.

Janey opened up a cake tin and handed round generously sized slices of Millionaire's shortbread.

'I saw the forecast last night after the news and thought these might cheer us up.'

'You made these late last night?' Grace was incredulous. 'It must have taken you ages.'

'Of course,' was the mumbled reply as Janey's mouth was full. 'It was simple.' To her, any time of day was the right time to cook or eat cake.

'Well, thank you. It looks delicious.'

Grace paused to wonder if she might ever be able to emulate such domesticity and concluded that probably not. Try as she might, it was impossible to conjure up the vision of her in an apron, with a mixing bowl cradled in the crook of one arm and wooden spoon in the other hand.

'Harry, do you want to share a piece, they're quite large?'

Harry's heart skipped a beat at the thought of sharing something with Grace. He nodded eagerly; his exaggerated movement making the light blue mice on his navy tie appear to jump up and down. He carefully accepted a chunk of cake, strands of caramel looping from beneath the chocolate topping.

Janey swallowed hard. 'So, let's get down to business. Andrew's doing an extra surgery to try to cope with all the extras who think they must be seen today. Bless him but one of us had to do it. Why don't we divide the calls up geographically to make it as easy as possible? I know that means we might not see some patients who have specifically requested a particular doctor if possible but looking at them, it doesn't make sense.'

'Good plan,' agreed Harry. He grimaced. 'Especially when we've all agreed to start early this afternoon. Why are there so many?'

'It's always the same. This rain makes everyone grumpy and fed up.'

She licked the last of the caramel off her fingers, toyed wistfully with the idea of a second wedge but replaced the lid firmly.

'We'll save that for when we get back. Something to look forward to.'

Grace felt about as dismal as the outlook that greeted her as she left the building, splashing her way across the puddles to her car and wishing that she'd put on some more suitable shoes. Resignedly, she set off to her first call. The only way to get them finished was to make a start; wishing they didn't exist wouldn't achieve anything other than make her feel even more irritated by her own negativity.

An elderly couple with chest infections, a diabetic with a nastily infected leg ulcer, a child with diarrhoea and vomiting who showed no signs of being unwell whatsoever saw her halfway through her mission. At the bizarrely named Serendipity Nursing home, a new patient had arrived and wanted to meet the doctor to talk about medications, another resident had a possible urinary infection and a third was feeling melancholy.

That makes two of us, thought Grace, nevertheless smiling away, emitting reassuring words and writing a prescription for antidepressants.

Just one more to go and her stomach was rumbling badly despite the substantial elevenses. The call sounded simple, which was why she'd left it until last, plus it was furthest away, down a long undulating country lane peppered with pot holes to one of the many converted barns in the area. The front door was ajar, as promised. In the circular hall, Grace called out to announce her presence and followed the answering voice up the wide staircase and into a vast bedroom, decorated in candy pink and white. The occupant of the four poster bed, Mrs Gwendoline Foyle, was half hidden by open magazines, frilly cushions and three Pekinese dogs which yapped and growled wildly, giving Grace a good view of their yellowing teeth. Beside her on the pristine carpet lay the tell-tale washing up bowl. She dramatically gesticulated to Grace to come nearer.

'About time! It's my bloody gallstones again! Just give me some pain relief and I'll be fine.'

The speaker was a squat female in her mid fifties with a hairstyle and facial features, including the prognathous jaw, that matched her dogs. All four of them even had tiny pink bows in their fringes.

'Shush, Teeny and Tiny. Quiet, Peeky. This nice lady's come to help Mummy.'

Marvelling at the unoriginality of the dogs' names, Grace affixed another friendly smile on her face, cooed a few noises at the animals and set about taking a history and making the appropriate examination, which had to be conducted largely through the flimsy negligee that Mrs Foyle's corpulent body was swaddled in and around the nosy dogs who, taking the role of guardians very seriously, refused to allow her unrestricted access to their mistress. Mercifully, gallstones indeed seemed to be the problem and the previous history of identical episodes added weight to her diagnosis.

'I usually have an injection and that settles me down. It's my fault entirely. I knew this would happen after I was stupid enough to have lobster Thermidor last night for supper and then, because it was my husband's birthday, I'd done a steamed jam sponge and custard for him. Could I resist having some? No. It was delicious and I had two helpings, so now I have to pay the price for my greed. Normally I can prevent any symptoms by sticking to a low-fat diet. And don't even mention surgery. I can see that you were about to. No way do I want an operation. Peeky's mother went into hospital to have an operation and died. Fit as a trout, she was when she went in. Dead as a dodo two days later. The same would happen to me. I know it would. I'm very like her.'

Grace opened her mouth to speak.

'No, don't even bother to start! Your lot have all done it before and you're not going to change my mind. I usually see Dr Janey and she understands.'

'Well, at the end of the day, it's your choice,' Grace agreed, 'so I'll get you something for the pain right away. If it doesn't work as it usually does, you must ring back and then we'll need to reassess you.'

'It'll work.' Mrs Foyle and her dogs growled in harmony.

Grace opened her bag and found a syringe and needle, which she pulled from their packaging and assembled. In the lid of her bag were her drugs for emergencies, a neat row of tiny vials containing treatments for heart failure, heart attacks, severe pain, vomiting, allergic reaction and anxiety. She was a stickler for organisation and liked to have them in alphabetical order. Pulling out a vial she checked its contents only to find that it was not what she needed. Nor was the one next to it. Bemused she studied them all. For some reason their arrangement was haphazard which was weird enough but the painkillers had disappeared completely.

What? Why? Last week she had given her bag to Leah, the practice nurse, as she did every three months, so that it could be checked thoroughly, items replaced, out-of-date drugs thrown away and replenished but this had never happened before. Leah was efficient and reliable. She had been at the practice for years, knew well how Grace liked her bag to be precise and had never failed to return it restored to perfection before. Perhaps she had delegated the job to one of the other practice nurses this time who was less experienced. Grace made a mental note to have a word on her return.

That, however, did not resolve the situation she found herself in at that moment. What was she going to do? Try as she might and her rummaging became more frenetic, she knew that she was not going to find what she needed. Mrs Foyle's large black eyes were following her every move. In desperation, it briefly occurred to her that she pretend to be giving the correct drug but in fact give water and hope for a placebo effect. A non-starter.

Honesty was the only way forward.

'I'm sorry,' she started, 'I don't seem to have any painkilling injections. I must have used up the last one and forgotten to replace it. I'm so, so sorry.'

'Well, that's useless of you, if you don't mind me saying. Here I am in agony and you can't do anything to help. I knew I should have insisted that Dr Janey came to see me. She's always well prepared and she likes the puppies.' Cue much stroking of the dogs.

'I can only apologise profusely and I'll get some as soon as I can. Let me make a phone call or two.'

More embarrassed that she had been for a long time, Grace moved over to the window, ostensibly to get a better signal on her mobile but really to get away from Mrs Foyle. She had two options. One, go back to the surgery and pick up the drugs and come back; two, phone Janey and Harry and see if, by chance, they were anywhere nearby so that they could come and bail her out.

Janey's phone went straight to voice mail, but Harry picked up immediately, recognising the number.

'Hi, Grace. Everything ok?'

'No, something awful's happened,' whispered Grace, rapidly telling him of the problem.

'No worries, I'm on my way. I'm about five minutes from you. Don't panic. It can easily happen. It did to me once…' he tried to reassure her but Grace was unconvinced. It might happen to Harry but it did not happen to her.

In reality Harry was back at the surgery, drying out and writing up his notes. Ever ready to help a damsel in distress, especially one called Grace, he pushed his half-eaten ham sandwich back into the bag and left his much-needed cup of tea to go cold. Opportunities to come to her rescue did not come along frequently. Without collecting his coat – it was soaking wet anyway, so of little use – he ran out into the rain, leapt into his car and ignored all the speed limits to meet Grace on the front doorstep exactly eight minutes later.

'I can't thank you enough, Harry. You've really saved my bacon here. I just don't know how this could have happened.'

'Go and sort out Mrs Foyle and we'll talk about it when you get back. She'll be fine once she's had her injection. I've met her before and that's all she wants. Why she doesn't just get rid of her gall bladder once and for all beats me but I know she has all manner of reasons why not.'

'See you later, Harry. And, thanks again. I owe you one.'

Harry glowed. He really wanted to hug her. He hated seeing her looking upset, her usually pretty face pinched by worry. She needed someone like him to look after her. On the verge of speaking, he watched forlornly as she ran back in and up the stairs.

Grace deftly administered the injection. 'There, that'll soon start working and you'll feel better. I am so sorry about the delay.'

Mrs Foyle, appeased now that she was in receipt of her main objective, was looking much more relaxed, one dog tucked under each arm, the third curled up on the pillow beside her head. With a flourish, she dismissed Grace and as she took her leave, Grace had to admit that there was such an uncanny resemblance in all four faces that it was hard to tell which was which.

Leah was in the treatment room, clearing up at the end of the day. Her long grey hair had partly escaped from her slide and she was repeatedly curling it behind her ears while she worked. Unlike many of the practice staff, she had stood the test of time and stayed with them for many years. She loved the job and had grown with it, relishing the challenge of teaching the junior nurses and taking on more responsibility. Hers was a tight ship and nobody was allowed to upset that.

Nearly home time and what a relief. Her back ached after bending down to renew a difficult dressing, made even harder because the patient kept moving and her head ached from listening to a succession of other patients confessing their woes. The weekend finally loomed large and she was so excited. Her husband was whisking her off to visit their son and daughter-in-law plus the beautiful new twin girls. She couldn't wait to see them for the first time, cuddle them close and breathe in that unmistakable baby aroma. Bethany and Cicely. Such pretty names. Unusual but not too off the wall like some of the children registered at the practice.

Grace knocked on the door and marched in, not waiting for an answer.

'Hello, Grace! What can I do for you?' She arched her back, rubbing it as she did so.

'The drugs in my bag, Leah. What did you do last week? They were all out of order and there were no painkillers.'

Leah shook her head. 'Everything was fine when I handed it back to you. As I always do. I know just how you like it.'

'But it was all wrong,' Grace persisted.

Leah's hackles started to stir. 'Well, that's nothing to do with me, Grace. I assure you that when you took your bag from me last Tuesday, its contents were as you like them to be. Have I ever made a mistake before?'

Grace had to admit that she hadn't. 'Well, I'm baffled then. I'm sorry to accuse you, Leah, but I cannot understand what's been going on. It was so awkward, there in front of the patient.

Luckily Harry was nearby and helped me out.'

'I'll check with the others, Grace, but I'm sure neither Liz nor Cathy has touched your bag. They've enough work on as it is plus they know it's my job.'

There was nothing more she could do and Grace returned to her room, opened up her bag again and carefully positioned all the contents exactly as she liked them. Luckily no one had come to any harm which was the most important aspect, she supposed, but it was all decidedly odd.

Putting her concern to one side, she tried to make a start on some referral letters that really had to go out in the post that evening. Her heart was not in it. She sighed and fiddled with pens on her desk and pretended to tidy some envelopes. How she hated not having explanations.

A knock on the door preceded Harry's friendly face peering around it. 'Bad day eh? You look exhausted. Fancy a quick drink on the way home?'

Grace knew that Gideon was going to be late. He always was on clinic days, which meant that she would return to an empty house and in addition it was supposed to be her turn to cook. She did not want to be on her own any more than she wanted to dice onions and peppers into impossibly small chunks. A far better idea was to accept Harry's offer and then text Gideon to let him know which pub they were in and invite him to join them when he had finished.

'That'd be lovely, Harry, thanks. Give me a few minutes to finish off here. Shall I meet you there? The usual place?'

'Sure – the Dog and Gun. I'll get the first round in. White wine?'

'Perfect,' agreed Grace.

'I'll make it a large one. I think you need it!'

Harry had Grace all to himself for over an hour before Gideon burst in and sat down with them. He listened empathically to Grace going over her day, only too aware of her perfectionist streak when it came to work and her inability to cope when anything stood in the way of this. While he was able to make her laugh with stories of his own mishaps (most of which were either embroidered or totally fictitious just to make her feel better) he knew that she was still worried and upset.

He was pretending that they were not in the lounge bar but the sitting room of their house, that their two children were upstairs sleeping like angels, their Labrador (or would it be two, one yellow, one black?) were flaked out on the rug in front of the fire and that it was only a matter of time before they would put out the lights, lock the doors and go up together to bed.

His reverie of romanticism was popped like a balloon colliding with a pin when Gideon appeared, raindrops glistening in his hair, coat collar turned up against the still dreadful weather. His heart sank as he saw the change in Grace's features. It was though she had been switched on. Her smile was radiant, her eyes bright and adoring as she turned her face up to be kissed. Harry's joy dissipated in a second. With immediate effect he felt he had been relegated to the bottom of the pile. How could he ever compete with, let alone beat, someone this good looking, articulate and intelligent who exerted such an effect on Grace?

Gideon gave Grace a perfunctory peck on the cheek and shook Harry by the hand. A rather watery handshake, Harry thought, not that befitting a real man, such as he! He asked for a gin and tonic. Harry laughed inwardly. A girl's drink. Any proper bloke would take advantage of the local ale. And how could he possibly not envelop the fabulous Grace in a full-blown hug and lip-smacking kiss? To hell with the fact they were in public.

If Grace were his, Harry knew how proud he would be and how he would want the whole universe to know and share in his happiness. Maybe after all, there were chinks in Gideon's armour.

Definitely encouraged by these irrefutable signs that the man was not the shining example he originally thought, Harry lifted his pint glass and took a long, manly draft.

Chapter Eleven

With something less than a flourish, a subdued Sylvia came home, finally discharged after two trial home visits that had been deemed to be successful, even though she had spent most of the time sitting in front of the television. Douglas, elated, did his best to have the house looking as spotless as possible. He enrolled Grace's help and together they beavered away until it was time to leave to pick Sylvia up, proud of their hard work but knowing that, most likely, they had failed to reach her high standards.

Fortunately, if she did notice, she refrained from comment. She allowed Douglas to open the door for her, bent down to scoop Charnley up into her arms and squeezed him so tightly that he yelped.

'I never thought I'd see my home again,' she gulped into Charnley's neck dramatically while the little dog licked her face rapturously.

'Come on, Mum, let's go and sit down. The kettle's on. I know we need a cup of tea and I'm sure you're ready for one. You can unpack your clothes any time.'

'Oh, please. I'm really thirsty. Are there any biscuits? I'm so hungry. Your dad looks as if he's lost weight. I'd better start feeding him up.'

'I'll be fine, now I've got you back. You know I've never been one for eating much on my own.' Douglas planted a smacking kiss on her cheek, hoping that neither his wife nor daughter noticed him wiping away a tear of joy.

He forced the tiny voice that was whispering 'Here we go again' to the furthest recesses of his brain, determined to concentrate on the present.

One day at a time.

It was so wonderful to have Sylvia back. He had convinced himself that she looked well. There was no denying that the new medication was continuing to control her moods. For weeks there had been not so much as a hint of elaborate ideas, delusional thoughts or flights of fancy. Nor, mercifully had they noticed any suggestion of nihilism, anhedonia or negativity.

Everything, however, comes at a price and, whilst Douglas might be unaware, Sylvia knew full well of how she had to pay. The longer she had been on this new cocktail of drugs the worse it seemed to get. Weight had piled on as her appetite became extraordinary. No amount of food satisfied her. She craved it to a degree that was pathological. What was left of her waist had long disappeared, replaced by a roll of undesirable, doughy fat, like a life belt around her middle. It wobbled uncomfortably and made it impossible to do up any of her blouses or skirts. Her legs looked, to her, elephantine, her ankles were swollen and her bloated feet would not fit into her shoes. She had even been forced to cut the top of her slippers so make more room. For someone who had always taken pride in her appearance, even if it had on more than several occasions been beyond exotic, such bodily changes were anathema to her.

Maybe she would learn to live with her new shape in time

but she doubted that she would ever learn to live with the numbing of her thoughts, where nothing was entirely coherent and everything seemed indistinct. She felt automated, unreal, stifled. It was as though as soon as a thought began it was snatched away from her, before it could develop and lead to another one. Making decisions was horrendous. Logic had been taken over by horrible feelings of being drugged and her soul had been leeched of all personality. All she seemed to do was sleep, get up, eat, nod off in a chair, eat and go to bed. Little interested her. Her powers of concentration were blunted. Half an hour of television – if she stayed awake that long – was more than she wanted to cope with and reading a book, even a light, fluffy novel, was hopeless as even if she did reach the end of the first chapter, she was confused about which character was which and what was happening.

However delighted Douglas and Grace were with her progress, Sylvia was unable to join in their celebrations. This wasn't her. She struggled to remember the past but little images spontaneously flashed into her mind, only momentarily but long enough for her to yearn to be the way she had been, when she had been allowed to feel, think, laugh, and emote.

Still, she was so glad to be home and to have all her possessions around her. Never in a million years would anyone realise how much she hated that ward, the weird characters that haunted the corridors and came into her room uninvited, the cacophony of voices, the mixed-up smells of bodies, cooking, illness and – ugh – the food. She shivered reflexively.

To observe her homecoming, she was wearing a new but shapeless dress, striped in red and gold, which had become very creased from sitting in the car, accessorised with a collection of necklaces and bangles. The only clues that she had just been discharged from hospital were the identity bracelet around her left wrist and the slippers on her feet. They belonged to someone else. Still clutching a now wriggly Charnley she flopped onto the settee with a sigh of relief. The dog jumped down and Douglas was quick to take over the space beside her and put his arm around her shoulders.

'Home sweet home, eh? It's so good to have you back, my darling. Ah, here's Grace with the tea.'

Grace watched her mother's hand shaking as she reached for the proffered cup, which then rattled around in the saucer. She hurried through to the kitchen and came back with a mug.

'Here. This'll be easier for you. And it's bigger so you can have a larger drink.'

'Thank you, dear. My tablets give me such a dry mouth. Are there any more biscuits? These seem to have been finished.'

She seemed unaware of the chocolate around her mouth and the crumbs on her chest.

'I'll get some, Mum.'

Douglas, determined to be cheerful, chortled. 'Didn't they feed you in hospital?'

'Yes, the food was lovely,' Sylvia lied, simply. She slurped her tea noisily. 'Ugh, there's no sugar!'

'You don't take sugar, Mum,' Grace reminded her.

'I do now. Two lumps please.'

Between them they did their best, forced jolly conversation about inanities, silly tales of what Charnley had done on a walk, how Douglas was wondering if they should get some decorating done, brighten the house up a little bit, maybe even get some new furniture but nothing, not even the mention of Gideon, produced anything resembling a sparkle from Sylvia. Her replies were polite, dutiful and largely monosyllabic. Never once did she volunteer any information or ask about anything other than where the biscuits were and what was for tea. Emptying her mug with one last gulp, Sylvia leaned back in her chair and within seconds her chin was lolling on her chest and she was snoring loudly.

'She's exhausted, poor love,' exclaimed Douglas. 'Thank goodness she's able to sleep. I bet she was awake all last night with excitement. Don't worry, Grace. She'll be a bit better tomorrow and even better the day after. It's a huge change for her to come home, even though she's had a couple of practice runs. She's probably really nervous in case something goes wrong.'

'But she seems so different, Dad,' Grace murmured. 'Sort of flat. Deflated. Hollow.'

'It's fine, just fine. Phillip said they'd had to increase the dose of her drugs last week as a precaution, so she's most likely getting used to that. I've told you, don't worry, love.'

Grace returned to the kitchen to wash up. She'd seen her mother in more states of emotion than she cared to remember over the years, up, down, happy, sad, feral, verging on catatonic but never like this and this was how it was intended that she would stay.

A vestige of her real self, a parody of a human being.

It was nothing short of tragic.

At Grace's behest, Harry popped in to see Sylvia a few days later, ostensibly to check how she was settling in. Douglas, having shown Harry into the sitting room, tactfully took his leave, saying that he was going to brush Charnley, who was filthy after digging down a rabbit hole in the woods.

She seemed pleased to see him. Memories of their last meeting had been completely eradicated and she held out both hands to him and clutched them warmly, before turning back to her monotonous dusting of the photographs.

'So, how are you?' asked Harry, taking off his tweed jacket, as it was so warm in the room. He carefully tucked his tie, dark grey with lighter grey cats and kittens, into his belt.

Sylvia carefully pushed her yellow duster into the corners of a frame, contemplating her reply. 'Look at this one,' she waved the photo at Harry, 'it's Grace's first day at school! Look at those cute little socks with frills and that huge blazer which comes down to her knees. You can barely see her hands, the sleeves are so long. That great big bag was full of her teddies.'

Harry thought that Grace looked adorable, even at the tender age of five.

'And here she is when she passed her first piano exam. She hated those lessons, I'm afraid.' Sylvia moved round the room, pointing as she did so. 'This is her first day at secondary school, this, her first school disco. Just look at that dress! How short is that? This one is her first red rosette at the local show. Willow was the pony's name. Doesn't she look proud?'

'Indeed,' agreed Harry. 'Chuffed to bits.'

'That one over there, is her graduation. The official photo of course, in her gown and mortar board. The one next to it is her being silly with her friends. They all look so happy.'

She looked at Harry wistfully. 'I missed every one of these events, Harry. Can you believe it? For each of these and many more, I was in hospital, ill. Douglas took all these photos and brought them to me, so that I could feel as far as possible that I was part of it. But it was never enough. I wasn't there for her when I should've been. What sort of mother does that make me?'

'Sylvia, you've always done your best. Look how Grace has turned out. She's a credit to you – beautiful, clever...' He stopped abruptly not wanting to give his feelings away. 'Regardless of how you've been, your love for her has known no bounds and Grace knows that. You didn't ask to be bipolar.'

'No, I didn't. Harry, please will you speak to Phillip for me about this medication? I hate it so much. I can more or less cope with the dry mouth, shaking hands and constipation but I've turned into a giant suet pudding and I feel so detached from real life. It's as though I'm wandering around in a dream where there's fog all around me. My feelings aren't working. I can know I'm sad but can't even cry, and when someone says something funny, I can't laugh. At least with the other drugs, I had the energy to do things and the clarity to think for myself. All I do now is sleep, get fatter and sit like a huge fatty blob that's neither use nor ornament.'

'That's grim, Sylvia. I can't imagine what that must be like. But there must be some positives?'

'Such as?' She tilted her head to one side, challenging him to come up with one.

'Well,' he thought quickly, 'the new drugs have got you well enough to come home. You're sleeping well at night...' He was running out of ideas.

'See what I mean?' Sylvia commented. 'I think you'll agree that those couple of things are far outweighed by the negatives ones. I know I wasn't brilliant with the last drugs but at least I could feel. If I really have to stay on this drug, how about reducing the dose? Please, Harry, will you speak to him for me?'

'Of course I will. I'll try to explain how you're feeling. When is your out-patient appointment?'

'I can't remember. Not long. Douglas will have written it down on the calendar, like he always does. I'd be lost without him.'

'I'll ring him today,' Harry promised.

'Thank you, so much,' breathed Sylvia. 'I feel I've someone on my side, when I talk to you.'

'You know I'll do whatever I can for you. Shall I give Douglas a call when I've had a word with Phillip?'

Sylvia's eyes darted towards the closed door. 'No, no, don't say anything to him. I don't want to worry him. It's been so terrible for him recently, I want to spare him any more stress than I have to.'

'As you wish. I'll call in tomorrow then, all being well.'

'You're a good man, Harry. You care. I can see that and I thank you from the bottom of my heart. Oh, I think I can hear Charnley so Douglas won't be far behind. Tell me how my lovely Grace is getting on at work.'

Harry drew in a large breath. Where to start?

'She's doing splendidly well. Her patients love her, she works hard, she's committed to the practice and I love working with her. What more can I say?'

Sylvia looked pleased. Her face relaxed and she smiled. 'She's so like her father. He used to work every hour of the day and night sometimes. So devoted to his job and yet he still found time for me. What a remarkable pair they are.'

Sensing the possibility of an ally, Harry ventured, 'Does Grace seem happy to you?'

Sylvia pondered and moved on to another photo frame to dust. 'I think so. She's got quite a nice boyfriend at the moment. Gideon, he's called. Have you met him?'

Harry ground his back teeth and grimaced in what he hoped looked like a charming smile. 'Yes, I have. He seems like an all-round nice chap.'

'Good. That's good to hear. I do worry about her. I'd love to see her settled down but it has to be with someone who's right for her.'

Harry nodded, in total agreement.

'Someone like you, really. You'd be so good for her.'

Chapter Twelve

'Thanks, Grace.' Harry handed over the cat carrier to her, poking his finger in between the bars to stroke Thadeus's' nose one last time. 'You be good and don't scratch the furniture like you did last time,' he addressed the cat.

'It's a pleasure, you know it is. He's always very good. I expect he'll be a bit miffed that Gideon is now on the side of the bed that he likes.' Grace laughed and Harry chose to ignore her. He preferred not to think about such things.

'I'll be back on Sunday. Just popping over to the east coast to see some friends. I'll ring tomorrow to make sure all's well.'

'He'll be fine, Harry. You enjoy yourself. You never seem to go away much.'

'I'm happy at home,' he replied, simply. 'By the way, how's your mother with that slightly lower dose of medication?'

'Much the same though a bit less sleepy during the day. She still doesn't have much motivation to do anything. And she's still eating for England. But don't even think about her for the weekend. Concentrate on enjoying yourself.'

Spontaneously, she leant forward and gave him a quick hug but had released him before he had time to reciprocate. Joy exploded in his chest.

'Thank you for all you do for mum, Harry. I know it's not easy looking after friends' relatives.'

'My pleasure. Well, I'd best be off. I promised I'd be there in time for dinner. See you Sunday!'

She waved him off from the door before closing it and then releasing a rather cross Thadeus who stomped his way across the hall, indignant tail held vertically, and promptly vomited on the carpet.

'Thadeus!'

Grace knew he was not a good traveller but usually it didn't have this effect. Sighing, she went in search of a mop and bucket.

She was not having a good day. Come to think of it, she wasn't having a good week, or even fortnight. Since Sylvia had come home, there had been a catalogue of minor irritations, one after the other. Stupid things, which when viewed in isolation seemed laughable but in conjunction led to a rather nasty feeling of being ill at ease and an undercurrent of concern about whatever was going to happen next. Trying to explain how she felt to Gideon had not been helpful. He hadn't taken her as seriously as she felt he ought to have done. To begin with, she'd had to shout to get his attention and then he'd barely even looked up from the journal he was reading.

Everybody has bad days, that's life, he had told her, dismissively, when she had tried to have a discussion with him. He had them all the time but never bothered to over analyse them and Grace would do well to do the same. She would do well to concentrate on the good days instead. Grace supposed that he was trying to be reassuring in his little way and he perhaps he was right, perhaps she was making a range of mountains out of a field full of molehills but his rather flippant comments failed this time to make her feel any better.

Sitting on her own, that evening, waiting for him to come home, she at last had the opportunity to make sense of all that had happened by writing a list. She liked lists. Like her mother did. Not just shopping lists and what to buy people for Christmas. Lists had always helped her organise her life, home and work. Seeing what needed to be done in black and white focussed her mind and there was a delightful sense of satisfaction when items that had been completed were scored out. Lists also helped her sort her thoughts out, prioritise, banish needless worries and make sense of muddle. They helped her sort out difficult patients too; it all made so much more sense when she could see it in front of her, a map of symptoms, test results, chronologically arranged and as a result her diary, which was too big to fit into any of her bags, was crammed with her tiny handwriting on more or less every day.

To one side was a glass of red wine and a pile of cheese on toast, splattered with plenty of brown sauce on the top. To the other, Thadeus, remarkably recovered from his earlier incident, was curled up on the arm of her chair, purring softly. He was a large ginger cat, with a white splash above his nose, which made him look as if he had just had a drink of milk.

The curtains were closed, the heating on and the television played quietly in the background, more for company than entertainment. Outside, winter had really taken a grip, strong winds were whipping the trees from side to side and the temperature had plummeted over the last few days. The house was creaking and next door's gate, which was unlatched and hanging off one hinge, kept banging against the wall of her house, making her jump.

Gideon was eating out, at some neurological society do. He was presenting a paper and had been preparing for days which meant that he had been spending nearly all of every evening in the spare room, which he had commandeered for his study, suggesting to Grace that it would be nicer for her to do her work downstairs where it was warmer.

The cheese on toast was delicious. Her out-and-out favourite since a child. Simple, hot but tasty. She crunched her way through the first half slice hungrily and then concentrated her thoughts. Right, so what had been happening?

There were the lost house keys. A creature of habit, she always hung them up on a hook by the coat stand. It was a habit, a ritual even that she did before taking off her coat. Their place was next to the spare car keys, which were next to the garage door key and the key to her parents' house. The other morning they had not been there and Gideon swore that he'd not seen them. They still hadn't turned up, despite her turning the house, her car and her consulting room upside down.

On going to empty the washing machine, as the door opened a projectile of dirty water spouted onto her feet, ruining her slippers. The kitchen floor was awash before she was able to think of closing the door or reaching for a towel and took forever to mop dry and then, even worse, she was left with a sodden heap of half-washed laundry that she had to finish by hand. And what a job that had been. Wrestling with a king-size duvet cover and being comprehensively conquered by it had ended up revisiting her student days and heading for the local launderette where at least she could spin and partly dry everything before draping it all around the house, much to Gideon's annoyance.

Somehow the back kitchen window had been broken. No big problem as Douglas had trotted across the road and fixed it while she was at work but the fact remained that she didn't know why it had happened. Like most people Grace liked logical explanations. It was the unknown that frightened her for this supplied her fertile imagination with the chance to run amok and conjure up often ridiculous scenarios that poured fuel onto her ability to worry. Douglas suggested that the pane of glass had been loose anyway, from all the slamming of the back door and perhaps a sudden gust of wind was all that it had taken to produce the final crack. It was a solution, Grace supposed, but not one that felt right.

She sucked the end of her pen, thinking. There had been more weird phone calls. Silence greeted her when she picked up the receiver. It had happened that evening already but also a couple of nights ago when Gideon had answered. He had shouted angrily down the phone, subjecting whoever was at the other end of the line to a vituperative string of obscenities and Grace had hoped that such an action coupled with a man's voice might put an end to the calls but sadly not. He was confident, however, that whoever it was would soon get fed up and stop, probably opting for a different, more vulnerable target.

She had mislaid a bracelet. Nothing expensive, in fact quite the opposite. A cheap piece of jewellery picked up in a craft shop in the Dales on a day out but it was entrancingly pretty with tiny clear hexagonal stones that reflected spectra of light in all directions. Grace wore it most days, only taking it off at bedtimes and if she was doing some procedure or other at work, for example removing a toenail or incising a juicy boil. Again, Gideon had been less than sympathetic. Such a trifle was replaced in a trice and he promised to replace it with something more expensive. The money wasn't the point though, Grace knew. It was a possession that she loved largely for its simplicity and to her it was irreplaceable. She wondered if she had literally worn it out and the string had snapped when she hadn't noticed.

It could be anywhere, shame really.

Today, there had been that peculiar house call. A request from a woman, staying temporarily in the area with acute low back pain, so bad that she was unable to move off the floor. The caller had stated that she was the mother of a two year old who was screaming in its cot and there was no way she was going to be able to reach it. Harry was still seeing his last patient, so Grace had rushed to the address, only to find that while numbers one to fifty-four Canterbury Lane existed, number sixty-one was nowhere to be found and the phone number was said to be unobtainable. Puzzled she had returned to the practice and told the others what had happened. There was nothing else that they could do but wait and see, which they did and they had heard nothing more.

Reading back her list out loud to Thadeus, she realised that it looked pathetic. Gideon was right. She was over-reacting. It was nothing more than a run of bad luck and people who thought it was funny to make hoax calls to doctors deserved to be shot at dawn. There were far more important things in life. Work had been grim of late. Amber had been off sick, which meant that they had to divide her workload up between them. Grace had been leaving her house early, getting home late and then calling in on her parents to see that all was well before she finally made it through her own front door. Sometimes there had been no time for anything other than a quick snack, hot drink and then bath and bed. Whichever way she looked there was stress, at work, with her mother and with her father who was as usual trying to convince her that all was well. Trying to juggle too many balls at once, that was how Sylvia referred to it. She knew it wasn't a good idea. She'd tried before and it had invariably been a disaster. Foolishly, she had thought, with the comforting presence of Gideon in the background, she would be a better juggler. Obviously not. And of course he was busy too. His clinics were full to bursting, there was more than enough work for one consultant and he was trying desperately hard to keep up with his research in what little spare time he had. It was selfish of her to expect him to pander to her silly whims and ideas.

With a few deft strokes of her Biro, she scribbled through all she had written, snapped her diary shut and turned the volume up on the television, ready to watch a comedy programme which she knew always made her laugh. Placing the plate of remaining cheese on toast on her lap and sipping on her wine, she settled down to try to forget all her troubles, glad for Thadeus's' company. Stroking his soft fur was definitely soothing. The telephone rang and she ignored it, secretly rather proud of herself.

Gideon was home a little earlier than expected and Grace was pleased to hear the sound of his key in the lock. He looked frozen to the core, his wool overcoat buttoned up tight, his red nose peeping over the fawn scarf that was wrapped around his neck. He was blowing on his hands as he came into the lounge to announce his arrival.

'God, it's bitter out there,' he gasped. 'What's that?' He pointed at Thadeus.

'Eeek,' cried Grace, feeling his chilly cheek against her warm one. 'Come in and get warm. He's Harry's cat. I told you he was coming for the weekend. I'll put the kettle on, or would you prefer a glass of wine? How was your supper?'

'Quite delicious. And yes, wine please. How's your evening been?'

'Fine,' Grace replied emphatically. 'We've been watching TV most of the time and relaxing. I wish they'd fix the gate next door, it's been driving me crazy.'

Gideon looked puzzled. Thadeus blinked slowly at him, disapproving of his presence.

'But they have! I noticed tonight as I got out of the car. They've even got a brand-new gate.'

'Well, good about that because it's been a long time coming, but there must be someone else with one loose. Maybe it's mine, I mean ours. Could you check please?'

Gideon disappeared and came back with the good news that their gate was also intact and fastened securely.

'Weird,' decided Grace. 'It must just have been the wind blowing something about. I'll get your wine...'

'Don't worry, you stay there, nice and comfy. I'll get it.'

'Gideon?' Grace called through to the kitchen.

'Yup?'

'Could you just feed Thadeus? His food's in a tin on the worktop, along with his bowl.'

'OK, how much does he have? All of it?'

'Yes, thanks. There you are, Thadeus, off you go, tea's ready.'

Predictably, at the sound of the tin being opened, Thadeus pricked up his ears and sauntered leisurely through to find his food. There was a little strangled meow, followed by the sound of Gideon apologising for his clumsiness. Nice domesticated sounds, which made Grace feel happy. Perhaps they ought to get a couple of kittens... The sort of thing that couples did.

She woke with a start, wondering what had disturbed her. Gideon, on his back, was snoring gently, one arm hooked around his head, the other across his chest as though he were performing a Scottish country dance. Grace sat up and looked around. No sign of Thadeus who had obviously taken umbrage and stalked out of the bedroom, bristly tailed, not wanting to share his usual space with Gideon. All seemed still and quiet. Even the wind had dropped.

Unable to get back to sleep, Grace slipped out of bed and wrapped her dressing gown about her. She didn't want to disturb Gideon by moving about too much under the bedclothes trying to get comfy or by putting the light on to read. A better plan was to take her book and sit downstairs, with a mug of cocoa, making her peace with Thadeus at the same time. At the foot of the stairs, she stepped into something unidentifiable but cold and wet. She found the light switch and flicked it on. Thadeus, surrounded by evidence of several further vomiting episodes was flat on his side. Grace rushed to him. Her hand stroked damp, cold and flattened fur. Little flecks of saliva glistened on his lips. His breathing was shallow and rapid.

'Thadeus, oh, your poor thing, what's happened to you?'

Grabbing a fleece from a coat hook she covered the sick animal in an attempt to warm him up.

'Don't worry, I'll get help,' she said softly before screeching at the top of her voice, 'Gideon, come quickly. Now!'

Grace was on the phone to the vet before a blurry eyed Gideon appeared halfway down the stairs.

'What's up?' he yawned.

'Quick get the car out. We've to take him round to the surgery now. The vet'll meet us there.'

'What? Why?'

'Gideon,' Grace demanded. 'It's Thadeus. He's really, really sick.'

'So I see.' Gideon looked with disdain at the carpet around him.

'No, ill! Unwell! Dying for all I know. He needs help. Please get dressed.'

'Oh, let's just wrap him up and keep him cosy. Give him some water. He'll be fine. We can take him in the morning if he's no better.'

Grace turned back to the pathetic creature at her side. 'I don't think he can wait that long. I can't leave him. What would Harry think? He loves him desperately. He's left me to look after him. I can't let him down.'

'All right. Give me a moment.'

To be fair, he did return quickly, in jeans and a huge jersey, carrying similar clothes plus some underwear for Grace. Not wanting to leave Thadeus without human contact, Grace scuttled into her clothes, scooped him up carefully into her arms, wrapped yet another blanket around him and gently cradled him as she went out to the car.

'Go carefully, Gideon, please but hurry!'

'I'll try but the road's really bumpy.'

Grace was relieved to see the welcoming lights at the veterinary practice waiting for them. Before Gideon had time to switch the engine off, she was up the path and banging on the door, which was immediately answered by a friendly face, which was what she needed more than anything.

Pamela Harewood showed no signs of having been fast asleep less than half an hour earlier. Wearing an Aran sweater over dark green cord trousers, she had pulled her hair back into a ponytail, out of the way. Tenderly, which Grace noted with approval, she unwrapped Thadeus, all the while taking a history about what had been happening. A grim expression came over her face as she commenced her examination. She looked up momentarily when Gideon slipped into the room and put his arm around Grace.

'He's extremely ill,' Pamela pronounced. 'Poisoning of some

sort would be my guess. We've had a few cats and dogs in recently with similar symptoms. Some hideous person is out there thinking it's all a bit of a lark to play tricks on unsuspecting animals. If I could get my hands on them I'd make them eat their own poison.'

'Will he be OK?' Grace plucked up the courage to ask nervously.

'It's a bit early to say. He's a high fever, rapid pulse and looks jaundiced. All the vomiting has made him dehydrated. Possibly kidney failure. He'll have to stay in of course, he needs a drip set up, some bloods sent off. Is that all right?'

'Anything. Oh, please do all you can. I'll have to ring Harry. He'll want to know.'

Gideon gave her a squeeze. 'Look, there's nothing we can do, so let's go home, get some sleep and you can ring first thing after breakfast.'

Grace turned on him, horrified. 'I can't leave him now.'

'But he's in good hands,' Gideon argued. 'The best, I'm sure. And he's not even our cat, at the end of the day. Harry will understand. Send him a text.'

'How could you? I have to stay for Harry's sake. And Thadeus's' sake. The least he deserves is someone with him that he knows. You go if you want. I'll get a taxi when I'm ready.' She glared at him.

Pamela cleared her throat and clattered some equipment around to avert a full-scale row. Gideon shook his head and rolled his eyes at her but kissed Grace on the cheek, told her to ring him when she wanted a lift home and, after an enormous yawn, backed out of the room.

'Not an animal lover, eh?' asked Pamela.

'Apparently not. I never realised before. I expect he didn't appreciate being woken up in the middle of the night.'

'Hmmm. That's never stopped me caring before and I guess it's the same for you. Now, let's get to work on this wee soul. Can you hold him still while I give this injection? Some antibiotics. I'm afraid the next few hours are going to be crucial.'

Chapter Thirteen

'A single yellow rose, I think' gulped Harry, his eyelids swollen from much crying and a similar amount of trying not to cry, 'and I'll bury him in the garden. He liked to lie under the rose bush in the summer.'

He looked out of the window of his little cottage, planning a suitable spot for the grave.

Grace was crying too. The sight of Harry so exposed and upset cut her to the quick. Women cried, sobbed and wailed in front of her on a daily basis but men crying, well that was a different kettle of fish altogether. Thadeus had died not long after arriving at the vet's, Grace by his side as he took his very last tiny gasp. The antibiotics had no chance to start working. Pamela, whilst incandescent at losing another animal for such a vile reason, had hugged Grace and made them both hot sweet tea. Grace had sat repeatedly stroking the lovely ginger coat, incredulous at what had happened and wondering if Harry would ever forgive her. Texting him was out of the question. Maybe emotionally deprived people used this as a way to break bad news but she didn't.

She had phoned him as early as she dared and he had had no second thoughts about returning instantly to be with them both.

He'd been crying when he arrived but the sight of Thadeus's' still, perfect body was more than he was able to bear. Together, they had brought him home, where he belonged. Grace had driven Harry's car, so that he could be with his beloved pet.

'He looks as though he's asleep, bless him.'

They had carefully laid Thadeus in a large box on the kitchen table. Next to him, Harry placed a toy mouse with a bell on its tail, a packet of cat treats and a tin of pilchards in tomato sauce.

'His favourites,' gulped Harry, wiping away a fresh flood of tears and blowing his nose on a handful of squashed tissues that he found in his pocket. 'I'm going to wrap the box in Christmas wrapping paper. He loved Christmas, hiding in all the paper, batting down the decorations from the tree. I think he'd like that.'

Grace half-smiled. 'I'm sure he would, Harry. Try to remember all the happy parts of his life. That'll make it easier for you. I'm so sorry I didn't do more.'

'Stop apologising, Grace. It wasn't your fault. No one else would have done that much. I'm just so pleased you were with him. He'd like that too. You were his second favourite person in the world.'

With the greatest reverence, Grace stood, holding the box in her arms while Harry puffed a lot and dug a deep hole. Grace then helped Harry lay Thadeus to rest in the garden under the yellow rose bush. It seemed only natural for them to have their arms around each other, united in their loss, but Harry was too lost in his grief to notice what was happening.

Driven back inside by an icy wind, she made them both a strong coffee and added brandy, for medicinal purposes. They sat, sipping synchronously, neither wanting the biscuits that Grace had found in a tin.

'You'll get another cat, won't you, Harry?' Grace asked after a few minutes silence.

He sniffed. 'I'll see. It will seem quiet without him though.'

'Good. I think you should.'

Harry turned to her. 'If I do, you will look after it if I go away, won't you?'

'Oh, Harry, of course I will, if that's what you want.'

'Thanks.'

Grace kissed him affectionately on the cheek and laid her head on his shoulder. Harry reached up and stroked her hair.

'You're such a good friend, Grace. I don't know what I'd do without you.'

Dusk was starting to fall when Grace opened her own front door, reluctant to leave Harry until she was sure that he was calmer. They had spent the afternoon looking at photos of Thadeus as a kitten, tidying up his many toys and then watching a comedy film on television, which had made them both laugh. Gideon was sitting reading in the lounge. He jumped up and kissed her.

'I've been waiting all day for you to ring me. Where have you been?'

'With Harry,' she replied simply. 'He dropped me off. He's popped in to see Mum while he's here.'

'Dare I ask? How's the cat? Is it all right?'

Grace shook her head. 'He,' she stated with emphasis, 'or rather Thadeus died about an hour after you left.'

'Oh, I'm sorry. Still you did all you could have done. Let me get you a drink. Shall we go out for dinner? I can easily book us a table somewhere nice.'

Grace shook her head again. 'Yes to the drink, please but thanks and no to the going out. It wouldn't be right.'

106

'What are you talking about? Why wouldn't it be right?'

Grace sighed. 'It's been a long, sad day. I've seen one of my best friends distraught with grief and now I'd like to toast Thadeus with a glass of wine and chill out a bit. Perhaps we could have a take-away later if you fancy it.'

She wandered into the kitchen and took a bottle of wine out of the fridge.

'Thanks for clearing up all the mess,' she said, returning to the lounge and noticing how spotless the hall was.

'I was hardly going to leave it like that.'

Gideon sat next to Grace on the sofa and they touched glasses.

'Here's to Thomas,' he announced.

'Thadeus,' Grace corrected him, sternly.

'OK, then, Thadeus. May he be happy in cat heaven for ever more, chasing mice to his heart's content.'

They raised their glasses and drank. As the alcohol soothed her jangled nerves, Grace realised how exhausted she was. Allowing her eyes to close, her head on Gideon's lap, she wondered for a moment how Harry was, all alone and hoped that he wasn't crying or getting upset again. The thought of him with nobody to look after him was suddenly really distressing. Before she fell asleep, she promised herself that she would phone him in the morning and check on how he was. Inviting him for supper was an idea, Sunday roast with all the trimmings but somehow she knew that Gideon did not treat the situation with the same gravity as Harry and the two of them meeting might not be as harmonious as it usually was.

Chapter Fourteen

⤜⤐❧⤑⤛

'I'm sorry, Grace,' began Andrew, 'but we've had a letter of complaint about you.'

A lead weight plummeted in Grace's heart, instantly afraid she had missed a serious diagnosis.

'Oh no! What was it about?' She was wracking her brain trying to think of something recent where she had felt unsure or had been extra worried. Try as she might, nothing came to mind in particular. On the whole she felt that work had been going well, that she had been on top of things, in control but obviously not.

Andrew, ever sensible, watched her reaction. Her hands starting to tremble, her repeated swallowing to relieve the dry mouth and the colour draining from her face. His heart went out to her, knowing how personally she responded to complaints. Mostly, he was able to acknowledge that these moments were just part and parcel of the job, none the less unpleasant for all that, but in this day and age unwelcome moments that punctuated working life occasionally.

He rustled through some papers and produced a type-written letter.

'It's from a temporary resident who saw you last month. She says you were impatient with her, didn't listen and didn't give her enough time.'

'What name was it?' Grace was puzzled.

'Mary Baker. Ring any bells?'

'No, if I'm honest. Let me look on the computer. Oh, here she is. It's all a bit odd, if I'm honest. I had a word with reception to see if there'd been a difficulty with her appointment but they said the only thing was that she specifically asked to see me, rather than take an earlier appointment with Janey or you.'

There was silence while they both looked at the notes Grace had written.

'I'm baffled,' confessed Grace. 'I do remember her now. Large hat and scarf and a shopping bag on wheels. She'd forgotten her medication and needed some to last her over her visit here. There was nothing extraordinary about it. She was in and out in a few moments. She led the whole consultation, rushing through. I distinctly recall asking her if there was anything else I could do for her because I felt it was all so quick but she said no and got up and left.'

'Don't worry about it, Grace. We'll concoct a letter back and then forget about it. None of her complaints sound like you, to begin with. You've done nothing wrong. She was probably having a bad day and took her wrath out on us. I'm sure we'd have all done exactly the same thing. Let's face it, how much of a relief is it to get an easy consultation in amongst all the hard ones?'

'Sorry, Andrew. I don't want to upset anyone here.' Grace looked penitent.

'You haven't. Now, seriously, don't worry. I know what you're like, remember, and there is no need. Promise me?'

'I'll try,' Grace half smiled. 'I hate this, more than I can say. I try so hard all the time. At least I haven't made a clinical mistake but I do feel that my personality has been violated.'

'Ignore it, Grace... keep on consulting the way you always have done. Don't try changing anything because of one strange encounter.'

'I'll go and write the letter now, Andrew. I'd like to get it done.'

'Good idea. Keep it short and let me see it before you send it. Now, the delights of Serendipity Nursing Home await me, so if you're all right, I'll see you later...'

He looked quizzically at her and she nodded in return, looking more confident than she felt.

Grace found Janey in the coffee room, sat down next to her but refused a slice of coffee and walnut cake. As expected Janey was as sympathetic and reassuring as Andrew had been.

'You did nothing wrong, Grace,' she repeated. 'It's just one of those perks of the job. Never forget to put work in perspective and remember all those many, many cards and presents you get from your faithful followers.'

'I know and I don't know why I take it so badly. I'm daft as a brush.'

Janey laughed. 'That's better! And we love you the way you are so don't change. Ah, here's Harry. Cake?'

Harry cut a slice, while Janey tutted in disgust at his modesty.

'Have a bigger bit than that Harry,' she coaxed.

He shook his head. 'Grace, I'm glad I've found you. I need to talk to you about your mum.'

'Is there a problem?' Instantly alert, Grace sat up.

'No, no, just need to keep you up to speed with what's going on. Two points. I've been to see her this morning and she asked me to explain to you what's happening. Phillip rang me after her clinic visit and suggested a change to her dosage. He thinks she's still over sedated so he's suggested that we decrease her tablets down to three in the morning of the mood stabiliser and two of the antidepressants.'

'OK, if that's what he thinks. I bet Mum was pleased, wasn't she? I get the impression she hates the way the drugs make her feel. She's certainly not as well as she has been in the past, even though Dad has convinced himself that she's so much better.'

Harry confirmed that Sylvia had been delighted.

'It might help her appetite as well,' Grace mused, optimistically.

'Which neatly brings me to the other point. I'm afraid it looks as though she's become diabetic.'

'No!' Grace's initial reaction was one of horror. As if her mother didn't have enough to contend with.

'Her bloods confirm it. Whether it's do to with the drugs – it might be, or her weight gain, or a bit of both, I don't know but we need to look after the physical side of her health as well.'

'Of course,' agreed Grace, hurriedly. 'What did she have to say about the diabetes?'

'Not pleased. I think she saw is as another millstone around her neck. But I'll go and see her again in a couple of days and talk it through again. I've told Phillip and we're both hopeful that if her mood's a bit brighter, she'll be more motivated to accept the diabetes and try to help herself in whatever way she can.'

'Hmmmm,' Grace was unconvinced. 'And Dad? What did he say?'

'What do you think? He was his usual, cheery, optimistic self. "nothing's a problem", "everything will be all right" etc., etc.'

'But she'll never cope with insulin, will she? Not on her own. That's more responsibility for Dad and he's starting to crack under the strain as it is.'

'You know the score, Grace. We'll try and see if she'll stick to a diet first, then add tablets and see how she gets on. I'm not optimistic about the trial of diet alone though...'

'Not a chance,' agreed Grace, who continued to be amazed by the amounts of food her mother was eating, predominantly those of a sugary base. She put her head in her hands and gazed sadly at her knees. Just one trouble after another. Spotting the start of tears in her eyes when she looked up, Harry tactfully started chatting to Janey, giving Grace a chance to regain some composure.

Secretly he was dreading the effect that the diagnosis of diabetes would have on Sylvia. His conversations with Phillip had confirmed their mutual worry for her well-being and fear for her future. The new medication was not turning out to be the success that Phillip had hoped for. Finding the optimal dose was proving to be a challenge worse than balancing on a tight rope. Too much or too little of the drug and she was likely to spiral out of control again and be back on the ward. Douglas was turning into an ostrich with its head in the sand. He saw what he wanted to see and heard what he wanted to hear. No blame could be put on him for this. Like any person emotionally involved, his love overrode the clinical picture and the love he felt for his wife was unshakable and infinite.

Harry felt dichotomous about how to approach Grace with regard to her mother. He wanted to be honest but he wanted to protect her. It was one of the hardest situations he had been faced with at work for a long time.

Chapter Fifteen

*D*ouglas and Charnley were out walking. Well, Douglas was marching along in the manner of a soldier leading a route march and Charnley was charging around him in all directions, following promising scents, snuffling in piles of crispy dead leaves and rolling in unmentionable detritus that meant a bath on their return home was inevitable. The winter sun was shining through the bare tree branches and the sky was a vivid icy blue.

Glad to be out in the fresh air, no matter how frosty it was, Douglas, well wrapped up against the cold, in a tweed jacket and deerstalker, watched his freezing breath escape from his mouth as he ploughed onwards and up the gentle incline. This particular walk took exactly forty-five minutes and while he covered three miles of woodland paths and field tracks, Charnley ran perhaps three times as far.

Sylvia had been left at home, reading a magazine and dozing. Douglas had supervised her breakfast, a banana sliced onto a bowl of porridge and one small slice of brown toast. Two cups of coffee to wash it down. Good enough for anyone to set them up for the day. It had then been agreed that she would see to the washing up while he went and changed into his quilted walking trousers and warm jumper. The transition into his outdoor outfit had taken minutes only but when he came back to the kitchen, Sylvia had consumed half a loaf of bread with butter and jam and had made good headway into the biscuit tin. She looked up guiltily, hearing his entrance, half a biscuit in one hand, tell-tale crumbs around her mouth.

'I did try,' she blurted out, apologetically. 'Really I did.'

'Of course you did,' he agreed, giving her a hug, instantly forgiving her but replacing the tin lid firmly and putting it right to the back of the cupboard.

There was no point in trying to convince her otherwise. The insatiable appetite was none of her doing; it was a monster inside her, some unidentifiable parasite living off her in the most disastrous manner. He had tried hiding food but she always seemed to find it, even when he resorted to the most ridiculous places thinkable, such as the washing machine or the china cabinet in the rarely used dining room. Somehow she had an infallible antenna designed to locate all edible objects, come what may.

Together with Grace, he had discussed strategies to cope with the food problem, shopping for small amounts daily, banning all sugary products from the house but Sylvia was quite capable of popping down the road and round the corner to the nearby garage and buying – and consuming – to her heart's desire. Gideon suggested they asked the staff in the garage to refuse to serve her but Douglas was outraged and barked that was how you treated alcoholics and drug addicts and his wife was never to be placed in that sort of category.

The reduction of her tablets had resulted in a modicum of success. Sylvia was decidedly less soporific but yet lacked any sense of purpose and had to be guided in most decision making and aspects of daily living. Douglas, though he never admitted this, was finding this beyond hard. He missed the vibrant, wildly exciting and unpredictable woman he married all those years ago. Her crazy sense of colour, her palpable love of life and her passion for all things, especially him, had him head over heels in love within days of their first meeting. What followed were such amazing adventures in their courtship and the early years of their marriage. Happy, fun times with parties, travel when work permitted, good friends, joy and much laughter.

It was hard not to reminisce and yearn for times past. He was spending more and more time dwelling on the past these days. Probably this was the reason he was able to keep on going. If he concentrated intently on all the good times and in the evenings, after she had gone to bed, spent hours gazing at the photos of how she used to look then he could pretend not to see what was happening now, how she had metamorphosed into a different species and how much she hated it. And that was without doubt the hardest thing of all. Knowing how unhappy she was.

Under a large weeping willow tree, one night when the moon was full and she had accepted his proposal of marriage, he had promised her that she would always be happy.

He felt he had failed her.

Reaching the gate before his master, Charnley hurried back to him, worrying a stick, wagging his stumpy tail with delight. Douglas bent down to stroke and praise him. The little muddy dog jumped up onto his knee and snuggled into him.

'Time to get home, lad,' he sighed, attaching Charnley's lead to his collar.

These walks were his salvation. Away from home he could escape and dream. Only when he returned home did he succumb to the awfulness of what the future may hold.

Sylvia, in her fitter days, had found this walk. Between them, when Charnley first arrived, they had explored the local area and found that there was easy access to some fields and woods that provided the perfect terrain for dog walking. She had then gone on to establish three different walks which she had plotted on a map and then timed, so that she knew exactly how long Douglas would be, according to which route he had told her he was going to take. She used to be such a stickler for order, Douglas mused and now she doesn't seem to care less. Whilst her obsessional tidiness had driven him to distraction on more occasions than he cared to remember, it was infinitely preferable to the bland disinterest and ennui she exhibited now.

Back at the house, he wiped Charnley's paws and undercarriage, scrubbed off the malodorous deposit near his tail and gave him a bone-shaped biscuit. He made two cups of coffee and went into the lounge where Sylvia was still asleep, oblivious of the fact he had been out. He gently woke her and she spluttered back into the real world, smiling at him. His heart melted. Despite everything else, she still had the smile that had conquered his heart.

'No biscuits, OK?' he announced with mock sternness, wagging one finger.

She pouted then laughed a little. 'OK. You're the boss.'

'Exactly.' Douglas put his arm around Sylvia's shoulders and she leant her head against him.

'This is nice,' they agreed.

'Grace is coming across shortly,' Douglas told his wife. 'She promised last night.'

'Oh, that'll be lovely,' Sylvia looked up at him. 'It's so long since I've seen her. She's no time for me since she got that man in her life.'

Ignoring the fact that Grace had been for her lunch the day before yesterday, Douglas squeezed Sylvia's shoulder affectionately.

Their quiet moment of togetherness was broken by the ringing of the doorbell. Expectantly, Douglas got up to answer it. On the doorstep stood Gideon, blowing on his cold hands and stamping his feet.

'I've just had a phone call from Grace. She's been held up at the surgery. Someone collapsed in the waiting area so she asked me to call round and see if you need anything.'

'Come in, come in. I'll get you a coffee, warm you up. We're just having one. You look frozen. Make your way into the lounge – Sylvia's in there.'

When he returned with the mug of steaming brew, Sylvia was looking less than pleased. Gideon was trying to coax some conversation from her but she was having none of it.

'Where's Grace? I want to see her. You told me she was coming.'

Gideon looked perplexed. 'I've explained to her….' he began, apologetically.

'Don't worry.' Douglas made Sylvia look at him. 'She's coming as soon as she can. It's nice that Gideon came to tell us, isn't it?'

'No. I want to see Grace. I'm going to phone her now and ask her where she is and when she's coming.'

She started to get up but struggled to raise her large form from the chair, where she had been settled for so long. Gideon tried to help but she pushed him away, Douglas reached out to her and she flapped her hand dismissively. With one almighty heave, Sylvia catapulted from the sofa, like a projectile from a battering ram, the two men tried to catch her as she fell forward and Charnley leapt off the armchair, where he had sneaked because he thought no one would notice and began to jump around and bark. The ensuing kerfuffle was inelegant and confused. Sylvia was shouting and shrieking, Douglas was trying to keep control and Gideon was doing his best though his vision was blocked by the flurry of arms and legs.

With a cry, someone fell to the floor.

There was an audibly loud snap.

'Bloody hell, I think I've fractured my hip,' moaned Douglas.

Chapter Sixteen

⁓⚬⚬⚬⁓

Whoever said that doctors and nurses make the worst patients was right. In the case of Douglas Dunstable, no description was more accurate. From the arrival of the paramedics, who both happened to be female, which did not go down well, to his being wheeled into Accident and Emergency he harrumphed, swore and groused about the irony of an orthopaedic surgeon falling victim to a common orthopaedic emergency.

'Why me?' he lambasted the tremulous junior doctor who admitted him. 'I walk miles every day. My bones must be as strong as scaffolding. Where are my x-rays? Let me look and check for myself. Are you sure my neck of femur's bust? And how long have you been qualified anyway? You don't look old enough to be a doctor. Where's the consultant? Tell him I demand to see him.'

Grace, who ran into the department having rushed from the surgery as soon as Gideon had telephoned, had no difficulty identifying which curtains her father was behind. He had just returned from radiology, ranting. Desperately she attempted to pour oil on troubled waters.

'Calm down, Dad. Don't be rude. Your x-rays are up on the

viewer. Even I can tell that your neck of femur's gone and I'm a humble GP. You look really pale. I expect you've lost a lot of blood. Shall I ask them to get you some pain relief?'

'About time. The stronger the better. Where's Sylvia?'

'Mum's in the waiting area with Gideon. She's shaken up but fine. No injuries.'

'I want to see her.'

'Sister says you're just about to go up to the ward, so let's get you sorted out and into bed and then you can see her there. You're the priority right at this moment. How on earth did this happen?'

He outlined events as best he could. 'I really don't know. We were trying to stop your mum from falling but in the mess, I was pushed over. What a disaster. This really is the final straw.'

He grimaced and repeatedly banged a clenched fist on the side of the trolley he was lying on.

Grace stroked his forehead. 'It's awful, I know. But we'll manage.'

'How? How will you manage? Your mum needs twenty-four-hour care and you've got a job to do. Oh, why did this have to happen?'

Grace almost winced at the sight of the pain in her father's eyes.

'Because we will. You'll have your surgery tomorrow and be back on your feet in no time. By the time you've been settled into your bed on the ward, I'll have a plan.'

'And your mother?'

The million-dollar question.

By the time Douglas and his entourage reached the ward, the hefty dose of analgesic was starting to work its magic. With the severity of his pain easing, some of his anxiety departed also and a decidedly calmer and more amenable patient allowed the porters to transfer him between the awaiting crisp white sheets while a very pretty student nurse asked him a barrage of questions. Grace and her mother came and sat by the bed once the formalities of admission had been completed, having waited in the day room skimming through dog-eared magazines while keeping one eye on the dreadful programme blaring out from the television.

Sylvia looked worried but composed. She took her husband's hand and held it, not wanting to let go.

'Hello, my darling!' he chirruped as cheerfully as he could muster. 'Don't look so afraid. Soon be as good as new! Better even as I'll have a new hip.'

'I am frightened for you Douglas,' she admitted. 'And I'm frightened for me too. What am I going to do without you? How will I manage?'

Grace swallowed hard and interrupted. 'You're going to come and stay with us, Mum. Gideon and I will look after you. I'll take some leave from work. I was going to be off the week after next anyway but my partners will understand and Gideon will jiggle his time about as well. You'll not be left on your own, I promise. Then, when Dad comes home, I'll come back to yours and look after both of you for as long as you need it. How about that?'

'That's such a relief to hear, Grace,' Sylvia breathed. 'I'll manage until I get your dad back if I've got you.'

'Then that's settled,' Grace smiled, wondering what Gideon, who had gone back to his office, would think to her hastily constructed plan. He had to agree. There was no alternative.

Footsteps clomped down the ward and Grace looked up to see Harry bearing down on them.

'News travels fast,' he greeted them. 'So sorry about this, Douglas.'

'Huh,' was the reply. 'I hate feeling helpless. I'm not using a bed pan and that's definite.'

'Mr Jensen will take excellent care of you. He's coming to see you shortly.'

'Jensen? Is he related to Keith Jensen that I trained with?'

Harry nodded. 'I do believe he is.'

Looking decidedly happier, Douglas managed a little curl of one edge of his mouth. 'I'd rather be looked after by someone who knows me, even if it's slightly tenuous.'

'You'll get along fine. He's a great guy. I think he's quite honoured to be taking care of someone who has such an illustrious career behind him.'

The other edge of Douglas's mouth agreed to smile and Sylvia, reassured, smiled too with the result that almost all the tension in the atmosphere around them dissipated in moments.

'Cup of tea, Grace?' suggested Harry, cocking his head towards the ward entrance. 'Let these two have a bit of time to themselves.'

'Good idea,' agreed Grace, gathering her bag up from under the bed and checking on her parents.

'We'll be back shortly.'

Sitting in the hospital restaurant, Grace reflected on how differently she felt compared to when she had last been there, full of anticipation, excitement and nervousness. Now her nerves were frazzled for reasons that were poles apart. Harry sat down opposite her with cappuccinos and a couple of Danish pastries, one of which he insisted she ate. She picked at it unenthusiastically and noticed Harry's tie of the day – dark brown with silver donkeys.

She sighed. 'Everything's going wrong. It's just one thing after another.'

'Don't worry, Grace, we can get through this,' Harry promised her, a little taken aback at how he had included himself in the promise without thinking about it. Not that he wasn't there to help Grace but he wondered if she might think it a little presumptuous of him.

'I really don't know what to think, Harry, 'she began. 'You and I both know how long it can take someone to get over a fractured hip. Some never recover in the sense that they don't walk properly or have chronic pain or…'

'Shush, Grace. You mustn't think like that. Your father's unique. He's not the sort of patient to give in. You mark my words, he'll be up and out of bed the day after his op. Be grateful that his physical health is so good. That'll stand him in good stead for the anaesthetic and for his recovery. Knowing him as I do, he's not going to let this get the better of him.'

'I hope you're right.' Grace sounded doubtful. 'I'm going to need some time off.'

'That's fine. Again, we'll manage. Amber's coming along quite nicely now, so she can step up and take a bit more responsibility and see some extras. I'll cancel the few days I was going to have--'

'I can't ask you to do that, Harry…!'

'Of course you can. I'd do anything for you. I was only going to tidy up the garden and potter about at home and I know the others will do whatever they can. When your dad's ready to come home, why not persuade him and your mum to go to convalesce somewhere for a couple of weeks. That way they can be together but both be looked after. '

'He'd never agree to that!'

'OK, then get some day care in for a few weeks.'

'He'll loathe that!'

'I know he will. But do it! Then you've got the reassurance of knowing the two of them are being looked after and can get back to work. Your life has to go on too, Grace. Your parents would expect that too.'

Harry made it all sound so easy, thought Grace. He was right. His advice was exactly what she had said to a patient in a comparable predicament but a fortnight ago. He had the ability to be objective whereas she did not.

'So you're taking your mum back to your house?'

'Yes,' Grace nodded. 'I think that's best. Then Gideon can help. He's doing quite a lot of research at the moment and he can do that from home. Mum doesn't need someone with her all the time, just someone around, in case.'

Harry bristled a little at the mention of his least favourite name. 'And he doesn't mind?'

Grace pulled a face. 'He doesn't actually know yet. But of course he won't mind. That's what it's all about, isn't it? Helping out, being there for each other whatever...I'd do it for him...'

She sounded almost wistful and Harry had to hold back an irresistible urge to kiss her.

'You're a wonderful person. I'll keep popping in too, if you like.'

Grace reached for his hand.'You are the best friend, Harry. Thank you for everything.'

Harry glowed with delight.

Which was more than Gideon did when he got home later that day to find Sylvia watching television in the lounge and Charnley curled up by the radiator. Sylvia's knitting was draped over her knees. Intermittently, she picked up the needles and did a few stitches. Grace had encouraged her to try, saying that Douglas would appreciate a nice rug for his legs. It was this incentive that had acted as the successful catalyst and Grace was pleased. She vowed to come up with some more ideas to encourage her mother.

Gideon found Grace in the kitchen, where she was scraping macaroni cheese from a pan into a dish, before topping with sliced tomato and extra cheese and putting it under the grill to brown. He walked over to the fridge, took out a bottle of white wine and poured a large glassful. Before speaking he downed over half of it in one swallow.

Grace smiled at him warmly. 'I'd love a glass of wine too please.'

'Just what is going on here, Grace?' He leant back against the worktop and crossed his arms.

'Mum's staying for a few days,' she answered simply. 'Tea'll be ready in a few minutes. Could you set the table for me?'

Without moving, Gideon finished his wine and refilled his glass. 'It's not really very convenient, is it? Having your mother here? Wouldn't it have been better for you to go and stay across the road?'

Realising that he was cross and not about to pour her any wine, Grace reached for her own glass and served herself.

'Why? This is my, or should I say our, home and I want to be in it. Mum's perfectly happy here. It's warm and cosy and we can both help her.'

'This is going to interfere with my work. I've a paper to write and submit before the end of the month. I've told you a thousand times….'

Grace tried to placate him. 'And you will. She doesn't need nursing. She just needs a presence in the house and an occasional chat. If you can just do this week then I'll be off work for the next week and by then Dad will be home.'

Gideon looked unconvinced.

'I'll come home every lunchtime, Harry's going to look in. The neighbours will help too. They all understand. So it won't be a big trouble to you. But I need your help for the first few days. Please....'

'I don't approve of this at all. It's a disaster waiting to happen.'

'Oh, it's not,' Grace pleaded. 'I'm sure she'll be on her best behaviour. Just make sure she takes her medication.'

'The best thing you could have done would have been to have left her at the hospital on the psych ward.'

Grace gasped, horrified, but Gideon was unrepentant. 'Put my supper on a tray please. I shall eat in my study.'

Chapter Seventeen

⸎

our days later and life at Grace's house had settled into a vague sort of contented routine. Gideon had apologised for his initial reaction, citing work pressure as an excuse and had proceeded to be the most welcoming host, much to Grace's relief. He had dutifully spent four days at home, working away in the study but stopping at regular intervals for a ten-minute chat with Sylvia to make sure all was well.

Sylvia in her turn seemed to have risen to the challenge. She was making supper for Gideon and Grace and although the portions were gargantuan and far more than they were used to, the food was more than passable and both appreciated her help. With a task in hand to focus on, Sylvia was able to see through the fog that had become her life and react with common sense. She surprised both Grace and Douglas with the way she coped. Each evening when they visited the increasingly belligerent patient, it was Sylvia who led the way on to the ward and Sylvia who gave the report of what they'd all been doing that day.

Douglas was doing nicely. His immediate post-operative course was soured by some confusion relating to the anaesthetic and he had spent a noisy night, singing 'hip hip hooray' and 'I'm very hippy because I've a new hip' much to the annoyance of the other in-patients who were consequently unable to sleep. Since then, however, his recovery had been near exemplary. Though his attempts to walk had been fraught, as he had point blank refused to use a walking frame, a compromise had been reached and he was getting the hang of using two sticks. Overall the physiotherapist was satisfied and so were the nurses and Mr Jensen. Plans for his discharge could be started.

As predicted, the idea of a nursing home for two weeks was anathema to both Douglas and Sylvia. Hand in hand they protested that, not only were they able to manage, they did not need any outside help coming in. When Grace announced that she had actually gone to a great deal of trouble and arranged for a really nice retired community nurse, who used to work for the practice and had terrific references, to come in for several hours each day, Douglas exploded and ordered her to cancel immediately. Gideon adding weight to Grace's cause achieved nothing other than a steely glare from them both and in desperation Grace rang Harry and begged him to come and make them see reason.

A summit meeting was held at the bedside. With Gideon on his ward round, Grace sat next to Harry on the bed, ignoring disapproving looks from the nursing staff, Sylvia and Douglas were in chairs beside each other creating a formidable force. Words were exchanged, views opined, arguments were dismissed by counter-arguments and a few sparks flew in all directions. It was agreed later by the other three patients in the same bay as Douglas (all knee replacements) that they had not had such an entertaining afternoon for a long time.

Conclusions were reached, however grudgingly. The nursing home idea was quashed. The retired community nurse was cancelled. Gideon would call in the mornings to make sure they were up and that medicines were taken. Grace would call at lunchtime, Harry promising to do some of her home visits if necessary and then she would be in after surgery and stay for most of the evening before going back to her own home. Jim from next door would walk Charnley when he was taking his own dog out. Plus Grace would sleep over for the first few nights and be on tap, should she be needed. It was the best solution they came up with that suited everyone as near as possible.

Contentment all around was achieved.

The day of Douglas's discharge was bitterly cold. Grace picked him up in a black taxicab, leaving Sylvia at home making scones as a welcome-home treat. As they were driven home Grace worried at how palely frail her father looked behind the facade he was presenting by talking incessantly. Shakily he managed, at the third attempt, to extract his body from the cab and stand upright, wobbling on his sticks. Grace paid the fare and took his arm. The effort it was taking him relayed down his arms to her hands. With a deep breath and a large, determined grunt, he set off quite steadily to the gate. Sylvia was waiting at the door, thrilled to bits, waving madly.

She called out to him and he looked up and without thinking waved one of his sticks in acknowledgement. In doing so he totally failed to notice the patch of ice on the path. His other stick shot across onto the little lawn, he tried desperately to save himself, much in the manner of an amateur ice skater, but tumbled to the ground.

Within two hours of leaving the ward, he was back, in the same bed, well sedated and waiting for Mr Jensen to come to reduce his dislocated new hip.

Chapter Eighteen

⚬⚬⚬

*T*wo groups of people were having supper simultaneously. After much ruminating, Harry had decided to ask Janey for her advice and had been invited for supper. They were all in the huge untidy farmhouse kitchen, sitting around the scrubbed pine table. There was a vast Welsh dresser, covered with photos, plates, piles of letters, paintings by the children. A dog was snoring in the corner, curled up in a beanbag bed. Wonderful aromas were coming from the range cooker on top of which a number of pans were puffing out steam. Janey was busy mashing root vegetables, warming plates and shrieking for the children to come to eat while Ben, her husband, was attacking the most enormous joint with a carving knife.

'Nearly ready,' Janey turned to Harry. 'Help yourself to more wine. There's another couple of bottles on the dresser if you need them! Eli! Bryony! Jack! Danny! Lottie! Now please! Put those guinea pigs back in their cage, turn off the TV and wash your hands.'

Suddenly the room was filled with children, all talking at once, excited at seeing Harry, hungry for their supper. With multitasking skills that Harry could never hope to aspire to, Janey extracted perfect Yorkshire puddings from the oven, poured gravy into a blue and white striped jug and spotted that two guinea pigs were peeping out of one of Jack's pockets.

'What did I say about those animals, Jack?' She gave him a look and he slunk out. 'How many times do I have to tell you?' she shouted at his retreating form. 'And don't forget to wash your hands.'

Turning back to the table with a contented smile, Janey sat down and surveyed all around her with pride. She looked hot from her hard work, her red, flushed cheeks clashing with her eye-popping candy pink dress. Ben kissed her passionately on the lips and laid a huge plate of food in front of her.

'Ugh!' the children sang in unison.

'Harry, it's a free for all at our table. Go for it but be warned, these little locusts of ours eat very quickly.'

'This is fabulous,' Harry thanked her, tucking in with gusto. 'Proper roast dinner. I can't remember the last time I had one. Mmmm delicious.'

Being part of such domesticity warmed Harry's heart. This is what he and Grace could have one day. Well, perhaps not five children. Looking around him he decided that might be a bit excessive. And perhaps their house would be rather tidier. Quite how Janey managed to stay so laid back was baffling to him.

Uncertain how to bring the subject round to Grace, Harry decided to do justice to his supper first. Second helpings followed and what had seemed like an invincible tower of roast potatoes was consumed along with everything else bar the broccoli.

Apple crumble followed with ice cream or custard and Harry was transported back to his childhood. This was paradise on a plate. Replete, he thanks his hosts effusively and started to get up to clear the table. Janey told him to sit down and, in an instant, five small people jumped to attention and between them made short work of the clearing up.

'Thank you, sweet things,' called Janey as her brood disappeared back into the recesses of the house and the sound of the television was heard blaring out. 'Let me make some coffee and then we can talk.'

No longer able to put off the main reason for his being there Harry was beset with nerves. How to start? What to say? How much to admit? Tongue tied he looked helplessly at Janey and Ben.

'I thought so,' concluded Janey, after summing up the look on his face. 'It's Grace, isn't it?'

Harry choked a little on his coffee.

'How did you know?'

'It's plain for all to see,' Janey informed him, 'that you are hopelessly in love with her.'

'Well...'started Harry, on the verge of trying to deny it.

'Just admit it,' Janey said. 'You'll feel so much better for a start.'

Ben nodded. 'She's right. She always is.'

Harry chewed the side of his mouth and took another mint chocolate from the bowl in front of him. After a pause, he nodded in slow motion.

'She is right. I am hopelessly in love. Grace is quite simply the most wonderful being I have ever set eyes on. Every moment we spend together is bliss. Even the hard times. It sounds the most terrible thing to say but all this business with her parents has been a boon to me because it's given me all the more reason to speak to her and go round to her house.' He paused and looked at the couple opposite. 'How ridiculous do I sound?'

'Not at all,' admonished Janey. 'I think you're made for each other.'

'That's made me so happy to hear. It makes me think I'm not going mad. But what am I going to do about it?'

'Tell her,' suggested Janey, simply.

'How? Plus of course there's that huge fly in the ointment called Gideon, who she thinks the sun shines out of and who can do no wrong. I really liked him when I first met him but now I can't stand the sight of him. Do you know, last week, when Mr Nichols came in with that weird gait that I thought might be a sensory ataxia, I actually rang the neurologists in Leeds to discuss it, as I couldn't bear the thought of speaking to Gideon. How stupid is that?'

Bryony came in with a doll, head in one hand, body in the other and plonked it on Harry's knee.

'Can you mend her please?'

She's adorable, thought Harry, loving her dark, messy curls and equally dark but huge eyes. He took the two pieces from her and snapped them back together.

'There you are. I've got to make her see me in a different way. We're good friends, there's no doubt about that but she doesn't think of me romantically.'

Bryony cocked her head on one side and studied him. With a wisdom far beyond her tender years, she announced, 'What you need is a makeover, like they have on telly.'

In a dark corner of a tapas bar, Gideon was showering Grace with compliments. For the first time in weeks, they had come out together, to enjoy each other's company. Grace however was finding it hard to relax. Unlike Gideon, she was unable simply to switch off. Her mobile phone was beside her on the table, next to a bowl of chorizo and chicken, much to Gideon's disapproval as he had told her that no calls were going to be forthcoming.

Douglas's second stay in hospital had been mercifully brief.

His dislocated joint had clunked back into place and no more damage had been done. Now back at home for a week, an uneasy calm had settled in the house. Sylvia was still doing her best, supervising the meals, and in her case the snacks in between meals, keeping the house tolerably tidy and making sure that her husband was comfortable and safe.

Grace had stayed over with them but after three nights of what they referred to as far too much fussing, she had unwillingly agreed to return home and, so far, all seemed to be going well.

Gideon had ordered champagne.

'It's a celebration in a way,' he told her. 'Our first night out for a long time.'

He was determined to talk about anything except her parents. She needed to have her mind taken away from the worries of home life, so he was concentrating on making plans for their future. He suggested holidays, not just weekends away at cosy pubs or statuesque hotels but longer trips abroad, perhaps a really long break to the antipodes if they could wangle the time off. Using all his charm, he made the prospects of travel sound exciting and tempting but Grace knew she that she must not commit to anything at the moment. Too much was going on in the present to think about the future, she told him.

He refused to give up. Ordering more drinks and more food, he painted such a rosy picture of their future as a couple that she ached deep inside, wanting it so much. Part of her though wanted Gideon to be more understanding of her predicament now. His general assumption was that now Douglas was home and he and Sylvia were wobbling along in a fairly satisfactory way then that dilemma was over, done with, finito. Why was he unable to see what Grace saw?

'This is lovely, isn't it?' he started eagerly. 'Are you enjoying it?'

Grace nodded, biting her lip, wondering if she should nip out and phone her parents. Reading her mind, Gideon reached for her mobile and slipped it into his pocket.

'Relax. They're fine. You've got to let go, Grace, leave them to it.'

'I know,' replied Grace. 'But they seem so frail....'

'I don't think that's a word that is applicable to your mother, the size she is.'

Grace glared at him. 'That's unkind, Gideon. You know it is. She's emotionally frail and as for Dad, well! He's putting on the brave face but he's not doing well. His right leg was very swollen this afternoon.'

'It will be. He's just had surgery to the hip on that side. It happens to them all. You can be exasperating at times. You go looking for problems when there aren't any.'

'I don't!' Grace was indignant. 'I just care. They're my parents.'

'You've got to fly the nest at some point.'

Grace looked close to tears and he speedily capitulated.

'I'm sorry. Let's not argue. I hate to see you so troubled. I want you to be happy. Here, have some more champagne. Let's just chill for a bit.'

'I need to go to the Ladies. I won't be a moment.'

Grace excused herself and disappeared even further back into the building. Gideon felt her phone vibrating in his pocket and ignored it. He was busy thinking hard. Something must be done and quickly. Grace was going to end up exhausted and ill. He had noticed how little she had eaten so far and how her eyes were darting around the room. He doubted she had absorbed much of all he had suggested about travelling.

She was back before long and he noticed she had gone to the trouble of freshening up her make up and combing her hair.

Sinking back into her seat, he slid along to be closer to her. He nuzzled her neck and the sensation of his soft and warm breath on her skin sent shivers all over her body. Turning to him, she looked into his eyes and wondered what she had done to deserve such a perfect boyfriend. They kissed tenderly, lingering over the delicious taste of each other's lips, infinitely more sensual than any of the food.

'Will you marry me, Grace?' he whispered.

'I keep ringing but there's no answer!' Sylvia turned to Douglas. 'Where can she be?'

'Try…again…'

Douglas was sitting on the edge of the bed, bent over, legs dangling. His left hand was holding the right side of his lower chest, the other hand clutched at the bedclothes. His breathing was stertorous and rapid. The colour had drained from his face apart from a cyanotic hue to his lips. Charnley was whimpering at his feet, instinctively aware something was very wrong.

They had been watching a film on television, both of them enjoying it, both laughing and singing along to all the songs they knew when a sudden thud hit him in the chest. Worse when he took a deep breath in, the physician within knew that he was having a pulmonary embolism but he was unprepared for how difficult his breathing was to become. He hadn't wanted to worry Sylvia and somehow the two of them had got up to bed and switched off the light. But settling down was impossible. Lying flat exacerbated his symptoms and his restlessness woke Sylvia who was horrified when she put the light back on and saw the state he was in.

'I'll try once more and if she doesn't answer, then I'm calling an ambulance. You need help and quickly.'

Her shaking fingers dialled the numbers again and impatiently she shook the phone while listening to the ringing tone. Angrily, she ended the call and dialled 999.

Which was why the newly engaged Grace, in a state of euphoria, arrived home to find an ambulance at her parents' door, her father on a stretcher with an oxygen mask on his face and a heart monitor attached to his chest while her mother, overnight bag in her hand, was locking up the house.

Chapter Nineteen

*H*arry had finished an interesting surgery. A couple of new and less run-of-the-mill diagnoses, the return of a depressed patient much improved, some cheery toddlers with copious amounts of green snot had all enlivened an otherwise routine morning. An eighty-nine-year-old lady had given him two toffees and admired his tie, elephants walking one behind the other, trunks and tails intertwined. He was ready for a drink and hopefully one of Janey's cakes. He wondered if Grace would be in the coffee room as he made his way up the stairs. He had heard about Douglas and instantly his concern had been for Grace and how she was bearing up under yet more strain.

The door was a little ajar and his pulse quickened as he heard Grace's voice. He stood for a while, listening.

'A pulmonary embolus?' Janey was horrified. Grace was telling her about the current disaster that had befallen her family. 'Hadn't they put him on blood thinners after his hip op?'

'Yes, but he'd stopped them. You know what he's like. Thinks he knows better than everyone else. To be fair he was becoming very mobile and was only due to keep having the injections for another week. I doubt that made any difference.'

'I can't believe what your poor dad has been through.' Janey was shaking her head while she opened up the tin of chocolate-chip flapjacks she had brought in. Grace accepted one gratefully.

'So what's happening now?'

Grace chewed and swallowed. The stickiness of the flapjacks did not encourage easy speech as her teeth were coated with oats.

'He's on the medical ward now. Causing havoc as you can imagine. Started on warfarin and they hope he'll be home in a few days but his chest x-ray shows a possible infection, so he's on antibiotics for that.'

'And your mum?'

'She's back at ours. She's upset but seems to be doing OK, bless her.'

'How's Gideon with that?'

'OK. He's doing his best. I know he doesn't like it though. He asked me to marry him, did I tell you?'

'Whoa!' Janey was aghast. 'When did this happen and what did you say?'

'The night of the PE. We were out having dinner. It was a bit of a funny evening really. The idea was that we were having some time for us. We deserve it after all. I was worried about Dad's swollen leg and he was dismissive totally. He confiscated my phone because he was sick of me looking at it, waiting for calls and then of course Mum kept on ringing me and I didn't know. I feel so bad about that and cross with Gideon. He must have known that calls were coming in but ignored them and that's hard to forgive. He says he had no idea. I thought he cared about Mum and Dad but that suggests he doesn't, so really I don't know what to do. He's sent flowers and apologised since, profusely and said he'd had too much to drink but, oh... I just don't know.'

'So you didn't give him an answer, then?'

'Oh, I did. I said yes but then all the rest happened. We've not talked about it since.'

'How exciting!' Janey tried her best to sound cheerful.

'Well, I think it is. I do love him but with so much else going on, I feel so mixed up.'

Outside the door, Harry was immobilised. A tear trickled down his face, disappearing into his beard. Taking a couple of steps back, he knew he couldn't face the two women. He crept back to his surgery and sat at his desk, reliving what he had heard. A handful of words that had destroyed his hopes and dreams in an instant. His heart was shattered into a trillion painful shards. Only Grace had the ability to mend it. The thought of Gideon made his flesh creep; the thought of Grace made him want to cry out loud; the thought of them together made him retch with despair.

The worst of it was that her voice lacked conviction. He was sure she had doubts about Gideon but did not realise. Harry knew, incontrovertibly, Grace did not love Gideon. She merely thought that she did. He had appeared on the scene, dazzled her with presents and flattery and then been there when her life had spiralled into turmoil. He had seemed dependable when she was naive and gullible, vulnerable in her worry. He had inveigled his way into her affections using his oozing charm and good looks. Harry was panic stricken. Nobody was going to take advantage of Grace, over his dead body.

Fury replaced his despair. Determination started to well in his spleen. Now was the time to act and do something. Faint heart never won fair lady. Right, it was time to act. Not just to make a plan and think about it but to carry it out. He thought back to all Janey and Ben had advised him as they had sat, long into the night, drinking good wine, eating chocolates and discussing tactics. Gradually, like an ugly duckling turning into an exquisite swan, it came to him, what he had to do.

Chapter Twenty

*S*ylvia was enjoying life, for the first time in as long as she could recall. Whether it was the reduction in her medication or perhaps that her body was simply becoming accustomed to it, she cared not, for the bonus was some energy and, joy of joys, a clearer mind. Worried that she was a burden to Grace and Gideon, she now found that she was able to be a useful visitor. Gideon always ensured that she took her drugs in the morning and then after the two of them went off to work, Sylvia cleared up the breakfast pots and justified her existence by polishing, dusting and hoovering for most of the morning. Rather than waiting for Grace to come in and make lunch, Sylvia had sandwiches and soup ready for her daughter, or jacket potatoes and a hot filling, the kettle boiling, fresh fruit for dessert. Her appetite was slowly receding and the weighing scales proclaimed good news each time she ventured onto them.

Her afternoons were spent washing and ironing then knitting and talking to Charnley, who was enjoying long walks every morning. Perhaps she did sneak in a little nap when it was quiet but woke with plenty of time to change, prepare something that would cook slowly in the oven and get ready to go and visit Douglas.

The chest infection had turned to pneumonia. Not life threatening but enough to protract his stay as the first antibiotics had been ineffective so an alternative had to be found. Like many other elderly patients, he had become institutionalised. He knew every moment of the daily routine, from the first cup of tea to the last cup of cocoa. He knew which nurses could be cajoled into finding him biscuits, which ones were up for a laugh or a joke and which ones took life very seriously and were not to be messed with. He had swapped life stories with the other longer-stay patients, watched with intrigue as new ones settled in and tried very hard to ignore the occasional poor soul who died and had to be wheeled away in a trolley that looked empty but had a hidden compartment.

The highlight of his day was Sylvia's visit. Despite his own health problems, he was not unaware of the change in her. She had a new air of self-worth and confidence. The little weight she had lost showed in her face, taking away the bloated, unhealthy look and her eyes were alive again. His friends in neighbouring beds looked at her with keen interest rather than pity. The pride he felt was the biggest impetus to recovery in the world.

With a feeling of déjà vu, Grace planned for her father's home coming.

Third time lucky, surely.

The onus on his body of two further major insults was considerable and Grace was fearful for her parents' future. Again, they refused all offers of professional help and the same routine as before was reinstated. Grace prayed that it would prove to be enough.

Gideon was happy to help out. He liked to get up early, often to be found studying for a couple of hours before he set off to the hospital, so it made sense for him to pop across the road and perform the morning check, thereby taking some pressure off Grace. He offered to do the evening check as well; it was as though nothing was too much trouble.

His change in demeanour aborted an embryonic worry in Grace's heart. He must at times be wondering what on earth he had got himself into. There had hardly been any opportunity to concrete the initial phase of their relationship before he had been sucked into the maelstrom of dependent parents and family illness, plus the interminable duties of an only child.

On the day that Douglas was due to come home, Gideon presented Grace with a small box from the jewellers. They were across the road, making final preparations, turning on the heating, changing the sheets, stocking up the cupboards.

'I hope you hadn't forgotten about this,' he muttered, dropping to one knee.

Maybe not the most romantic place for a proposal, the kitchen, thought Grace as she took the box from him, rendered speechless by surprise. Opening it she was stunned by a behemoth of a solitaire diamond winking at her. It was gorgeous, of course, and must have cost an impossibly large amount of money but, if she were honest, it was not what she would have chosen. She had hoped that they would go shopping together, knowing exactly which shop she wanted to go to – a tiny working jewellers secreted up a ginnel to one side of a wine bar in the centre of town. In her imagination she knew precisely how her ring ought to look and try as she might, it wasn't like this. Fortunately Gideon misinterpreted her lack of words for shock – actually this bit was correct – and delight. He stood up and took the ring from its box and slipped the jewel onto the third finger on Grace's left hand.

'It's perfect, isn't it? Don't you love it?' he acclaimed.

'Y-y-yes. Lovely. I don't know what to say! I don't think I've ever seen such a huge diamond in real life.'

'I wanted you to have something really extra special. You deserve it, with all that you've been through and all that you do for everyone else.'

'Wow!' Grace wafted her hand about, trying to accept the unaccustomed feel. 'I can't get over how large it is. And heavy!'

'The biggest in the shop!' was the proud reply. 'I'm going to ask your father for his permission when he gets home and then we can show them the ring immediately. It'll make his day very special!'

She hugged him tightly and felt happy and safe in their close proximity. Who cared about the ring she had planned in her mind? She would soon love this one, she loved Gideon and the thought of their future together was exciting, wonderful, fascinating. Surely this was the turning point and life was going to start to improve?

A shadow of his former self, Douglas feebly settled into an armchair by the fire. Walking from the front door, where he had climbed out of a wheelchair, had expended what little stamina he had. Like a tortoise from its shell, his scrawny head and neck protruded from his collar. The hands that had deftly performed so much surgery lay still in his lap. Sensing that he was cold, Sylvia wrapped her recently finished blanket around his shoulders, pulling it snugly up under his chin. Charnley, ecstatic but sensing that he had to be good, sat very close and leant against his master's leg. Happy that he was more or less settled, Sylvia departed to the kitchen and came bustling back with a pot of freshly brewed tea and a Victoria sponge cake, freshly baked and a little lopsided.

'What a lovely welcome,' Douglas said, accepting a piece and biting into it. 'Ah, this is what I'm needing, some good home cooking to help me get my strength back. Thank goodness, a proper cup of tea. That excuse they give you in hospital is undrinkable. Thank you, my darling. You've gone to a lot of trouble for your doddery old husband.'

'I'm just so pleased and relieved to have you home. This time to stay. You'll soon improve now I'm looking after you.'

'I'm sure I will. You do look so much better.'

'I feel it,' she agreed.

When Grace walked in a little later, her first thought was that she had stumbled into a Dickensian melodrama. The sight that met her eyes was pitiful and she had to fight back tears. Huddled up around the fire, covered by reams of roughly knitted material with a small ragged dog at their feet were her parents. An eerie glow flickered as they had only bothered to put one small reading light on and Douglas was by now even wearing some fingerless gloves to keep his hands warm, plus a woolly hat.

Business-like, she switched on the overhead light and checked that the radiators were warm. They were stone cold.

'For goodness sake, you two, the heating's not on. No wonder you're freezing. Right, let's get you sorted. I bet you haven't eaten either, have you?'

'We were just enjoying being back together,' Sylvia explained. 'I hadn't realised what time it was.'

'I wish you'd let me get someone to come in and look after you for a few days,' Grace pleaded. 'Look at the two of you. If I hadn't come in, how long would you have sat there?'

It was hopeless, she knew but she was exasperated. Not wanting to have a row she went into the kitchen, checked the boiler and started to heat up soup she had brought with her and a homemade (so the box said) chicken pie. Sylvia came to join her and peeled some potatoes and looked out some peas from the freezer.

'This looks good,' she said, trying to make her peace with Grace, who she knew was annoyed. 'Thank you.'

Grace hugged her mother. 'You two will be the death of me! I'm not cross I just worry so much about you.'

'I know. But we'll be fine this time, I promise.'

'I hope so.' Never was a comment said with such feeling.

By the time that Gideon arrived, the house was snug and warm, Charnley full of his dinner and back by his master's side. Douglas had agreed that the hat and gloves were no longer necessary and had more colour to his cheeks. They all ate well, Douglas having a second helping while Sylvia refused not only this but also the sponge pudding (also out of a box) and custard, saying that she must stick to her diet and have fruit. Grace was impressed. By the time she was scraping the last of her custard from the bottom of her bowl, she had considerably more confidence that maybe there was a chance that her parents would manage after all.

Their announcement was timed to coincide with coffee. Grace had made no bones about the fact that if the moment was not right, then they were to postpone it, despite Gideon's insistence that news of this magnitude must be shared and enjoyed by all as soon as possible. When it came to it, though, Sylvia pre-empted them by noticing the ring on her daughter's finger. Well, it was hard not to.

They were delighted. Douglas was gracious in his acceptance of Gideon's formal request for Grace's hand in marriage and Grace adored his being so traditional about such an important landmark in their lives. Gideon was always so thoughtful. Rather than bringing champagne, which might interfere with medication, he brought an organic sparkling elderflower drink, which tasted totally different to the way it smelled but after a few sips seemed an entirely suitable substitute.

Maybe they might have been a little more effusive with their congratulations and joy, Grace thought, but they had their reasons. It might have been better to leave their announcement for a few more days. News like this though, she wanted to shout from the rooftops and let the whole world know. Moreover, she calculated that the good news and prospect of wedding planning provided more good reasons to recover quickly.

The rest of the evening passed convivially, drawing to a close early. Douglas climbed the stairs to bed ('Nobody's putting my bed in the dining room,' he had dictated), gripping the banister on one side and Gideon on the other. Once at the top, he waited a while to get his breath back and then agreed that Sylvia was the one to help with a wash and change into pyjamas. Grace waited until she saw that her father was comfortably in bed, Charnley in place nearby and Sylvia doing some final tidying up before heading to join him.

'I really think it's going to be fine,' she told Gideon as arm in arm they ran across the road in the cold night air.

'I'm sure it is,' he agreed, hurrying to unlock the door and appreciate the warmth that greeted them.

'Let's wait until Dad's a bit stronger,' Grace suggested, 'and then have a party, here, for family and friends. Not a huge number, just people we're close to, whom we want to share our happiness with.'

'Good idea. Judging by the way he's come on this evening, it won't be long.'

'I wish there were some of your relatives to invite.' Grace felt sad for her fiancé.

'Not to worry, now I've all your family to enjoy.'

'Mum loved my ring,' Grace twirled Gideon around the hall, giddy with happiness.

'Not as much as I love you.' Gideon pulled her towards him and set about showing her just how much he cared.

Chapter Twenty-One

I wonder if this is the worst day of my life, mused Harry. I can't believe that I have just done what I have. Every cell in my body was screaming at me not to do it but still I did. Why do I have to be so nice perpetually? Why haven't I the balls to say what I think and give my opinions and have people listen and take notice of me?

Day in and day out I listen to folk, empathise, sympathise, do my job. I shoulder everyone else's problems and worries and they leave feeling better while I feel worse. I don't even have Thadeus any more to talk to. I never moan or complain, I'm always offering to cover for the others, or swap or do their duties if there's a problem.

I'm a good person. I don't smoke, I don't drink excessively and I've never used drugs. I try to eat five portions of fruit and vegetables every day of the week. Admittedly I only manage that about once a week but I walk to the supermarket and back and dig the garden. I accept there is room for improvement in these areas but at least I try.

So why can't I have some luck in life and love?

Every day I try to be a good friend. I'm lucky in that they reciprocate and are good friends to me. After my evening with

Janey and Ben I honestly believed that I had constructed a plan of campaign to win Grace's heart. Before I had so much as a chance to put phase one into place I am once again cowed into submission and dare not make a move. Perhaps it'd be better if I simply gave up.

Harry burst into floods of tears in the privacy of his consulting room. Moments before, they had all been up having coffee, laughing and chatting as usual, comparing notes from the morning, sharing out home visits and then the most terrible thing happened...

Grace had told them all of her engagement to Gideon and flashed the ring around for all to see. Without a perceptible qualm she had allowed Harry to take her left hand for a closer look at the diamond. He secretly thought it grotesque and probably not bona fide but said nothing. By switching to automatic pilot, he had heard his voice congratulating her; he had kissed her cheek chastely. Bless her, she had not been satisfied with that. The others had hugged her and she expected the same from him. So he had squeezed her tight in the hopes that by doing so his true feelings would transfer magically from his heart to hers.

Only when Andrew reminded Grace that she ought not to wear her ring at work for health and safety reasons, did Harry feel any better. At least he was not going to have a constant reminder shoved in his face every day.

There was to be, horror of horrors, a party. In a fortnight, at Grace's house. She had urged them all to come and Janey, typically, had offered to make some show-stopping desserts. To Harry the prospect was ludicrous. How in the world was he expected to go along, smile and make jokes for a whole evening? Unless he suddenly acquired a girlfriend, he would be on his own, the only person not in a couple. The only person with nobody to go home to, not even Thadeus.

Night had fallen before he felt minimally less distressed. Once home, he pulled the heavy curtains together, locked the door and poured a glass of red wine. He opened a packet of crisps, morosely crunching his way through them without stopping until they were all gone. A second packet was obligatory.

With a heavy heart, he wrote his acceptance for the party. However he felt, this was not a time to let his standards slip. Now it was vital that Grace suspected nothing. Of paramount importance was her happiness and if it had to be with Gideon then so be it. Harry metaphorically raised a white flag and refilled his glass. Silently he toasted the love of his life, now far out of his reach and unattainable.

No question, he decided, it was, without doubt, the worst day of his life.

Chapter Twenty-Two

in and yang
While Harry's life was on a downward spiral, Grace's luck was definitely in the ascendant. After weeks of worry and emotional upheaval, some force of nature saw fit to grant her some respite. So, buoyant in her newly acquired status of affianced woman, suddenly her problems melted away before her like ice on a sunny day and recent events dissolved into the recesses of time.

Gideon was perfect in all ways. Attentive, always showering her with affection and love, generous and understanding. A paragon, rather like her ring, which she was slowly growing to cherish. He continued to help look after her parents, without a whimper or moan and a couple of days ago had been seen walking Charnley up and down the road, an event hitherto unseen. He wasn't the world's greatest animal lover, Grace had realised. When questioned, he cited some bite by a large, hairy dog with huge teeth as a child, which had needed stitches and a painful tetanus booster and an allergy to cats' fur as his reasons he preferred to keep pets at arm's length but Grace secretly hoped that in the future, when they had their own family, he might be persuaded to have a puppy and learn to love it from the beginning.

Work was going well too. She had completed an audit on diabetic care at the practice, inspired by her mother's diagnosis, and presented it to all her partners. It had been well received and they all concurred that while the diabetic care at the practice was overall good, certain areas could be improved upon, to the benefit of the patients. With Janey's encouragement, she had spent some time with Amber, teaching her about contraception, letting her watch a coil being fitted and an implant inserted. Amber was a keen learner and the success of these tutorials made Grace start to consider the possibility of her becoming a trainer, which would be an arduous process but one that she thought would be enjoyable. She remembered her own training days with affection, apart from that awful day when the elderly lady had had a heart attack in the lounge and nothing could be done to save her. A tiny bit of Grace still took the blame for this. With hindsight, she wished that she had thought about the chance of heart disease when she had seen her the week before but then everything was so much clearer when you had more information. Her own trainer had been supportive and told her she was too hard on herself, that all they were able to do was make decisions at the time but it was a long, long time before Grace's angst started to wane.

So, work was good, Gideon was better than good. What of Douglas and Sylvia? Like a couple of phoenixes they were beginning to flourish. With plenty of good food Douglas's cheeks had filled out, he had more energy and his walking was improving daily. Together with neighbour Jim, he had started to walk little distances with Charnley, the little dog trotting along proudly, tail held high as though to alert all the residents in the road to the recrudescence of his best friend. Sylvia was responding positively to Douglas's progress. Though quiet, she had a daily routine of jobs which she carried out efficiently, if laboriously, and the house was tidy and clean. Both of them had suggested that Gideon's early-morning calls were no longer necessary but, the epitome of kindness, he had stressed that it was no trouble and probably best if he continued for the time being.

No wonder Grace felt as though she was wrapped up snugly in a warm cosy blanket. All aspects of her existence were running smoothly, a rare event but oh so welcome. Enjoy it while you can, she instructed herself.

The surgery was busy with winter ailments and all the partners were seeing extras to cope with the demand. Surgeries rarely ran to time but between them they were such a smoothly running machine that each simply got on with the work to be done. The times they met up together were rarer and shorter when they did occur, which made it easier for Harry to bury his head in the sand and play a ridiculous game in his head in which nothing had changed with Grace. It was so much easier that way, pretending, rather than facing up to the truth. How he loathed his own cowardice.

He had been out and bought some new clothes. Pathetically, he had hoped at Grace might be impressed if he looked a lot smarter. Some hope! Still, grudgingly he accepted there was nothing wrong with some new trousers, a jacket that matched and a new, thick overcoat to protect him from the elements. The shop assistant was keen to show him a selection of ties, discrete, dark with stripes or tiny dots (quite boring in Harry's opinion), promising him that these were all the rage now and that really ties with animal motifs had had their day.

While he acknowledged that the clothes were a big improve-

ment, Harry had no intention of changing his ties. In a show of
defiance, he went to the market and bought a purple one with
badgers on it.

Ironically, Grace had noticed his new clothes, well, the trousers
and the overcoat. She and Harry had simultaneously arrived in
the coffee room one morning and it had been hard not to stay
and have a cup of something with her. He had noted how lovely
she was looking. Her skin was clear and her eyes sparkling. She
had on a fitted red dress which emphasised her trim waist and
coordinating court shoes with a little heel. Her hair was a little
different too but try as he might, he could not decide why.

What a waste, he had snarled inwardly before reminding
himself that she was now off limits and it was time for him
to move on. His anger was such a negative emotion, a waste of
energy and he was determined to rise above it.

Grace had been complimentary and impressed by the trousers
which made him wonder just how bad the old ones had been.
Harry had tried to drink his tea with unnecessary haste but she
was keen to chat, needing a break before the next task of the day.

'We've not had a chance to talk for days, any of us, have we?'
she started.

'No,' he agreed, burning his tongue.

'Work's been terrible, hasn't it?' she tried.

'All part of the job,' Harry replied dismissively. 'It's that time
of the year.'

Grace put her head on one side and looked at him. 'You look
sad, Harry. What's wrong? Is it still Thadeus?'

If only she knew.

'No, it's nothing. Maybe I'm a little tired. All this work, you
know.' Blustering was never one of Harry's strong points.

'Have you thought about that kitten yet?'

'Not really.' He downed what was left of his tea, wishing he hadn't as his throat was scalded.

'I'm sure it would help,' Grace coaxed. 'You know I'll always come with you if you wanted to go and look at some...'

'Very kind of you. But, oh my! Look at the time. I must get on. I don't know about you but I've lots of visits.'

He plucked his overcoat off the hook and put it on.

'Oh, a new coat too!' exclaimed Grace. 'You have been busy. It's lovely. It really suits you...'

Harry felt like strutting up and down, preening.

'Gideon's got one that's identical! What good taste you both have.'

Harry exited as fast as he deemed to be polite, ran to his car, slammed the door shut behind him and sat shaking. Suddenly he hated his coat. It had cost what he considered to be a small fortune, a mix of wool and cashmere, dark blue, almost black and it felt like a dream to wear. After that comment, the chances of him wearing it again were slim. At that moment, given the chance he would have ripped it into a million shreds, set fire to it and jumped on the ashes.

Chapter Twenty-Three

*T*he day of the party was still cold and icy with the promise of snow after lunch. Clouds too heavy to move filled the sky, allowing little daylight through. There was little chance of turning off the lights that day.

Sylvia was sitting gazing out of the window; still in her nightdress in the middle of the morning, waiting for Douglas who had gone shopping with the ever-helpful Jim. They had both suggested that perhaps she might like to go too and look for a new dress for the party but she had said no. For the last few days, she really hadn't been bothered about getting up or making breakfast. It all seemed like such a chore and the less she ate, the less appetite she had, which was good in one way, she supposed, as Harry kept on and on at her to get some weight off.

A robin was balanced on the fence, watching a handful of other birds devouring nuts from a hanging container and swinging from fat balls. Next door's cat was contemplating using their garden as a toilet but not having much luck at digging up the frozen soil. Indignantly, it stalked off, snub nosed, offended, back towards the house.

She wasn't really in a party mood. A quiet evening in was a far more attractive idea. Some television, early bed. Climbing into bed and shutting out the world for twelve hours was such a relief. She wasn't sleeping very well at the moment; waking early and watching the clock go round until Douglas stirred. Still, being cocooned under a duvet and wrapped up in the darkness provided a protective shield from the world.

Spotting the top of Jim's car some hundred yards away, Sylvia reluctantly came away from the window and removed her nightdress. Disgusted, she surveyed herself in the mirror, barely able to look. Her breasts drooped; flaps of redundant skin, previously overstretched by fat, fell off her torso like some bizarre fashion statement. Cellulite pocked her thighs. She prodded it and sighed – once upon a time she had had such wonderful legs... Douglas had loved them.

Closing her eyes against the abhorrent sight of her body, Sylva pulled on yesterday's underwear, black leggings and a long dark grey pullover, once Douglas's but never the same after a turn in the washing machine at too high a temperature. Padding downstairs in old slippers, she made her way to the kitchen, put on the kettle and sat down again. There were the breakfast pots still waiting to be washed but they could wait a bit longer until there were the elevenses' mugs to go with them and maybe the lunch plates too.

Douglas was triumphant. 'I went twice as far as yesterday! Across the precinct and all the way round the supermarket without relying on the trolley too much. Jim thinks I'm ready to go out on my own and I agree! Only on the pavements to start with but in no time at all I'll be ready for the woods and rougher terrain.'

'That's marvellous, darling. I'm so pleased for you. Cup of something to warm you?'

'Please, coffee, I think and I could murder a couple of pieces of that shortbread that Grace brought over. You know the box that one of her patients gave her?'

'Of course, I'll get it out.'

'Only if you don't mind. I feel awful eating things you can't have.'

'No, honestly, it's fine. You enjoy it. All this dieting has quite put me off sweet stuff.'

'You're doing so well. I'm sure that you've cracked this diabetes business and Harry will be congratulating you when he sees you next. Didn't he say he'd pop in today?'

'Yes, I think he did,' Sylvia smiled in a watery fashion. 'I'm sure he doesn't need to come in so often now. He must have more important patients to see to. I'll suggest it when he comes.'

'No one is more important than you.' Douglas planted a cold, wet kiss on her cheek, reminding Sylvia of Charnley's nose.

Harry turned up at lunchtime. Tactfully, Douglas retreated to another room bribing Charnley with some cheese to follow him and so leaving the two of them alone together. Contrary to his decision, Harry was wearing his new coat; there was no disputing the fact that it was extremely warm and that day it was truly bitter. He half expected Sylvia to comment but she didn't, even when he removed it in a rather showy fashion, trying to draw her attention to it. He noted she looked a little distracted, less spontaneously chatty, a bit flat. Gone were the flamboyantly coloured clothes, hairpieces and jewellery. He needed to find out more.

'How are you?'

'Fine,' she sighed.

'You look a bit down, if you don't mind me saying.'

'Do I?' Sylvia sounded surprised.

'Yes. Do you want to tell me about it?'

'About what? There's nothing to tell, Harry dear. I promise.'

He looked unconvinced.

'Honestly! There's a lot going on. There's a lot that has been going on. You know that.'

'Of course.' Harry heaved a thankful sigh that Sylvia hadn't latched on to the topic of her daughter's engagement. 'If you're sure…'

'I'm sure.' Sylvia avoided looking into his eyes.

'All right, then, well, let's talk about other matters. I've got your blood test results and they're really very good. The combination of the tablets plus your own fabulous efforts with diet and weight loss has been a great success. Your blood sugar control is very much better, so well done. I'm really pleased and impressed by how you've coped when so much else has been impacting on your life. You should be very proud of yourself.'

'Oh, that is good news. Thank you, Harry. You're always so sweet and reassuring. I had been worrying since you took the tests. It's a lot easier than it was now that I'm in a routine. But there's no denying it was a huge change for me.'

'I expect you feel better for the change.'

Sylvia pondered on this one. 'Maybe, yes I think so. No, definitely I do.'

'Then keep focussing on that and it'll help you carry on. I'll be in again to see you soon. Do you need a prescription today while I'm here?'

Shaking her head, Sylvia replied, 'No, Gideon arranges all my medicines. I really feel I could do it now but he says no, so I suppose it does make things easier, one less thing to think about each day.'

'Right then. I'd better be off. I'll see you tonight, I guess. You must be looking forward to it.' Harry hoped he sounded suitably excited himself.

'Oh, I'm not one for lots of noise and music and people,' Sylvia told him. 'Not now. Those days are gone, I'm afraid. It's better left to you young ones.'

'I bet you've something lovely to wear, though. That will cheer you up.' Subtle interrogation, thought Harry, let's see what she has to say to that.

'I expect I'll wear my purple dress and matching beads,' replied Sylvia without enthusiasm. 'We won't stay long. Pop in for a quick drink and then slip away. We don't like to leave Charnley alone for too long. Grace will understand.'

Grace thought that her home looked perfect for a celebration. She had spent all day with her preparations. Tiny fairy lights twinkled around the hall and doorways, low lights in the lounge created a warm, inviting ambience and a loop of her favourite music was playing, not too intrusively but identifiably, in the background. She planned to turn up the volume later for dancing. The kitchen table was covered with trays of canapés that had to be put in the oven for seven minutes. She had spent quite a while in the shop studying the cooking instructions, comparing temperatures and times, in order to make her preparations as easy as possible. Absentmindedly she nibbled on some nuts while she went through the checklist in her head. The fridge was full of champagne, getting nicely cold, nestled next to cheesecakes, profiteroles and pavlovas that Janey had dropped in earlier, while on the worktop there was a pile of pizzas and garlic bread to be cooked later on. She congratulated herself on her organisational skills. She had even managed to delegate duties as well. Gideon was in charge of drinks, Janey and Andrew's wife Leonie had offered to act as waitresses to take some of the workload. So kind and so ideal, freeing her up to mingle and chat.

She wallowed in a long bath, enjoying the hot water with scented oil she had added, doggedly determined to enjoy every second of the day. Gideon popped his head around the door and passed her a glass of fizz, threatened to join her but they decided, laughing, that if he did that then the party would probably never happen as they would simply lock the doors and go to bed. Skin silky smooth, Grace looked stunning in an aquamarine shift that emphasised her figure and was short enough to show off her legs. Her hair was gleaming and her eyes sparkling to match her ring. She felt happy enough to burst, hardly able to believe that this was actually happening to her.

A little dizzy from the champagne, she ran downstairs as best she could in her high heels, high enough to receive Janey's approval but very hard to walk in. But they had seemed appropriate in the shop where she had bought the dress and the persuasive, slick-tongued assistant had convinced her that they were a must buy. She knew that she looked fabulous, she felt fabulous and Gideon's confirmation of this fact when she found him surreptitiously trying out the mini toad-in-the-holes was the cherry on top of her ice-cream sundae. He was as keyed up as she was and they jigged about to the music, roaring with hysterical laughter, waiting for the first chime of the doorbell.

Before long the house was alive with people, chattering, drinking and eating. A supremely happy feeling hung in the air. Corks popped, glasses chinked together, wonderful aromas wafted from one room to another. It was a joyous occasion, as befitting such a celebration and, for once, Grace enjoyed being the centre of attention, of having Gideon's arm draped around her shoulder or his hand on her bottom as they worked the room. We're a good team, she thought, her face hurting from all the smiling and giggling.

Sylvia and Douglas were amongst the last to arrive. When the time came to get ready, Douglas had needed to use all his powers of persuasion to shoe-horn his wife out of her chair and off to get changed and then it was an age before she returned. The purple dress had been eschewed, she had opted for black instead, safely shapeless with long sleeves. A string of pearls hung around her neck.

'You'll need some shoes, darling,' he chuckled, pointing at her slippered feet.

She looked down. 'Oh, silly me. I won't be a minute, Douglas.' At the door she turned back to him, 'We don't need to stay long, do we?'

Douglas looked puzzled. 'Not if you don't want to, but I'd have thought you'd want to be there for Grace.'

'Yes, maybe. But she's all her friends there. She's not got time for us. This is her moment.'

Douglas went over and put a hand on each of her shoulders. 'I understand but I do think she wants us there. Tell you what, we'll play it by ear. We'll stay an hour and then have a chat and see how you're feeling. If it's too much for you, give me a nudge and we can escape to the kitchen and do some washing up or something. How about that?'

'Thank you. Nowadays I like to be quiet. It's best when it's us and nobody else.'

Grace, with the best part of a bottle of champagne inside her squealed when they arrived, ushered them in, peeling off their coats as she did so. 'I think you know everyone. Gideon's going to bring you a drink and don't be shy about having something to eat. There's plenty.'

'Can we do anything to help?' asked Sylvia, hopefully.

'Definitely not. You're our guests this evening and I intend to spoil you. It's the least I can do after all you do for me. Go on, a tiny glass of champagne isn't going to hurt. Oh, and try one of these tiny Scotch eggs or a walnut and cheese sablé. Try both! Don't worry about your diet for one evening, Mum.'

Perhaps it was the drink, perhaps it was the phenomenon of being carried away by an atmosphere but Sylvia found she was having fun. Harry and Janey came to talk to her while Andrew monopolised Douglas in one corner. Harry was looking stressed and drinking too much. He kept taking furtive glances at his watch. She noticed that he was avoiding Gideon at all costs. Sylvia felt very sorry for him. He was a lovely, charming, warm man regardless of being an excellent doctor and he more than deserved some good fortune.

As the evening wore on, in spite of her assurance that her parents were not to lift a finger, Grace began to struggle in the kitchen. Having carried out their individually assigned tasks for the first hour or so, her delegates had slipped out of their roles. As the party warmed up and guests relaxed and began to enjoy themselves, it was generally accepted that they were perfectly able to help themselves to food and drink. Now they were starting to bay for something more substantial than bite-sized replicas of well-known classics and Grace, with a decidedly woozy head, needed help.

Sylvia had no hesitation in volunteering and invited Harry to go with her, sensing that he was in need of being rescued. Gratefully he followed her and they gasped at the carnage in the kitchen. Glasses and crumbs everywhere, half-eaten snacks secreted in corners and amongst the mess, Grace looking bewildered and trying to rip the covering off a pizza.

'Oh dear!' cried Sylvia. 'Right, Grace, sit down for a few

minutes and have a coffee. I'll put the pizzas in, Harry, you start to tidy up.'

'Thanks, Mum. My head's thumping. I need something to eat. We need clean plates too. Look I tell you what – I'll wash, Harry, and then if you'd be so sweet as to dry up then we can all sit down and have some food.' So saying she wriggled the ring off her finger, placed it with care on the windowsill and turned on the hot tap.

The hot cheesy and meaty pizzas were received with a cheer by all, torn apart and devoured along with a mountain of garlic bread, salad and more wine. Grace and Gideon sat together, alternately feeding each other which made Harry feel so sick he had to go back to the washing up. He had just about finished as much as he could do when, to his horror, Gideon came in with a pile of plates.

'Hey, Harry, forget that! Come and join us. Desserts are up next. Janey made them. They're fantastic.'

Composing his features into a pleasant mode, Harry managed to be suitably polite and even helped Gideon lay the desserts out on the table and summon everyone to come and dig in. He needed to get away though as soon as he could without looking rude. His assessment of the raucous states of all around him brought him to the conclusion that he could leave any time and not be missed. On the verge of going, someone, and he wasn't sure who, stuffed a plate, piled high with gooey puddings, into his hands, along with a spoon. Well, they did look good and Janey's cooking was not to be turned down, so he decided to do his best and then go home. He wandered back into the lounge and joined Ben by the window.

'Janey's done us proud as usual,' he said, mouth full of cream. 'Delicious... You're so lucky to have...'

Why he was so lucky, Ben was not to discover as an ear-shattering scream came from the kitchen, silencing the entire party in a trice.

Grace came running in, face pallid and terrified, tears streaming, arms waving.

'It's gone! I've lost it! My ring!!!!!'

Chapter Twenty-Four

*W*ell, thought Harry, gradually coming to the next morning with the worst headache and a tongue adherent to the roof of his mouth; that was the most abrupt end to a party I've ever known. Off went the music, up went the lights and in what might have been misinterpreted as a strange party game, the hunt for the ring began. Cushions were turned over, ornaments moved, the rubbish bin searched, the plughole and u-bend checked; even the downstairs cloakroom and bookshelves. None of these places revealed the ring despite intense inspection. Grace was inconsolable, wailing over and over that she had left it on the windowsill and not seen it since, having forgotten to put it back on when she returned to her guests. Sylvia had tried to comfort her, unsuccessfully, while Douglas joined in the hunt.

After an hour or more of frantic rummaging, Gideon had started to encourage the guests to leave, apologising profusely for the precipitate end to the party, herding them to the door like a well-trained sheepdog, promising to let them all know as soon as the ring was found. In the resulting melee, Harry had grabbed his coat and gone with the flow, glad of the offer of a lift from Andrew and Leonie who would pass his cottage on their way home.

His second thought was for Grace. How his heart had ached as he watched her despair. Her pain was his pain. How almost dismissive Gideon had been, looking for the ring. How did he dare call himself her fiancé? He ought to have been hugging her close, reassuring her that material things did not matter, loving her and telling her that all would be well.

Shaking his head was not a good idea, he decided, getting up and heading for a restorative shower. A little invigorated, he fried some bacon and made a pile of sandwiches together with a large pot of tea. Full and feeling much better, he rang Grace.

'No, it's not turned up.' She sounded worn out. He suspected that she'd been up most of the night looking for it.

'I'm so sorry. Do you want me to come round and help you look?'

'I don't think it will help. I've searched everywhere. Now Gideon's suggesting that perhaps someone took it, but I can't believe that's a possibility.'

'Surely not. That's a ridiculous idea.'

'I know but he keeps going on about it and how much it cost. I'm afraid we've had a bit of a row and he's gone out in a huff. He says I should have put it somewhere safer.'

'He's panicking. Don't worry. I bet you're both exhausted.'

'We are. There was all the clearing up to do as well. I didn't go to bed until four and then I couldn't sleep. It's all turned into a dreadful nightmare.'

It was clear that she was crying again.

'Please try not to be so upset. There's every chance it'll turn up. Look, I'm just slipping out for the Sunday paper and then I'll be at home all day, so if you want me to come round, or if you want to come round here, then shout. I mean it. It might even be a good idea for you to get away for a bit.'

'Thank you so much, Harry. I'll be fine, I'm sure. I'd better wait here for Gideon anyway...'

She rang off, leaving Harry feeling not one jot happier than he had been doing.

Outside, it was snowing. Already the ground was becoming covered as large, ungainly flakes fell silently but with intent. Harry pulled on his boots and grabbed his coat. Doing up the buttons, it felt tight around his middle, which was odd. It wasn't as though he was wearing a particularly thick sweater either. He ignored the slightly uncomfortable feel and trudged down the lane. Within seconds his hair and beard were speckled with snow. His hands were bitterly cold and he wished he had bought his gloves. He plunged them deep into the pockets then stopped abruptly. With one hand he pulled out some papers, hospital parking tickets and a reminder of a neurological conference. His brow furrowed.

Oh, it was Gideon's coat. That explained it! No wonder it didn't fit. An easy mistake to make when they were all being shuffled out of the house at speed. He hadn't occurred to him to check. Understandably he'd grabbed the first dark blue overcoat that caught his eye off the hook and left. If Grace didn't get in touch that day, they could swap back at the surgery tomorrow.

He set off again, stopping after only two steps. Hang on! What was that in the other pocket? Right at the bottom. Surely not!

His trembling fingers told him he was right and so it came as no surprise when Grace's engagement ring appeared, stuck on the end of his thumb, still sparkling as the snowflakes fell around it.

By teatime, the Sunday papers lay in a heap by Harry's armchair, unread. He spent his day instead pondering over the meaning of his discovery in Gideon's coat pocket. Much as he wanted to end Grace's suffering, he also wanted to think through in his own mind what was going on, before letting her know. Various explanations came and were shelved. Had Grace put the ring there herself for safe-keeping but then forgotten in her intoxicated state? Hardly likely. Had Sylvia done likewise? No, because she hadn't been drunk. Had one of the guests done it for a joke? Pretty weird sort of joke.

Or had Gideon done it? By mistake or on purpose and if so, why? Had Gideon believed that it was Harry's coat?

Harry felt somewhat ashamed as his active imagination ran riot, fuelled by his unconcealed hatred for Gideon. Worse still, what if there even one iota of truth in some of it?

Chapter Twenty-Five

*In the end, Harry decided to do absolutely nothing but wait and see. Consequently, he put the ring back into the pocket (he told himself not to be stupid and that it really was a step too far when he considered wiping his fingerprints off it) and sent a text to Grace asking her to bring his coat with her to work the following day.

She still looked dreadful that Monday morning. Washed out and wan with eyelids heavy from crying, she insisted that she was fit to work. She wanted to work, to take her mind off her misery. Unusually, she had paid little attention to her appearance, which suggested that she had crawled out of bed, scraped her hair back and thrown on a dark brown, rather unflattering wraparound dress, black tights and nondescript shoes. No jewellery, no makeup. Looking as though she had the whole world's problems on her shoulders, she listlessly toyed with a tea bag in a mug while making a cup of tea and admitted that she had not eaten for over a day.

I can't bear it, thought Harry. I cannot bear to see her like this, when I know that, in an instant, I can make her so happy by telling her about the ring. But if I do, she'll want to know why I didn't tell her yesterday and then I don't know what I'd say.

Grace slumped off to her room leaving Harry with his dilemma. Talking to Janey was an option but he felt unready for this yet. He had more thinking to do first. The responsibility was his to come up with a solution.

By lunchtime, Grace was the first to admit that her morning was a disaster, from start to finish. All the patients had lists of problems and expected her not only to listen to them all but sort them all in one sitting. They seemed oblivious of the fact that she was half-crying, apart from one who advised her to take something for her bad cold before she passed it on to anyone. Every five minutes she checked her phone and emails in case there was a message from Gideon. She had sent him innumerable texts, trying as many approaches as she could think of, some sad, some funny and some apologetic, veering close to grovelling but received nothing in return.

Home had not been a comfortable place to be since the party. The heating was fully turned up but the air was cold as ice. They were barely talking, apart from the merest civilities, further searching had been futile and he had not touched or kissed her for over twenty-four hours. Not that she was counting, of course.

As if that wasn't enough to have on her conscience, she spilled coffee down her dress which left a large damp patch as though she had wet herself and then found that she had a flat tyre and had to ask the others to take her home visits as well as their own so that she could get that seen to. In desperation she rang Gideon's office but his secretary, Hattie, highly skilled in deflecting unwanted callers, said pointedly that he was at a meeting and then had a full clinic ahead of him which he was already late starting.

Hopeless.

Grace gave up and turned instead to the faith that he would

come home that evening, when they might have a chance to sit and talk and make friends again. She had to trust him or else she had nothing. Their relationship was not ideal at times, she knew that. After the initial euphoria, they had shared some very hard times and had a few bumpy rides. He had revealed traits that she was not so enamoured of but then expected that she had too. She knew that he thought her to be too sensitive and too quick to over react. Nobody was perfect. And that was what love was all about, being with one person, without whom life was unimaginable, warts and all. At the moment there seemed to be an awful lot of warts unfortunately.

Unbeknown to Grace, Harry ordered the receptionists to block off some of her appointments for the afternoon, promising to see extra himself to make up the shortfall. He simply told them she was unwell, which was not far from the truth and one look at her was enough for them to know this was the case. It seemed to help though. He kept an eye on her progress on the computer as the day wore on and easing off the pressure for her meant that she was nearly running on time for one thing. Catching up with her at the close of play, when she looked very relieved to have survived the day, he offered to take her out for a bowl of pasta.

'Come on, it'll do you good. You need to eat. We haven't been to Barolo for ages. You know you love their crab linguine. A portion of that, some garlic bread, a couple of glasses of house red and you'll sleep like a top. Tomorrow the world will seem a brighter place, I promise.'

She refused predictably.

'I can't, Harry, I'm sorry. I have to get back to see Gideon. I can't live with this tension between us. It's dreadful. I hate it. I will eat, I promise you and let's hope, as you say, tomorrow will be better.'

She looked totally unconvinced.

'None of this is your fault, Grace. Let him wait. Let him worry where you are for a change. Come out for an hour and then I'll see you home.'

Shaking her head sadly, 'I can't,' she repeated. 'I've got to go. And it is my fault. If I hadn't taken my ring off, none of this would have happened.'

Taking Gideon's coat and hugging it to her face, hoping for a whiff of his cologne, Grace walked sadly to her car. Harry watched her go, willing her to look in the pockets but she tossed it onto the back seat without a thought, revved up the engine and screeched out of the car park.

Harry half expected to see her grinning from ear to ear the next morning but no, she was still pale and drawn, wearing the same dress and shoes. He saw her walking across the car park from his window. She dropped her bag and had to bend down to gather up the contents which had rolled in all directions. Her dress looked suspiciously creased at the back and he guessed she had slept in it, perhaps finally dropping off in a chair in the lounge, waiting for Gideon to turn up. He allowed her a little time to go to her surgery and then knocked tentatively on the door.

'Hi, how's things?' Did he really need to ask? She looked haggard.

'No better,' she replied simply. 'He came home about nine thirty, made a coffee and disappeared up to bed without a word. I was going to go after him but if I'm honest, Harry, I was so tired I knew all that I wanted to say would come out wrong and I'd just make everything worse, rather than better.'

Harry sat down in the patient's chair, thinking how different the world looked from this angle and surprised at how vulnerable he felt.

'I've barely slept,' she went on. 'I wanted to be awake in case he came down to see me, but he didn't. I heard him go to the bathroom and then get up this morning. He went over to Mum and Dad as usual. That must mean that he cares. I mean, if this really was the end, he wouldn't do that would he? And then he roared off in his car, no breakfast, not even a drink. Obviously avoiding me and a possible confrontation. What am I going to do?'

Harry thought for a second. 'Firstly, you are going home. Remember it's your house. You are not fit – no don't interrupt – I'll say again, you are not fit to work. Quite apart from anything else, you look worse than any patient. Go home, unplug the phone, turn your mobile off and go to bed. Everything appears so much worse when you're tired out. It all becomes black and doom laden and you can't see the way out. How often do you tell patients that? Exactly. Now do as I say.'

Grace started to protest but Harry quelled her with a stern look. 'Go home. I'm going to see your mother later this morning, so I will come to see you as well and you can make me a sandwich for lunch – and one for yourself, which you will eat while I watch. Right?'

She nodded, reluctantly, with a half laugh.

'That's settled then. Switch off for a bit, promise me. I'll see you later.'

Without thinking he held his arms out and she came to him for a close hug. It was quite simply the natural gesture to make, regardless of how blooming wonderful it was to have her so close.

Harry was astonished by his sudden command of the situation.

Had he ever taken charge with such an authoritative air before? Secretly he was rather proud of his assertive reaction and the way he had taken control. He hoped that Grace was similarly impressed too.

He felt pleasantly good as he strolled off with a bit of a swagger to call in his first patient, looking forward to lunch.

Chapter Twenty-Six

ouglas was sitting with his head buried in his hands. Nausea played havoc with his guts which were already in knots. Charnley, full of concern, was sitting beside him, nudging him with a cold nose, uttering an occasional soft, sympathetic whimper. Distractedly, Douglas stretched down with one hand to pat his friend on the head, amazed at the intuitive nature of one so small and furry.

He was angry. Angry at his own selfishness and his preoccupation with his own problems. Having had to learn to walk again, taking umpteen painkillers each day to abate the pain as he did so and then counteract the inevitable side effects with laxatives by the gallon, he had taken his eye off the ball. So intent had he been on his own welfare that he had let his guard slip and that was unforgivable. For nearly forty years he had watched Sylvia constantly, assessed her mood, kept an eye open for any hints, signs and subtle nuances in her behaviour to suggest that she was changing. Until the last few weeks.

Overwhelmed by the entire experience of being a patient, he had allowed his watchfulness to relax; he had put his confidence in the new medication and the positive way she seemed to respond to it. He hadn't realised that she was slipping, spiralling out of control again. Every cell in his body was curdled by remorse, his brain weighed down by guilty conscience.

She never altered suddenly, there were always plenty of warning signs that he was attuned to and this time he had missed them. Reprehensible.

Ironically, when he most needed her, his partner in diagnosis, his second pair of eyes, otherwise known as Grace, was less use than a stethoscope with the earpieces missing. The run-up to the party and then the subsequent debacle with the missing ring meant that she too had other thoughts which took priority to the exclusion of all others. He had no idea what was going on across the road right now. Gideon had been monosyllabic that morning. In and out before they drew breath. Then he had seen Grace draw up in her car earlier, when by rights she ought to have been in surgery. She had run into the house before he'd had time to call out to her and before he had time to cross the road he saw the bedroom curtains being closed with an air of finality. Something about her demeanour told him not to interfere and he knew, inevitably, she would come to him and tell him what was happening.

Until then, he had to cope on his own. He wondered what time Harry was due to arrive.

In the lounge, Sylvia had done the unthinkable. Overnight while he had slept, every one of the photographs had been taken out of the frames and torn into a thousand pieces, strewn around the carpet. Having done this, she had laid down on the settee where she still was and had been for hours. Her black leggings and sweater were the ones she had changed back into immediately when they got back from the party. Her hair was lank and unwashed; her body was beginning to smell. As soon as he had opened the door to the room that morning, he had been hit by the smell of stale sweat and urine and her desperate need for a bath. Trying to rouse her had not been successful beyond her pushing him away and sobbing that she wanted to be left alone. He had ignored her naturally and hugged and kissed her but her response was frigid.

Why had this happened? The question went through his head over and over. It was literally decades since she had plummeted into such depths of despair. Yes, they'd had more than their fair share of manic episodes but rarely depression. When Grace was eight, Sylvia had taken an overdose. Not a large one but Grace had never been told about this. She had thought it fun when she was taken round to her best friend's house for a sleepover, not one night but three, not knowing that her father was keeping a constant vigil by her mother's hospital bed and more electroconvulsive treatment had to be employed.

Spare us from more of that, he prayed. It had to be the new medication. The dose had been reduced a little but not by much. Perhaps she was just resistant to it now. At least he had the reassurance that her compliance had been perfect, thanks to Gideon who had never once failed to appear before breakfast and watch her swallow the handful of tablets. He was taking the task so seriously that he even kept the tablets at Grace's, thereby making sure that Sylvia had no chance of self-medicating. He was a true godsend, thought Douglas, reliable and responsible.

Sylvia's world was the same colour as her clothes. No matter where she looked, which dark recesses of her brain she plumbed into, there was no hope. She knew she ought to count her blessings but this no longer helped. What was the point? She was a worthless individual, of no use to anyone, a waste of space and a parasite on society.

All she was able to do was cry, cry until her throat muscles were so sore that they screamed at her to stop. Her limbs were leaden and she was oh, so tired.

Douglas's attempts to soothe and love her had the opposite effect, they made her feel more of a failure, undeserving of his devotion. He was just doing it to be nice. There was nothing about her that was lovable. She was pitiful. From her hideous physique to her twisted, tortured mind, she was grotesque.

She was unsure sometimes which was worse. The horrendous thoughts which terrified her as it was incredible that she was capable of such or the malignant way they stole every ounce of her energy so that she was rendered immobile with no desire to eat or drink. Any innate yen to survive had abandoned her. Contemplating days ahead being like this was not viable. The world would not mourn her; it would be a better place without her, it would celebrate her absence. Grace did not need a mother who was mad and unstable, Douglas did not deserve the worry and stress that she brought with her wherever she went. They were able to look after each other and maybe, with time, their memories of her would be good ones, of her happy days, though she was unable to remember any of that herself.

Sylvia heard Harry arriving at the door, hushed whispers in the hall as Douglas no doubt filled him in on how she was. She pushed up into a sitting position. The room was warm but she was shivering. It made no difference how many clothes she wore or how high the fire was turned up; she was cold, like stone, devoid of life.

Not even the sight of Harry's face cheered her up, as it tended to. He was another person she had let down. She gazed at the carpet, unable to meet his eyes, hugged the cushion close to her and pulled her sweater sleeves down over her hands, hiding away as best she could. Unfazed, Harry sat down next to her.

'Hello, Sylvia,' he began. 'Things aren't so good, Douglas tells me.'

Her shoulders heaved.

'What's happened to all the photos?'

'I'm not good enough to have a daughter. This way she doesn't have to look at me. And I don't have to be reminded of how I've failed as a mother.'

'That's nonsense. You're a fabulous mother. It's all down to you that Grace has turned out to be such a wonderful person and a wonderful doctor.'

'You're only saying that because you have to.'

'How long have things been this bad?'

'For always.'

'Has anything happened to disturb you?'

'No.'

'You seemed quite bright at Grace's party...'Harry ventured.

'I didn't want to go. Douglas knew that but he insisted.'

'And since then?'

'I don't know. I can't think any more. My brain hurts. The voices won't stop either. They won't let me rest or sleep.'

'Voices? Tell me more.'

'In my head. Constantly going on and on and on. They never stop, no matter how much I beg them to.'

'What are they saying?'

'What I already know. That I'm beyond help, worthless, a fool. That everyone hates me and is laughing at me for being an idiot.'

'When did they start?'

'A few days ago, maybe more. I can't remember.'

Harry's concern was growing steadily. Sylvia was very depressed indeed.

'I have to ask, Sylvia. Have you had any thoughts about

harming yourself?'

A dreadful silence hung menacingly between them.

'Sylvia? Answer me, please. I only want to help you get better.'

'All the time,' she whispered. 'I don't want to be here any more. I'm sorry I've let you all down.'

'You haven't. You're ill, Sylvia. It's the bipolar playing more tricks on you. But we'll get you right again, I promise. Have you been taking your tablets? Please don't tell me you've stopped them.'

Sylvia wiped her nose with her sleeve and then sniffed.

'Oh them! No, I've been taking them. I hate them. Gideon brings them every morning. Three white ones and two yellow ones. Like some prison guard he stands over me watching until he knows I've swallowed them. I tried once to hide them under my tongue – I was going to spit them out later, but he guessed and he was really cross. They don't seem to be working, do they?'

At this point she lay down again, exhausted by the effort of talking for so long.

'I think I'll ring Phillip, Sylvia. He needs to know.'

'Do what you want, what do I care? Just leave me alone.'

'He might suggest you go back to the ward for a few days. How would you feel about that?'

She shrugged. 'I'd rather not.'

Harry left the room to find Douglas, who was pacing in the kitchen. One look was all he needed to know how serious the situation was.

'She'll need to be admitted, I'm sure, but I'm optimistic we can avoid a section this time. She's so worn out, she's lost all her fight.'

'It's my fault, Harry, I'm so sorry.' Douglas filled the kettle, more to have something to do than because he wanted a drink.

'Stop trying to take the blame. You've lived with this long enough to know how unpredictable a condition it is. I'm going to get hold of Phillip. With any luck I'll be able to as it's lunchtime, so he might be free. Grace has promised me a sandwich so I'll be over there if you want me but of course I'll pop back and have a word before I go.'

Douglas caught Harry's arm as he walked to the door.

'That's my other worry. Grace. Is she OK?'

'I'll make sure she is.'

'Sometimes,' began Douglas, almost afraid of what he was about to say, 'I see so many reminders of her mother at that age. I'm afraid for her…'

Harry slapped him a couple of times on the shoulder. 'You have nothing to worry about on that score. She's vulnerable, I grant you but she's strong.'

Grace's reaction to the news was to be expected; like her father she felt culpable for her mother's downswing.

'Honestly, Harry, I thought things were getting better for us all. So much has gone wrong over the last few weeks that I hoped my engagement was a sign that change was on the way. And Mum – well, she seemed to be doing splendidly. Poor, poor Mum. Shall I go over there?'

'There's no rush. Your dad's with her and she's safe. He's trying to persuade her to have some lunch. What about my sandwich? I'm starving. Incidentally, you've obviously had some sleep and you look fractionally more alive than you did.'

Grace managed a watery laugh. 'Thanks for that. So, what filling would you like? I could rustle up a cheese and salad in granary for you. How'd that be?'

'Perfect, but no onions and while you're doing that, I'll try to get hold of Phillip.'

Phillip was by some stroke of good fortune in his office when Harry rang. He listened sympathetically, concern in his voice. 'What meds is she taking? Have you altered them?'

'No, I'd not do anything like that without discussing it with you first. The same as when you saw her in the clinic last month when she seemed to be doing well. You didn't make any changes so that's what she's still on, or, as she puts it, three white ones and two yellow ones.'

'Yellow ones? Which are they?'

'The antidepressants. The Vivial.'

'But they're not yellow, they're a green and red capsule… I'm looking at a packet of them on my desk that a patient left, as we speak.'

'Perhaps the local pharmacy got in a different brand,' suggested Harry.

'No,' Phillip stated firmly. 'That's not possible. There's only one drug company that makes them.'

'Oh my goodness,' a horrified Harry spluttered. 'Whatever has she been taking then?'

Chapter Twenty-Seven

*H*arry's mind was on a roller coaster. What had been going on? Where had Sylvia got these yellow tablets from and how long had she been on them? More to the point, if they weren't Vivial, then what on earth were they? He knew that the correct prescriptions had left the surgery because he had signed them personally. They were sent to the local pharmacy for Douglas to pick up. An efficient system that many patients used and were very satisfied with. It had been up and running for years now, along with home deliveries. Occasionally mistakes were made but very rarely and they were inevitably soon spotted and corrected.

Wait a minute, though, he had a sudden flash of brilliance, it wasn't Douglas who had been collecting the drugs and administering them, was it? No, it was the ever-wonderful Gideon who had been determined not to relinquish his daily task, come what may.

Surely not! He was a consultant neurologist, for goodness sake. Why would he behave like that? Was it possible that he had made a genuine mistake?

Grace called him through to the kitchen where lunch was ready. She looked at him expectantly and he wondered how much to tell her.

'Did you manage to get hold of him?'

'Yes, first go! He'll be round this afternoon.'

'Thank you, Harry. That sounds so inadequate but you've been such a star with my mum. With all of us.'

'Hey, you'll make me blush. That's what friends are for. Now, let's eat. I'm glad to see you've made yourself a sandwich too, even though it's not quite as huge as mine.'

They munched in silence, both lost in thought.

Harry swallowed hard. 'Anything from Gideon?' He rescued a piece of cucumber from his beard.

'Zilch. I checked my phone while you were ringing Phillip.'

'Sorry to hear that.'

'By the way, you've a blob of mayo on your tie. It matches the hamsters...'

Harry stood up and went over to the sink to remove the offending splash, hoping not to end up with a mark that was even worse.

'He's still helping with your mum's tablets, you said?'

'Yes. But if he's not coming back then, he'll stop that too.'

'Where does he keep them?' Harry hoped he sounded disinterested.

'In his briefcase I think. That way he's organised and can set off for the hospital as soon as he's been over to Mum. Why?'

'Oh, nothing. I needed to look at a dosage but I can do that when I'm back at work. Something that Phillip asked me to check.' The lies came easily.

'I'll check the cupboard... no, nothing. He must have them with him.'

'Not to worry.'

'Coffee?' asked Grace, jumping as her phone jingled.

She grabbed it and checked, her face breaking into a smile as she did so.

'It's from Gideon! He's says he's sorry and he'll be back at teatime, plus he loves me and...'

'Spare me the details,' Harry tried to look pleased for her.

'Oh, I'm so happy. I can't wait to see him. Sorry, Harry, I'll get your coffee and there are some chocolate biscuits somewhere too. Suddenly I'm famished!'

She looked twenty years younger, thought Harry, cut to the quick. I wish I had that effect on her. I will do, one day, but there's something very odd going on and I need to get to the bottom of it first and I need to act fast.

Grace was prattling on while she poured out milk and opened a box of biscuits.

'He'll be so upset to hear about Mum. Do you think I should text him, or would phoning him be better?'

Harry gave some thought to the question. 'Just text him, no! Wait! Don't do that. Leave it until this evening. No need to distress him if he's in clinic, eh?'

'You're right. Much better that we talk about her face to face. Harry? You are a saviour. I'll never be able to thank you enough.'

But Harry was not listening for once to her compliments. He was hatching a plan and wondering if he was daring enough to carry it out.

Back across the road, Grace took one look at her mother's expressionless face and burst into tears. Sylvia was crying too and apologising. It was all too much for Douglas who felt hopelessly out of control and retreated to the garden under the pretext of filling up the bird feeders. Before long, Sylvia would be back in hospital, back in that inhospitable ward and his days would be planned around visiting times once more. He filled his lungs with sharp cold air and gently exhaled.

Here we go again, he thought, wretchedly.

He was still outside when Phillip arrived, dressed in a black pin-stripe suit, black shirt, white tie and a black fedora. Douglas half expected him produce a trombone or to start tap-dancing.

He needed no more than minutes to know that Sylvia ought to be admitted. Preparing for a battle of wills, he was pleasantly relieved when she accepted his suggestion without a bleat and agreed to go in the car so long as Grace and Douglas went with her. The last indignity would be yet another ambulance arriving at the door.

Phillip checked his watch and rang the ward. After a one-sided conversation in which he became increasingly tetchy he snapped his phone off and turned to Douglas and Grace.

'I'm sorry, we've no beds until the day after tomorrow. Do you think you could manage two more nights?'

'Of course,' Douglas agreed readily. 'She might even be a little better tomorrow.'

'She's definitely being admitted. Hopefully not for long, all being well.'

'I can stay over, Dad, and help,' offered Grace.

Douglas wagged a finger at her. 'I am perfectly capable of looking after your mother. Now, I had arranged with Jim to go down to the Starbeck Arms for a pint and some dominoes tomorrow evening but I can easily put him off….'

'No don't do that, Dad. You go and I'll come and sit with Mum until you get back, then you take over. Go on, please. You need a break. Nothing's going to happen if I'm here.'

Douglas had a quick think and glanced at Sylvia, who nodded. 'All right then. Come across at seven thirty. I'll be back by ten.'

'Good, then all's settled. I'm so sorry I can't take her today. I've had my number of beds cut by a third in the last year but don't get me climbing on that soapbox. There will definitely be a bed for Sylvia on Friday morning, if you'd like to bring her up to the ward about nine.' Phillip stood up and patted Sylvia on the arm. 'I'll see you then, Sylvia, and I promise that I will sort out what's gone wrong and have you better as soon as possible.'

Sylvia rewarded him by actually looking directly at him, a pleading in her eyes that made Douglas cough self consciously to disguise his desire to cry. With Phillip gone, Harry departed soon afterwards, content that his patient was safe and sorted. Nothing would go wrong now.

Chapter Twenty-Eight

❦

*H*arry was ready. Better known for his skills in prevarication, he had surpassed himself this time. He wished he had someone to boast to but better he kept quiet until his mission was accomplished. What he had to do was scary but necessary. If his suspicions were correct then he would be opening a Pandora's box with potentially unthinkable consequences.

He was at the hospital, reading the notice board by the restaurant, having had a cup of tea and a slice of fruitcake. Luckily it was his half-day but this was so important that surgery paled into insignificance for the first time in his life. It was nearing six o'clock; outside it was pitch black and snowing again.

Harry turned his attention to the adverts. A course for sexually transmitted diseases? No. An update in congestive cardiac failure? He'd done that a year ago. An opportunity to share a three-bedroomed flat with two student nurses? That sounded the most promising of them all. Aha! A litter of kittens, five of them, assorted colours, only four weeks old, ready to leave their mother in another fortnight. Free to good homes.

A great believer in Fate, Harry jotted down the number, determined to ring later. He needed something to look forward to. Thadeus was irreplaceable – he still had a photo of him in his wallet – but there was more than enough room in his big heart for a tiny, totally dependent, squeaky kitten. Or maybe two, this time, so they had each other's company when he was at work. He was sure Grace would be happy to look after two if and when he went on holiday.

He was running out of posters to read when he heard footsteps coming down the corridor, looked up and saw Gideon, brief case in hand, dark blue overcoat neatly buttoned and a striped muffler around his neck and mouth.

They greeted each other in a friendly fashion.

'Good to see you, Harry,' boomed Gideon, through the woolly material.

'And you. Hardly had a chance to speak to you at the party, what with one thing and another. How's it going?'

'What a party that was! Fancy a drink? We could go to the doctor's mess. They've a really good guest beer on this week, Lambstrangle.'

You have just played right into my hands, thought Harry, beaming with delight and accepting the invitation with alacrity. No mention of rushing home to Grace to make amends, he noticed. What a bastard!

'Let me get the drinks in, Gideon, please,' Harry insisted. 'You go and sit over there and unravel that scarf. Lambstrangle for you is it?'

'Please.'

'Sounds good, I'll try it too.'

The mess was warm and inviting. Various groups of doctors were arranged around the room, discussing their day, washing away the horrors, trying to relax. As usual there was no one behind the bar. It was accepted that you poured your own drinks and left the money in the till, or ran up a tab.

Harry bent down to find two pint glasses, taking the opportunity to crumble a small beige tablet that he had in his pocket into one of them. Standing, he filled them both to the brim, allowed the froth to settle, topped them up and walked carefully over to the table, two packets of nuts clenched between his teeth.

'Thanks, mate,' said Gideon, ripping open one packet and diving in, before 'Cheers.'

'Cheers. Your good health!' replied Harry, sipping the brew which was strong enough to make his eyes water slightly. 'This is excellent, you're right.'

They swapped stories of patients, each one trying to outdo the other with the complexity of the diagnosis before moving onto hospital gossip which included the outrageous rumour that one of the junior doctors had been found in a patient's bed, while the patient was still in it. Harry shook his head. Things like that never happened in his hospital days.

Gideon refilled their glasses. The genial surroundings and salty snacks had resulted in quick drinking coupled with the fact that the beer was slipping down a treat.

'How's Grace?' asked Gideon, starting on his second pint with enthusiasm.

'She's had better days,' Harry answered truthfully. 'She's expecting you later.'

'I know,' Gideon nodded. 'We had a bit of a fall-out over that bloody ring. But it's all water under the bridge now.' He glanced at his watch. 'I'm supposed to be there by now but she'll forgive me, she always does.'

'Perhaps you ought to text her and tell her where you are?' Harry advised.

'Nah, no point. She'll wait for me. Hey, what about you, Harry.

You seeing anyone at the moment?'

'Not really.'

'Ah! What does that mean? Spill the beans, mate. Who is she?'

Harry assumed a mysterious look. 'Couldn't possibly say at this point in time. All a bit clandestine, if you know what I mean.' Harry tapped the side of his nose, meaningfully. 'Come on, drink up, you've time for another before we have to go.'

'Sure thing. Tell you what though, this beer goes right through you. I'll have to go and have a pee. Here's some money. Do you mind getting the drinks and I'll be back in a mo.'

This was the moment Harry had been waiting for. He watched Gideon staggering slightly across the room to the toilets, counted to ten after he had disappeared from view and then, heart thumping, he casually leant across and reached for the brief case.

Thank the Lord, it was unlocked. To anyone else in the mess, it looked as though Harry was simply checking his own bag. He rifled through some papers, grimaced at a brown apple core and dismissed a bunch of envelopes and a tendon hammer. Nothing. How infuriating. He was so sure.

Time was running out. Harry hastily attempted to put everything back in its place. And then he spotted them, wedged into a side compartment. Sylvia's medications. One box of mood stabilisers and...one bottle, unlabelled, of yellow shiny tablets. He took one and shoved it in his pocket, shut the briefcase and placed it back by Gideon's chair. Milliseconds to spare. He jumped up and hurried to the bar.

Gideon was back and eager to try to discover the identity of Harry's fictitious woman. He elegantly deflected the questions.

'Grace's mother being readmitted on Friday.'

'Sorry about that. Thought she was all right.'

'It's been very kind of you to help.'

'No problem, mate. It's been a pleasure.' He laughed out loud. 'Oh shit, I need another pee. What's wrong with this beer? It's only minutes since I peed more than a cart horse.'

Harry smiled benignly. 'How odd. I've not noticed a thing.'

But then, thought Harry, I didn't have a diuretic dissolved in mine!

Back at home, with the door locked and the curtains drawn, Harry examined the yellow tablet. He pushed it around with his finger and sniffed it. Fetching a knife from the kitchen drawer he attempted to cut it in half. With a snap, it half scooted across the table, the remains fragmented on the plate. The inside of the tablet was dark brown. Never seen that before, thought Harry. Mind you, I don't often do this sort of thing.

He carried out a further inspection and then timidly licked a bit with the tip of his tongue. Contrary to his expectations it was not bitter like most medications. He took another lick. No, it was sweet and not unpleasant at all. Now braver, he nibbled it. The crisp coating shattered under the impact of his teeth and he was left in no doubt whatsoever that the inside was chocolate. It was nothing more than a candy-coated sweet!

Chapter Twenty-Nine

Although he was unable to make head nor tail of what was going on, Harry knew that the first job to do was ring Phillip and inform him that Sylvia had not been on the correct medication for an unknown period of time. With any luck, restarting the correct antidepressants, which had been helping her previously, might negate the need for any electroconvulsive treatment which Harry had a feeling they were considering if all else failed. Rarely undertaken these days, it was very much a last resort with a lot of patients.

Phillip received the news with a mix of curiosity and displeasure. Harry, who did not want to discuss any details until he had worked them out for himself, simply advised that there must have been some sort of mix up and he promised to find out what.

'You better find out, Harry, and let me know. We're playing with a human life here. She's profoundly depressed, verging on catatonic. We cannot risk this happening again. If and when she's ready for discharge, I can't let her go until I know she's completely safe.'

'Of course, I realise all that and agree with you totally. I will find out, don't worry and I'll let you know. I've a few ideas and I need to ask one or two people one or two questions but I'll get to the bottom of it, trust me.'

'It's a puzzle, that's for sure. Let me know if I can do anything to help.'

Harry rang off. Carefully he put what remained of the so-called tablet into an envelope, sealed it up and placed it between the pages of a physiology textbook that he had kept since medical school. He went into the kitchen, poured a glass of red wine and smiled at the thought of Gideon enjoying an evening interrupted by frequent trips to empty his bursting bladder. Perhaps he had been a little bit unkind choosing that large dose of diuretic when a smaller one would have been just as quick acting but no, Gideon deserved all he got. In fact, so much so, Harry hoped fervently that the trips to the bathroom continued all through the night as well.

Chopping spring onions and baby sweet corn for a stir-fry, it was with a degree of peacefulness that Harry cooked his supper and then sat eating it, watching the news as he did so. He was filled with an immense sense of satisfaction that he had finally nailed Gideon, in theory to begin with, and uncharacteristically he was looking forward to coming face to face with him in the flesh.

Not yet though. He must have all his facts straight before the confrontation or else Gideon would try to extract himself slimily with oleaginous excuses and perfectly possible arguments. The big question was why? Why Grace? And why Grace's mother?

While Harry was sipping away at his wine, poring over every angle of his conundrum Gideon had returned home to Grace. Trying to conduct a serious conversation when one person is already quite drunk is doomed before it has even begun and Grace was understandably frustrated by her lovely fiancé who wanted to get even more drunk and shower her with wet sloppy kisses and suggestive comments about how he was able to think of far better ways to spend the evening than talking. As he tried to put his hand up her jumper, Grace was torn. On the one hand she wanted to demand that they get all their problems out in the open and have an adult and frank discussion. She had spent every minute since she had received his text rehearsing for this moment and was of the opinion that she had come up with some blistering one-liners and highly intelligent suggestions. On the other, he was so gorgeous, was obviously so sorry to have upset her – he'd even had to have a drink before he came home to pluck up courage – that she longed to melt into his arms and submit to his love making. Try as she might, it was very difficult, verging on impossible to keep a straight face when he was whispering fabulously sentimental and sensuous words in her ear and his warm breath was melting her resolve.

It was no contest. She went into the kitchen, opened a bottle of rosé wine and took two glasses from the cupboard, returned to Gideon's open arms and prepared to surrender to his charms.

Chapter Thirty

It might have been the whole bottle of rosé that she had consumed, for they had succumbed to the temptations of a second bottle, or it might have been the takeaway they ordered in, both too tired and drunk to contemplate cooking for themselves, but a decidedly seedy Grace emerged from her front door the following day and set off for work. Pale green around the gills, with a bottle of water an arm's length away, she dragged her way through another day, feeling worse as each hour passed, rather than better. Janey suggested she try something solid at lunchtime but the plain sandwich – just ham and tomato – did nothing to improve the heaving in her guts and the thumping headache. Her skin felt prickly and her bones started to ache. That awful solid feeling at the back of the nose started, intimating that she was developing a cold and this was quickly followed by its partner in crime, a sore throat. This was definitely more than a hangover. This was an evil virus that, by teatime, had rendered her incapable of much more than driving home, shivering constantly and crawling into the house, up the stairs and into bed.

Gideon was full of concern. He helped her undress and found her a clean nightdress. He brought her iced water, orange juice and a hot-water bottle. Tenderly he stroked her forehead with a cool flannel, which was blissfully soothing and told her how she still managed to look beautiful when pale and sweaty. Amidst the waves of fever, Grace considered that perhaps this was not the best compliment she had ever received or perhaps it was. Her brain hurt too much to analyse his words further.

'Gideon?' she croaked, her throat on fire.

'Yes, my love,' he answered dutifully.

'Can you ring Dad please? I'd promised to go over and sit with Mum so that he could go out for a few hours but there's no way I can go in this state. Tell him I'm really, really sorry.'

'OK, I'll do that right away. Can I get you anything else?'

'Thanks, but no. I'm going to try to have a nap, though I don't want to sleep too much as that'll mean I won't sleep tonight.'

'You need lots of sleep. It'll make you better. I'm going to bring you two paracetamol now. Get that fever down. You feel like a furnace.'

He blew her a kiss and went downstairs, humming. He picked the phone up, began dialling but then hung up. Something rather clever had occurred to him. He went over to the corner where the coats were hung, opened his medical bag and after a little fumbling found exactly what it was he was looking for. Pressing two tablets out of their bubble pack, he sniggered a little. How convenient it was that there were so many drugs that were white and round tablets. Usually it was a source of great annoyance to him.

'What tablets do you take?' He would ask his patients in the out patients clinic.

'Oh, you know, the white ones.' this reply was heard frequently. How could people be so ignorant and disinterested in their own health?

200

Five minutes later he was back upstairs, sitting on the edge of her bed, smiling adoringly at her.

'Here you are, take these now. Let me hand you a drink. There you go.'

He handed her the two tablets. She lurched up onto one elbow and swallowed them obediently without giving them as much as a thought. She grimaced at the bitter taste.

'You lie back now and close your eyes. With any luck, you'll sleep until the morning and wake up feeling so much better.'

'What did Dad say? Did he mind?'

'Of course not,' Gideon lied easily. 'He was concerned for you. Said for you to get well soon and sent his love.'

'You are wonderful, Gideon. I don't know what I'd do without you. I'm so sorry about my ring. What shall we do?'

'Shhhhh, don't think about a thing. We'll get another one, even better. Just happy thoughts now. Relax, be calm, feel your body beginning to float...'

'Where are you going to be?' she whispered, suddenly anxious. 'I don't want to be on my own.'

'I'll stay with you until you fall asleep. Then I'll be downstairs, watching a DVD I think, when I've done a bit of reading. Just call me and I'll come running.'

Grace squeezed his hand. 'OK. I love you so much.'

'Me too. And let me tell you how much.'

His voice was hypnotic. Through her fever, Grace thought there was almost a sinister tone she had not heard before but fatigue was overtaking her rapidly and deliciously. Better to put up no resistance, was her last thought as she drifted off into a dreamless sleep.

'Hello, Gideon!' Douglas was surprised to see the young man at the door.

'Evening, Douglas,' he replied heartily. 'Poor Grace. Struck down with a throat infection, so I've banished her to bed with the usual treatments and come over to sit with Sylvia so you can go out. Grace told me your plans. She's right. It'll do you good to have a bit of time off.'

'Well, that is kind of you. Don't expect Sylvia to be the best company. She's barely saying a word now. She just sits and stares at the television but I don't think she's taking it in. The sooner tomorrow comes the better.'

Gideon waved his briefcase. 'I've brought some work I can get on with. Here's Jim, off you go. See you later!'

'See if you can persuade her to have a drink –cup of tea is your best bet, milk and one sugar. She's barely had anything today.' Douglas looked worried as he buttoned up his coat.

'I will, now be off. See you soon.'

He virtually shoved Douglas across the threshold.

'Perhaps I shouldn't go,' were his last words before Gideon shut the door, firmly.

Sylvia did not look up as Gideon joined her, nor did she respond to his words of welcome. Sighing, she flicked from one channel to another before settling on one, quite randomly which, as far as Gideon was able to tell, appeared to be a shopping channel in an unidentifiable language. A good-looking man and an equally attractive woman were involved in an excitable chat about some unrecognisable household object. He made no comment but instead opened up his briefcase, got out a sheaf of papers, thus exposing a box of tablets.

Tutting, he shut one end of the box that was coming loose and replaced them tidily.

'Silly me,' he commented out loud. 'I meant to take those back to the pharmacy. That patient, Bruce Hill, gave them back to me this afternoon. Slapped them down in front of me, in a somewhat unnecessarily aggressive manner, I tell you, saying they were no bloody good. I'd have thought they'd have helped his pain, strong as they are, but apparently not. They'd fell an elephant usually.'

He settled down to read, pretending to ignore the annoying babble that was coming from the television. Halfway through the evening, he went and made Sylvia a cup of tea and poured himself a generous dram of Douglas's best whisky. Sylvia frowned and refused to touch her drink. It went cold and acquired a nasty skin on the top.

'If you don't want it, so be it. I'll go and wash up. Back in ten.'

He took the cup back into the kitchen. He had no intention of washing up but turned the tap on while he hung about for a few minutes, whistling loudly, clattering some crockery about and having a peep in all the cupboards and drawers to pass the time. After what he hoped was enough time, he returned, smiling, to Sylvia and resumed his reading. She glanced at him warily before poking at the remote control and swapping to a keep fit programme. Gideon decided the lissom lovelies in their thonged leotards were a big improvement.

Douglas returned punctually, having enjoyed his evening and had even managed to switch off for a little. Two and a half pints of beer inside him and fifty pence in his pocket that he had won all helped his good humour. The scene in the lounge was much as he had left it. Sylvia appeared not to have moved and Gideon was working away hard.

'All's well,' Gideon announced, 'I'd better get off and see how Grace is, if you can manage from here.'

'Yes, yes, fine. Thank you so much for your help. Give our love to Grace and we'll see her tomorrow.' If she's not well enough, tell her not to worry about coming to the hospital. I'll take her mum and she can visit later. And don't you worry about her medication. It's all going to change again, so missing the morning's dose won't make any difference.'

'Righto. Have a peaceful night. She looks ready for bed, doesn't she?'

'Perhaps. She hasn't slept well for ages. Anyway,' Douglas perked up a little, 'it'll soon be tomorrow and she can start getting better. Good night, Gideon, and thanks again.'

Gideon waved as he jogged across the road and quietly opened the front door, so as not to disturb Grace. He crept up the stairs and saw, to his relief, that she was sleeping soundly, so much so that she looked as though she had not moved from when he had left. On her back, mouth wide open, several adjectives sprung to mind to describe her and beautiful did not feature among them. Her breaths were deep and sonorous, with a half snore due to her catarrhal state. Perfect. Exactly as he had planned. Now there was one more detail to check.

There was no danger that Grace was going to wake up any time soon but despite this, Gideon returned to the lounge to open up his briefcase again, leaving the door open so he would hear if she woke and came down to find him. This time, however, studying was far from his thoughts. With any luck Sylvia, in her vulnerable state, would have taken his bait. Hands trembling he opened up the box of extra strong painkillers.

He punched the air triumphantly. Over half were missing. That was a couple of dozen tablets at least. Never mind fell an elephant, it was way more than enough to kill a human. Now all he had to do was pray and hope that she did exactly what he intended and took them...

Out for the count, Grace was oblivious to the screaming

ambulance sirens roaring down the road and screeching to a halt. Nor was she aware of the stroboscopic blue light that lit up her bedroom. If she did, she thought it was a dream, turned over and went back into a deep sleep. Gideon, watching between a tiny crack in the curtains, smiled and nodded slowly.

Bingo!

He saw the crew help a white-faced, frail-looking Douglas into the back of the vehicle. Briefly, he felt a flicker of remorse. Douglas was a nice bloke. He looked to have aged twenty years, poor git. Didn't deserve all this trouble in his life.

Douglas looked over at his daughter's house briefly, up at the bedroom window, which was in darkness and then disappeared from view as the doors closed and they sped off into the night to Accident and Emergency.

Chapter Thirty-One

I should never have left her but I had no idea this was going to happen. Where on earth did she get the tablets from? We've never had anything like that in the house. Even when I'd had my hip done, I only took paracetamol and codeine. And I know for sure that there weren't any of those in the house as I cleared them out. That's right, I gave them to Grace who was going to take them back to the pharmacy for me. I didn't want to take any risks you see. I am always so careful.'

Douglas was sitting on the intensive care unit by his wife's bed. Machines monitoring her vital signs blinked and winked and bleeped monotonously. Sylvia lay motionless, in an induced coma, an intravenous drip in each arm and a catheter bag hung from the rails of the cot sides. Dedicated, hard-working nurses were recording multiple observations and watching her like hawks.

'You know how it is Douglas,' began Scott Melanaphy, the consultant in charge of the unit. 'Patients like this find a way, when they're really determined.'

He looked casual in dark brown corduroy trousers and a short sleeved beige shirt. His hair was closely cropped and he kept pushing his glasses back up his nose. Douglas felt he looked far too young to be in charge.

'She must have had the tablets hidden somewhere. I took her up to bed. Looking back that was a bit odd as lately she's wanted to sit up all night but last night she told me she wanted to go upstairs. I thought that was a good sign, so I took her up, helped settle her and she genuinely looked so sleepy I left her, thinking I'd watch the news headlines with a small single malt and then join her. I'm ashamed to say I fell asleep and it was some hours before I went back. The empty packs were on the floor and on the duvet. She's maybe taken fifty, perhaps more. I don't know how many she had to start with.'

Scott pulled up a chair beside him.

'At least we know what it was that she took. Her bloods do show that she took a huge amount. We're doing all we can but the crucial thing is how her liver and kidneys withstand this insult. At the moment her tests are stable but the next forty-eight hours will be critical.'

'It's all my fault,' Douglas said, simply.

'You must not blame yourself,' Scott answered firmly. 'There was nothing you could have differently that would have prevented it. She'd have found a way, believe me.'

'I cannot bear to think that she was feeling so desperate. Why didn't she tell me? If I'd only got her through tonight, then she'd be on the ward and safe.'

'Every day of our lives is full of ifs, buts and maybes. For all you know she might have taken the tablets onto the ward, hidden in her bag and taken them later today. Try to stop thinking of what might have been. Concentrate on now and the future. We're taking it hour by hour. Currently, as I say, she's stable. Let's wait and see. Never stop hoping.'

'I need to tell Grace,' Douglas told Scott. 'I don't know how she'll react to this news. She's had such a hard time of it recently, what with one thing and another. In many ways she's so like her mother. And now she's in bed with a throat infection or flu. She'll want to come in...'

Scott shook his head. 'I don't want her on the ward if she's infectious. I'll happily talk to her and explain everything and she can ring me any time.'

'I understand but she'll want to be here...'

Douglas nodded and turned his gaze back to Sylva. How peaceful she looked with her regular breathing and closed eyes. For all the world she might be asleep. She was beautiful now. His very own sleeping beauty. The lines of angst and mental pain had melted from her face to be replaced by an expression of exquisite repose. Douglas took her hand. They were so close, their souls so entwined, he knew she was aware of his presence and his love. How simple would it be if all he had to do was kiss her and she would wake up? She had to live. She had to. He needed her for his own survival.

Outside a grimy dawn was starting to creep over the buildings on the skyline. Another hour and he would call Grace.

Waking, Grace felt momentarily disorientated, wondering where she was and what day and time it was. When was the last time she had slept so soundly and for so long? As she came to, she tentatively assessed her state of health. She felt quite cool and her throat, while still sore, was definitely better. Her head ached but she was thirsty and, to her surprise, hungry. Next to her the bed was empty. Probably for the best, she thought. Poor Gideon would have had a poor night if he had been next to her. Not a lot of fun trying to sleep next to a hot, burning up body who was restless and moving around a lot, tossing the covers on and off. No, it was sensible of him to have defected to the spare room.

She sat up and gulped down the orange juice and the water, now tepid, on her bedside table. Better. In need of the bathroom she tucked her feet into her slippers, wrapped her dressing gown around her and padded across the landing. The spare room door was closed and she decided to let him sleep. He'd need to be up soon to get ready for work. Automatically she looked across the road. Lights were on in her parents' house and she sighed, remembering that her mother was being admitted that morning. She pictured her father packing the suitcase.

Grace decided that toast and honey sounded good, after which she planned to ring her father and check all was well and apologise again for the previous night.

Not even the noise of the shower made Gideon appear. She stood, enjoying the warmth of the water and its rejuvenating effect on her body. Her hair desperately needed a wash, having stuck with sweat to the nape of her neck and her forehead. Towelling herself dry as she returned to her bedroom, she marvelled at Gideon's ability to sleep through. Hurriedly, to prevent getting cold, she dressed in grey jogging bottoms and a baggy navy jumper, the same one, she noticed ruefully, that she had worn when poor Thadeus had been ill.

She managed half a slice of toast before her own phone rang. A private number. Odd, she thought hoping it wasn't another of those stupid calls.

'Grace?' It was her father and she knew instantly that he was upset.

'What's happened, Dad? Where are you?'

'At the hospital with Mum. There's no easy way to tell you this. She's taken an overdose...'

'Of what?' Grace gasped.

'A drug called aspradirol. I'd never heard of it.'

'It's a morphine-based painkiller. Where did she get that from?'

'We've no idea.'

'How is she? How much did she take?'

'On Intensive Care. I'm afraid it's all very touch and go. She took an enormous dose. Grace? Grace are you still there?'

Grace, speechless, had the sudden ridiculous vision of her father shaking the phone and glaring at it, as if checking that it still worked.

'Dad, I can't believe this. I'm on my way.'

'Grace, you're not to come if you're ill. You might pass on an infection.'

'You can't stop me. I'm a lot better anyway. Honest.'

She slammed the phone down. Now her head was really throbbing and she felt so weak. Dragging a comb through her wet hair, she felt exhausted from such humdrum activity, a victim of viral illness lassitude. Steeling herself, she pulled on trainers and went into the spare room, bizarrely considering knocking before she did so.

It was empty. The bed was untouched, covers still elegantly crease free and the scatter cushions in the exact places that she liked them to be – three in a row and then two smaller ones on top. Where had he slept? Where was he now? Out running? Sometimes he did before work. Already at work? That was more likely, such was his conscientiousness. Should she ring him?

Now was not the time to prevaricate. She grabbed her bag, phone and car keys and ran out to the car.

When Grace crept onto intensive care, she saw her father leaning over her mother, talking away as if she were awake. Reluctant to interrupt, Grace stood some way from the bed watching, wondering what to say, wishing there was more she could do. Scott Melanaphy came up behind her.

'Your dad's an incredible person,' he said, in soft tones.

Grace turned to him.

'He is. Fair weather friends would have given up on my mum years ago, probably when she was first ill but not my dad. He's been with her, through the good, the bad and what seems to be a disproportionate share of the exceedingly ugly and never for a second has his love for her wavered.' She sighed. 'How is she?'

'Her renal function's deteriorating, I'm afraid. It was normal when she was admitted but the last result looks as though she's developing acute renal failure. It's going to get a lot worse, sadly before it gets better…if it gets better.'

Grace swallowed hard. 'It's really that bad?' It was a huge effort to utter those four words but it was going to be an even huger one to hear the answer.

'I'm sorry. We're doing all we can, I promise.'

'I know you are. Does my dad know how bad the outlook is?'

'I tried to have a talk with him a little while ago. I suspect he chose not to hear what I was saying, so I'll try again in a bit.'

'This is all like a bad dream. I keep thinking I'm about to wake up.' Grace wiped her eyes. 'I wish it were.'

Douglas was waving to her, beckoning her over, so she thanked Scott and made her way to the bed. Was the person lying there really her mother? Perhaps there had been some awful mistake…

She hugged her father and sat next to him. 'You look exhausted, Dad. Why don't you go home and get some rest. I'll stay here.'

'I'm never leaving her again. Look what happened the last time I did.'

Grace looked at him puzzled. 'What are you talking about?'

'I left her, yesterday evening to go and play dominoes and then she did this when I got back. If I'd been there I would have known what she was going to do. I would have recognised the signs, I'd have persuaded her not to, I'd…'

'Shhhhhh, Dad. Please don't get upset. I thought you'd cancel your dominoes when you knew I was ill.'

'Under normal circumstances, I would have, but Gideon arrived, told me about you and said he would sit with her. So I thought it was safe for me to go. And I enjoyed it, what's more but at what cost?'

'Hang on,' started Grace. 'I asked Gideon to ring you. He promised to stay with me as I was feeling so lousy.'

'Well, he didn't. He appeared at the door, said he'd brought some work to catch up with and almost pushed me into Jim's arms. Everything seemed as I'd left it when I got back. Gideon said your mum hadn't said a word.'

Try as she might, Grace was unable to make any sense out of all this information.

'How odd,' she muttered. 'Still, I'm sure you going out and this happening is no more than coincidence.'

'No, there's more to it. I know there is. I can feel it.' Douglas was angry.

'Dad, we've got to stay calm, for Mum's sake. Look, why don't we both go and get a cup of something in the restaurant. It's a stone's throw down the corridor. We don't need to be more than ten minutes and they've got my number if they want us urgently.'

'I'm not leaving her.'

Grace looked imploringly at the charge nurse who was filling in a large chart at the end of the bed and mouthed 'help, please'. He finished off what he was writing, snapped his pen shut and came to crouch by Douglas.

'Hi, I'm Joe. Started my shift five minutes ago. If I were you, don't bother with the restaurant. Way too busy and smells of gravy, even at this time of day. Go into our day room over there. You can make coffee, tea and even toast in there and still be able to see Sylvia from the door. How about that? You can use your mobile as well if wish.'

'I suppose,' Douglas acquiesced, grudgingly. He allowed his daughter and Joe to escort him the few yards to the relatives' room, whereupon he wearily sat down on the chair nearest to the door, having first demanded that it be turned around to face Sylvia.

Chapter Thirty-Two

~~~❧~~~

Twenty-four hours later, Grace had concocted a rough rota to make sure there was someone by Sylvia's bed at all times and someone taking care of Charnley, as Douglas had stipulated must be the case. Thanks to the kindness of Jim, Jim's wife Margie and Harry, with Janey and Andrew on standby to take the dog if required, Grace had successfully complied with this demand, at the same time ensuring that her father would have regular breaks.

The patient's progress was not good. True to prediction, she had developed renal failure and by the jaundiced appearance of her skin, Grace reckoned that it didn't take a specialist to diagnose concurrent liver problems in addition. Sylvia had needed dialysis and a blood transfusion, to which she had had a reaction with high fever and a rigor. Nothing could be done apart from watching and waiting and hoping that she would turn a corner and start to improve.

After another day of sitting alternating with pacing about, too much tea or an occasional coffee for a change, Grace was shattered when she got home and found Gideon waiting for her.

He took her in his arms. 'Oh, my darling. I had no idea or I'd have been at the hospital.'

'Where were you?' Grace had no energy left to argue. 'I needed you so much.'

'On that course I told you about.'

'What course?'

'You must have forgotten with all this going on. Totally understandable. I told you last week. Remember? In Manchester, staying overnight? Dinner? Me chairing the meeting?'

'I don't recall a thing,' Grace replied with complete honesty.

'Well, I'm back now. That's what matters eh? It went very well, as it happens and I'm going to be invited to speak at a meeting in New York. How about that? Maybe you can come with me. Now what on earth has been happening and how is your dear mother?'

Grace dissolved into sobs. It took several minutes before she was able to speak.

'Gideon, I'm so afraid she's going to die. Her blood results are disastrous at the last count, she's jaundiced, her urine output's next to nothing...'

'That sounds very worrying, I agree. She'd taken an overdose? How dreadful.'

'Which reminds me, why did you go over and sit with her? You promised to stay with me.'

'It sort of happened. I tried phoning but the phone didn't seem to be working, so I popped across and when I saw how let down your dad looked, I offered to help out. I knew you were out for the count. Talk about snoring! The roof nearly blew off.'

His attempt at humour fell flatter than an amoeba. He put on his serious face.

'She seemed OK while I was there. We had a chat, watched some nice TV – more her sort of stuff than mine – had a cup of tea and then your dad came back, so I scooted off back to my wonderful fiancée. If I'm honest, she seemed quite a bit brighter than she has been.'

'None of this makes any sense at all,' Grace agonised.

'I think I might be able to help you there,' Gideon suggested. 'Let's have a glass of wine and talk.'

He vanished into the kitchen and returned with drinks and a plate of snacks.

'Go on, drink,' he urged, pushing the full glass towards her. She took a small sip and shuddered.

'I'm not really in the mood. And before you ask, I've had enough tea and coffee to last a lifetime.'

'Try. For me. It'll help you unwind.'

Grace curled her feet up under her and rested her head on the back of the settee, closing her eyes. If only she could step off the world for a few hours and escape from everything and everyone. If only she had a switch on the side of her head that would stop the endless turmoil of thoughts for a while. What selfish thoughts they were. How was it possible for her to think like that when her father was at the hospital beside her mother who was in a coma, hovering terrifyingly near to death? I love them both dearly, thought Grace but I'm so tired that I can't think straight. I need to recharge. I don't want wine, I don't want to eat, I've talked so much today already, all I want is a bath and then bed.

Gideon, however, had other ideas. Sitting beside her, he put his arm around her neck and she gratefully snuggled against his chest, badly in need of comfort.

'What I have to say isn't going to be easy,' he began, carefully picking his words. He felt her body stiffen next to his. 'I have to say it though, even though this isn't a good time for you and it's partly for that reason why we have to have this chat now. Before anything else happens and because you are so precious to me.'

'What are you talking about?' Grace asked, sleepily.

'I've been doing a lot of thinking. Your knee-jerk reaction will be that this sounds preposterous but hear me out and you'll gradually realise that I'm talking sense.'

'Be quick, please. I want to go to bed.'

'Not before I've told you. I've had to pluck up all my courage for this.'

Grace sat up to look at him. His face was deadly serious. He had just said she was precious but was he about to dump her? If so, his timing left a lot to be desired.

As if reading her mind, Gideon, took her hands in his. 'Don't glare at me like that! I love you. This is about your mother. I'm very concerned.'

'We all are. Now please let me go and get some sleep. I've promised to be back to take over from Dad at the crack of dawn.'

'OK, bear with me for a little longer. It's hard to know where to start.' He drew her back onto his chest. 'A lot's been happening since we met and got together. The more I think about it, the more I think that there's more to it than a string of bad luck. Your car was damaged, the spooky phone calls, the lost keys and bracelet, that cat being poisoned, the drugs missing from your bag…'

'I know, it's been awful,' Grace had no hesitation in agreeing. 'So what? You told me I was over-reacting weeks ago.'

'I did and I apologise for now I understand that I was wrong.'

He took a deep breath in and tightened his grip around Grace. 'I suspect that your mother has been doing all these things…'

'What?' Grace was incredulous. She almost burst out laughing.

'Look at the evidence, Grace. As long as we've been together, her mental health has been like a yo-yo. One minute she was as high as a kite, now she's floundering in the pits of doom. It's obvious; she wants you all to herself and doesn't want to share with me. She wants you to suffer. Her warped mind...'

Grace pushed away from Gideon. 'My mother does not have a warped mind,' she cried. 'Nor would she ever, ever want me to suffer. Have some pity and compassion. She may well die. I do not need to hear this now.'

'Grace, Grace, I think you do,' Gideon cooed. 'It will help you cope. All the while, her bipolar has been making her act in a crazy fashion and, sadly, you have been the target.'

'I've never heard such rubbish in my life,' Grace spluttered.

'It all adds up. She has a key to the house, she had medical knowledge. She has a reputation for not taking her meds regularly and thus being unstable. She's a liability. I think she took your engagement ring too. She was in the kitchen, wasn't she, she saw you leave it on the window sill...'

'Enough! Do not say another word. I cannot take any more of these wild accusations. I'm going to bed. On. My. Own.'

With heavy emphasis on the last three words, she flounced out of the room, half furious, half in despair, running up to the bedroom and slamming the door. Leaning against it, she listened but there were no sounds to suggest he was following her. Good, she needed to be alone. She marvelled at his audacity to conjure up such theories, let alone vocalise them. How dare he? Angrily, she tore off her clothes and threw on a pair of pyjamas. Light out, she cocooned her body within the duvet and willed sleep to take her away from her thoughts. Her weariness forbade her to think about what Gideon had said. Sleep was vital to restore her rational thinking.

The sensation of Gideon climbing in beside her and reclaiming his share of the bedclothes did not help. She did not want him there but he had other plans. He spooned around her, motionless initially before starting to caress her body, slowly and lightly with his fingertips. He was not fooled by her attempt to feign sleep.

'I'm sorry,' he breathed. 'Forgive me. The words I chose were crass and insensitive. Please try to see past my tactlessness and give what I said some thought. I'm sure it's hellish for you to consider your mother has any part to play in your recent stresses as you only see the good in her, of which I am sure there is plenty when she's well...'

He kissed her neck and coaxed her to turn towards him. He knew she would submit to his carefully constructed show of affection. She always did and this time was no different. It was so easy, it was laughable.

Grace avoided Gideon when she woke with a jolt before the alarm had a chance to buzz. Unwinding his limbs that were wrapped around her, she slithered out of bed, showered, dressed and left for the hospital, leaving him dead to the world. The roads were deserted, as was the hospital car park and, for once, she was able to park close to the main entrance. She found Douglas in the visitors' room, nodding in the chair. Sylvia looked as she had done since she had been admitted, pale yellow and serene. Grace noticed there was slightly more urine in the catheter bag and hoped this was a positive sign but knew she had to be careful about making assumptions from too little information.

Douglas was awake in instant, attune to the sound of her step across the floor.

'How's she been?' asked Grace, kissing his cheek.

'The same, I suppose. They're giving her this and that. Drugs way beyond my ken but maybe they'd make more sense to you. At the last report, she wasn't any worse, so that's a small comfort.'

'Definitely. Now you go home and have some proper rest in a real bed. I'm here for the day and Harry's doing the evening shift.'

'You will ring, won't you? If there's the slightest change. One way or the other?'

'Dad, you know I will.'

'I'll go and phone a taxi then.'

'Good. Remember to have some food as well. Keep your strength up.'

'Jim and Margie have asked me for lunch,' he admitted with little enthusiasm.

'So take them up on the offer.'

Douglas gave her a withering look and trudged off the ward, head bowed, shoulders stooped by despondency. Grace took up position by her mother and gazed searchingly at her. Gideon's words haunted her. Was any of what he proposed possible? Looking at her now, it seemed illogical, absurd, and positively unimaginable. This was her mother he was talking about. Patients might behave like this but not her mother.

A nagging voice reminded her of an innate inability to detach from her emotions. How many times had she told patients that because you were emotionally involved it was so hard to be objective about loved ones and what was happening to them? More times than she cared to remember. The same advice applied to her. Her thoughts about her mother were biased. She could see no wrong there, no potential for wrong doing; her mother was not perfect but nobody was. Throughout Sylvia's years of illness, Grace had never once had cause to doubt the maternal love that shone through unerringly irrespective of whether her mood was up or down.

Over and over, while she sat at her vigil, she reconsidered

Gideon's theory from all angles. Like it or not, parts of it rang true, however appalling the prospect. Her mother's feelings for Gideon had been variable, from the first hysteria of knowing he existed to the lacklustre acceptance when she was discharged after her manic episode. Grace shuddered at the memory of the dining-room table piled high with food. Naturally, her mother had a key to the house. She had been a godsend. Always on tap to take in parcels, pop in and water plants, take over some baking, open windows on hot days and close curtains on dark, dank days. What was wrong with that? It was a bonus of having parents across the road. She did the same for them. Symbiosis at its best. Would it really occur to her to jeopardise Grace's career by meddling with the drugs in her bag? As for the idea that she had anything to do with Thadeus's' demise – no, Grace refused to go there. Sylvia adored the cat. Countless times had she commented that if they didn't have Charnley, then she would like to have a cat. Thinking about that evening and the poor suffering feline made her feel sick.

She was no further forward when the ward round came and went. Scott took Grace to one side and much like her father had reported, informed her that it was a mercy that her blood results, while deplorable, were no worse than the previous day.

'If she's going to respond, it should be soon,' he told her. 'I'm so sorry not to be the bearer of better news. Try to take comfort from the fact she's peaceful and has no pain. We're doing all we can.'

Grace thanked him. She was in awe of anyone who was sufficiently strong to work in such a high-pressure job, full time, where emotions ran high perpetually. Personally, she loved the palliative care side of her own job but knew that she was only able to do it well because she had all the many other facets of her job to dilute the strain and keep her balanced. Over the last five years, she'd seen all sorts, the seriously ill, the worried well and that funny lady who had just popped in to share her holiday photos. And wasn't it Harry who had had the patient who brought in an iguana for a second opinion?

One of the monitors beside her mother began to bleep more loudly and persistently; lights flashed, jerking Grace back to the present. She spun round, trying to work out what was happening. Suddenly the bed was surrounded by nurses, Scott and a couple of junior doctors who had introduced themselves earlier but she had no clue as to what their names were. Joe came up beside her.

'Let's pop into the visitors' room. A little hiccup. Scott'll come and have a word as soon as your mum's settled again.'

'What's happening. Please tell me! My dad, he'll want to know.'

'Her potassium is quite high. The lab's been on the phone. She's developed an arrhythmia of her heart because of that, we think, but it ought to respond to the medication she's being given now.'

'No! She might arrest!' screeched Grace.

'Not if we've got anything to do with it,' promised Joe. 'Trust me, this is a problem we see frequently and we put right. Bread and butter stuff. There, her ECG trace is looking better already... Can you see?'

'No! Oh yes! Oh thank goodness.'

The monitor returned to the now-familiar background bleep.

'Panic over,' announced Scott, coming into the room to join them. 'All's well now. Joe, she'll need U and Es in half an hour please and page me with the result if I'm not here. Grace, give the nurses a few minutes, they're having a quick tidy up.'

By the time Grace got back to the bedside it was as though

nothing had happened. The frenetic air had evaporated.

'Hello, Mum,' she murmured. 'Please don't give me any more frights like that. Please get better. Dad and I need you so very much.'

The sheets had been changed, straightened and smoothed; Sylvia's face was washed and her hair had even been brushed. The picture of innocence. Or was it?

Chapter Thirty-Three

❧

'*S*he's not coping,' Janey shared with Andrew and Harry, over cherry slices and coffee, one morning a fortnight later, not that they needed enlightening. 'She's trying to spread herself too thin and as a result is falling apart. Today I found a prescription she'd done, supposedly for penicillin but she'd clicked on penicillamine, a totally different drug and definitely not a cure for tonsillitis. Luckily the patient noticed, was understanding and so no harm done. It's an easy mistake to make if your eye's not on the ball.'

'Oh dear,' Andrew was equally worried. 'We can't have that. She'd hate to know something like that has happened. You know how meticulously fastidious she is. She'd be mortified.'

'Let's tell her to take a month off,' suggested Janey, to which the two men nodded in agreement. 'Compassionate leave. Hang the expense and let's get a locum in. It'll be one less thing for her to worry about and by then the overall picture might be clearer.'

'What is the latest news?' asked Andrew.

'I popped in yesterday evening,' reported Harry. 'Not a lot to say, really. Sylvia's still needing to be dialysed regularly and her liver function's poor. She's had a urinary infection but got over that. Remarkable I guess, as I don't think anyone thought she'd survive the initial phase. What the future holds? Who knows?'

'Poor Grace,' empathised Janey. 'It's very hard to imagine what she's going through.'

'She and Douglas have settled into a routine now. Douglas has finally been persuaded that someone does not need to be at Sylvia's bedside permanently, so they are both sleeping at home at night. Grace takes him back in the morning, then stays for a while before coming here, where she thinks she can work for a few hours. Then she goes back, stays the evening and takes Douglas home again. She'll not be sleeping well, despite being at home.'

'And she's lost weight,' added Janey. 'That skirt she had on this morning was hanging off her.'

'I'll speak to her,' promised Andrew.

'No, let me, please,' begged Harry, 'I feel it ought to be me who does this.'

'No problem. If that's what you'd like. Thank you. Keep me posted.'

The daily burden was indeed immeasurable. Weighed down by the fear for her mother, the deleterious effect the pressure was having on her father and the refusal of Gideon's comments to go away, Grace was feeling shockingly miserable. She felt that she had come to the end of the line; that finding the strength to go on even one more day was a hopeless task.

Each morning she woke, having slept fitfully, on tenterhooks in case the phone rang. On autopilot, she got ready, went across to make breakfast for her father, knowing that if she didn't do this, then he would go without and then took him to the hospital. More often than not, she parked in the same space. Each morning as they approached the ward, a tiny flame of optimism fluttered inside her. There may have been some change for the good overnight and Scott was waiting, looking forward to breaking cheerful news to them rather than none at all. But that never happened.

Other patients on the unit came and went; their stays only brief in comparison. The fortunate were moved to the wards, the unlucky to the mortuary. Grace and Douglas forged links with other relatives, all inextricably bound together in this microcosm of the hospital. They shared joy, despair, sorrow, even anger but throughout Sylvia stayed the same, motionless, emotionless and lost in some faraway world. I wonder what it's like, Grace considered frequently during the endless hours she sat there. Can she think? Can she hear? Can she feel?

Gideon was always waiting for Grace when she finally returned home, dead beat, fit for nothing more than bed. He was solicitous and kind, concerned for her welfare, supportive, never once referring to his previous conversation.

That night he had made a beef casserole and jacket potatoes. Grace disinterestedly pushed hers around the plate. She had arrived even later than usual and was looking particularly haggard and unhappy.

'Grace,' he started, 'I think perhaps you should go and see your GP.'

'Why?' She sounded alarmed.

'It's patently obvious, even to a neurologist, that you are depressed and need help.'

'I'm only tired. That's all. I'll be fine after a good night's sleep.'

Gideon was exasperated. 'Good God! Change the record. How many times have you said that? I don't know about you, but I've lost count. You never do sleep well. You twitch and turn over and mutter and grind your teeth. And then you wake at four and lie there, hoping that I don't realise you're awake.'

'It's hard to switch off,' she explained.

'You are depressed. Look at you. You've let yourself go...'

Grace cringed but he had only just begun.

'.... you don't eat, you cry all the time and you're flogging yourself to a miserable end by trying to be everything to all people and not taking care of your own needs.'

'I'll be fine when Mum's a bit better.'

'You won't be able to enjoy your mother being better if you're in the state you are now. You'll be in the next bed to hers. Please, for my sake, do something.'

He looked so troubled that Grace had to give in. What he said made sense.

'OK, I promise I'll go and have a chat. I don't want antidepressants though. Possibly a few sleeping tablets...'

'Take the advice you're given. Haven't you any insight? Honestly, you are so like your mother, it's uncanny!'

Chapter Thirty-Four

⟋⟍⟋⟍

*H*arry found Grace in floods of tears at the end of her surgery the next day. He had been waiting for her, watching her progress on the computer as she worked her way through the list of patients at a painfully slow pace, finishing very late. When she failed to turn up for coffee (and Danish pastries), he knew all was not well and went in search of her. There was no response to his knock on her door so he gently went in. The sight of her extreme grief tore his heart apart. If only he had the power to help. He was still mulling over the curious incident of Gideon and the tablets and wondering what it all meant. Discussing it with Phillip had led to the conclusion that the most likely solution was Sylvia swapping the tablets herself, thinking that she no longer needed them but wanting to appear to comply. Try as he might, Harry was unable to accept this. He was still sure that Gideon was involved. So much so that he had chosen a tie with snakes on that day.

She was dressed in a drab pinafore with a dark blouse beneath it. The latter seemed to have escaped the attentions of the iron. A stark contrast to the smart, businesslike persona she liked to exude. Her short hair was scraped back, viciously and pinned up after a fashion as many strands had tumbled around her face, accentuating her pallor and making her look very young.

'Grace, what is it? Have you had bad news from the hospital?'

She sniffed in an unladylike way and looked up at him, bleary, red-rimmed eyes giving away the truth that she had been crying for some time.

'No, she's still the same.'

'Then has something else upset you? A patient?'

'No, no. I don't know where to begin...I'm such a failure.'

Harry felt his own eyes starting to prickle. 'Hey, you're nothing of the sort. Whatever gives you that idea?'

She took a deep breath. 'I can't cope. I'm tired, fed up, worn out, not sleeping, not eating. How's that for a start?'

Harry smiled sympathetically. 'Pretty good if you ask me.'

Grace shook her head. She had lost the ability to smile, she decided.

'I'm hopeless, Harry. Why can't I cope? I ought to be able to.'

Harry sat down. 'Grace, listen to me. Have you taken a moment to sit back and think about what is going on in your life right now?'

Grace raised her eyebrows.

'My dear Grace, your mother is desperately ill as a result of extraordinary circumstances, you are trying to deal with that while taking care of your father whose pain knows no boundaries. Add to that, you are trying to be a competent GP and not let us or your patients down...'

She wasn't listening, too intent on confessing further. 'Gideon thinks I'm depressed and need treatment. He keeps nagging me to do something about it. Maybe I am and I can't see it. What do you think?'

'You might be, but if you are, then it's no fault of yours. Most folk, including the strong personalities, would have crumbled a long time ago.'

'He also thinks Mum is angry with me. He thinks she's responsible for all the things that have been going on – you know, my car, my ring…Thadeus. He thinks she pushed Dad over when he broke his hip as well. On purpose. And he thinks that she stopped her medication deliberately.'

Gideon thinks far too much, thought Harry, privately, but instead he asked, 'Why is she supposed to be angry with you of all people?'

'Because I've got Gideon in my life and I'm not paying her enough attention. He thinks it's all some sort of revenge. Is he right? Has Mum done all these things, because she's ill?'

'That's nothing short of outrageous.'

Grace blew her nose loudly. 'I thought that at first and then I started to wonder and the more I thought about it, the more it started to make sense. It all falls into place. And so now I'm terrified he might be right…'

Harry was lost for words. A rare event. But he could see that Grace had not finished and did not want to interrupt her flow of speech.

She reached out for his hand, which he gave, gladly. The pulse at her wrist was galloping. What little colour she had, drained from her face.

'I don't know how to say this, Harry, but Gideon has really, really petrified me.'

'He's wrong about your mum,' Harry placated her.

'Not just that. He says I'm like her. He suspects that I may be bipolar too.'

It's Gideon who's got the problem, deduced Harry. How dare he do this to Grace? What was behind his cold and calculating attempt to ruin this wonderful person's life? Harry was incandescent with rage. Given the chance, he would throttle the man, and the consequences be hanged. The priority was Grace however.

'Rubbish. He's trying to scare you. How long have you and I known each other?'

'Nearly six years.'

'And in all of that time, the thought has never once crossed my mind.'

'What am I going to do?' she wailed.

Harry thought quickly. 'He's playing with your mind. I'm almost certain of it.'

'What are you talking about?'

'Grace, there are things I must tell you, now. Gideon's said enough, it's my turn. It all seems inexplicable and random. You might laugh at me and never speak to me again. I've found out something that concerns both your mother and Gideon. Something very important.'

'Go on. I've heard so many outlandish claims that one more isn't going to make any difference. What are you going to come up with? That I was swapped at birth and my real mother is a trapeze artist in the Soviet Union? This is all madness, I tell you. But I do trust you, Harry, so tell me.'

As gently and succinctly as he could, Harry explained to Grace how he had discovered that some of Sylvia's medications had been swapped to sweets and how it could only have been Gideon that had done this because he had found the sweets in his briefcase. Grace listened, her mouth dropping open as she tried to make sense of what she was being told.

'But why would he do such a thing?'

'That's the bit I can't work out,' admitted Harry. 'I intend to find out though, as soon as I can. Is there anything at all that you can think of?'

'I haven't a clue,' a bemused Grace replied. 'I still cannot believe what you've told me.'

They sat quietly, absorbed in their thoughts. All at once Grace gasped and grabbed Harry.

'What is it?'

'I can hardly believe I'm going to say this. The night she took the overdose. He went round to the house and sat with her while Dad went out. I was going to go but was ill. He gave me some paracetamol – well he said that's what they were but now I'm becoming more and more suspicious that they were sleeping tablets to knock me out. He must have left the aspradirol for her to take, recognising that she was vulnerable and likely to be tempted. There's no other way she could have come by controlled drugs like that.'

'It fits, much as I hate to admit it,' Harry said, 'it all fits.'

He stood up and paced around, searching for inspiration. Grace watched him as he stopped by the window and gazed out at the cold winter's day. Trees were being buffeted about by a strong wind and dead leaves flew around the surgery car park. By now he was tapping his fingers on the glass. He turned.

'I don't want you being alone with him. Can you get him to go away for a few days?'

'How?'

'I haven't a clue. He's always going off on courses. Isn't there one of those coming up?'

'Not that I know of.'

'Then, maybe you'd be better off staying with your dad for a few days.'

'But Harry. It's my house! If what you say is true, then I'm afraid to leave him in it. What might he do next?'

'True. OK, cancel that plan and I'll come up with another.' He did some more pacing in a meaningful manner.

'Right! This is what we're going to…'

Chapter Thirty-Five

'I'm delighted to say, she's starting to respond.' Scott looked triumphantly at Douglas and Grace when they arrived on the ward.

Douglas enveloped his daughter in the biggest bear hug.

'Thank God,' he breathed. He looked over to where Sylvia lay.

'I know she doesn't look any different but her renal function has improved enormously and her liver function is more or less back to normal. I'm very pleased. The last few batches of tests have all shown sustained recovery. I'm hoping it won't be long before she's breathing on her own.'

No words were better than these. Grace felt as though a lead overcoat with matching trousers, boots, gloves and hat had been removed from her body. At last, some good news.

'Thank you so much,' she gushed. 'It sounds so inadequate but we do mean it.'

'I know. I'm as delighted as you are. There've been a few moments when I've thought that we'd lost her.'

'I'm so happy,' half laughed, half cried Grace.

'It's still a long haul,' Scott admonished her. 'And don't forget that when she leaves us, she'll be transferred to the psych unit and her recovery there may take many weeks.'

'I understand, we both do. It's just that we've been coming in every day at this time for what seems like forever, hoping for news like this and never getting it and now we have.'

'Enjoy your moment,' Scott gave in, 'but judiciously.'

Everyone on the ward looked happier today, thought Grace. The fluorescent lights looked brighter, the machines less threatening and there was even some glimmer of sunshine outside. The nurses, although to be fair they always had a warm welcome, had an extra sparkle about them and Sylvia, well, Grace was sensing that her conscious level seemed lighter. Douglas, rejuvenated, agreed and set about passing on all the news while he stroked her arms and forehead even more convinced that she could hear.

With no work to go to, Grace stayed for the day. There was no coaxing Douglas to take a break where Sylvia might be out of his sight. He was waiting, expecting now, for tangible signs of life. He wanted to be there when her fingers curled around his, when her eyelashes fluttered for the first time, when her head turned and she looked at him. Grace hadn't the heart to say that this would not happen while she was in an induced coma. It was so fabulous to see him looking and behaving like this, it was not for her to go and spoil things. She was perfectly happy simply being there, living for the moment, watching him watching Sylvia and wallowing in the fact that now there really was hope.

Chapter Thirty-Six

❧

'H i, Gideon.' Grace walked into the house followed by
Harry.

'Hello. Oh, hello, Harry. What brings you here?'

'A disaster,' was the dramatic reply. 'The last thing I needed.
All this cold weather and now I've a leaking pipe. My kitchen's
flooded.' Harry sounded distraught.

'Shame! Sorry, my friend. Well, you spend some time with us
this evening in the warm. There's a chicken dish in the oven, as
you can probably smell. Plenty for three.'

'Thanks. You're a mate. Actually,' Harry announced, sitting
down in one of the comfiest armchairs, making himself at home,
'Grace has kindly asked me to stay for a few days while it's all
sorted out at home.'

Was it Harry's vivid imagination or did a look of disgust track
across Gideon's features?

'Hey, no problem.' His reply was lacking spontaneity. 'Of
course you must stay. Fancy a beer? Have you no bags with
you?'

'I've still got to go and pick them up. I met Grace at the hospital,
she invited me for supper and a warm up, then I'll nip back and
get a few things. So, a beer maybe later, when I haven't got to

236

drive.'

'As you wish. There'll be a couple in the fridge for you later whenever you're ready. Just help yourself, don't wait to be asked. Grace?' Gideon yelled.

Her face popped round the door. 'Yes?'

'Chop the chorizo and add it to the chicken would you? Use it all as there's three of us. And do some rice.'

'All right.'

Harry bristled. There was no need to treat Grace as a doormat. An occasional please or thank you would not have gone amiss. Wishing he had an excuse to go and help Grace in the kitchen, Harry attempted to make light conversation with his host.

'How are things in the world of neurology?' was the best he could come up with. At least it was one of Gideon's favourite topics.

'Fascinating as always. Did I tell you about the patient I saw with lower motor neurone signs that the surgeons had completely missed?'

Under any other circumstances, Harry might have been quite intrigued. It was always good to parry medical case histories. A lot could be learned and it never failed to amaze him that he was continually surprised and picked up nuggets of information to put to good use in the future. Tongue loosened by the beer and several other beers before Grace and Harry arrived, Gideon was in his element, prattling along about the inadequacies of junior doctor training, how his was the only speciality with no middle-grade support, which was ridiculous in this day and age but he was 'this close' to persuading the board to appoint a second neurologist to help ease the considerable burden.

Supper was delicious. Even Harry was forced to admit that Gideon was a good cook. After a dessert of fruit and cheese,

Gideon sat back and patted his abdomen.

'Excellent, even though I do say so myself. Grace – you've barely eaten, as usual. I don't know how you manage to survive. You'll waste away.'

'Sorry,' Grace excused herself. 'It's really lovely but I'm not hungry.'

'As usual.' Gideon rolled his eyes at Harry, expecting his support. 'She doesn't eat enough to keep a bird alive. You tell her, Harry.'

'It's hard to do justice to food when you're innards are in a knot,' Harry remarked, slowly.

'Another bad day, eh?' Gideon turned to Grace. 'How is your mother today?'

'A little better,' she admitted. 'I get the feeling that Scott's feeling more optimistic.'

'That's good, darling. But don't get too excited. You know how these patients can change suddenly. She's not out of the woods yet. And if she does pass away then at least she won't be suffering any more.'

Harry choked a little on a cream cracker. Gideon talked about Sylvia as if she was an aged and much-loved spaniel. Grace got up and left the room, grabbing some dishes as she did but Harry knew she was going to hide the hurt she felt at the thoughtless comments.

'Well! That was all splendid. I can see I'm going to be spoiled rotten while I'm here. I'll grab my coat now, if you don't mind and head off back – feel free to leave the dishes for me. I'm a dab hand at the sink.'

'Don't you want coffee, Harry?' sniffed Grace, coming back in with a wad of tissues in her hand.

'Nope! If I get comfy, I won't want to go out in the cold again.

Shouldn't take me more than an hour. I'll have to check the post, phone, see what sort of a start the plumber's got off to. See you soon!'

So saying he sped from the table and Grace sat down beside Gideon. They heard the rattle of the letterbox as the front door closed. She gathered up some cutlery.

'You don't mind, do you? You know, about Harry staying?'

'No, why should I? I hope it's not for too long though. I like it best when it's the two of us on our own.'

He moved in closer to kiss her; his lips tasted of garlic, tomato, Stilton and beer and Grace tried to limit their touch.

'Not in the mood? Par for the course, I guess, these days. Another symptom of depression, loss of libido. Do I have to remind you of that?'

'Gideon, I know about depression. I see new cases of it every day. Anyway, you'll be pleased with me because I've made an appointment to go and see my GP and if she suggests antidepressants, then I'm prepared to give them a try. It's no fun feeling like this and it's not fair on you.'

'At last!' he cried, triumphantly. 'You've seen the light. When are you going?'

'The day after tomorrow.'

'Great. Whatever you do don't forget to tell her about your mother and all the problems she's had. There's a distinct possibility you may be bipolar as well, you know. I've been pondering on that for some time now.'

'I dread that,' Grace said, simply, hoping for reassurance.

'It would be devastating for you,' he declared, coldly. 'The consequences don't bear thinking about.'

Grace disappeared with more washing up, composed her features yet again, took some deep breaths and went back to

Gideon.

'I'd rather not talk about me, if you don't mind. Harry will be back soon and I don't want him to be privy to any of this. The fact is that I've had so much time to think while I've been sitting at the hospital next to Mum and I've sorted out some worries and made some decisions.'

'I'm all ears, my love.'

'When you first postulated that Mum could have had any involvement with things going wrong in my life, I wondered if it was you that had lost your mind and not her. Then I considered how ill I might be and I can assure you that I am only too aware of the increased risk I have of bipolar illness. So please, until we know, can you stop reminding me about that?

'I've always trusted you and listened to what you have to say. You always talk good sense, you can see clearly when I can't and you're wise beyond your years. We've had a fabulous time together these past months, despite my lurching from one trauma to another and I can't thank you enough for that.' She paused to peck his cheek. 'Gideon, it pains me to say this, but, I think you are right about Mum. I agree that it was most likely she scratched my car, hid my keys, made those phone calls and hid my engagement ring. Why? Who knows? Who will ever know what goes on in that head of hers?'

'I'm so pleased you've come to the right conclusion, darling. I know it's been hard for you. Very hard. She's a very sick woman.'

'I appreciate that now. I doubt that I'll ever come to terms with it properly but I'll try.'

'Well, you've got me to help you.'

Gideon leant over to pick up the remote control and turn on the television.

'Can you hang on a minute? I've not finished.'

Chapter Thirty-Six

'Oh? What more is there to discuss?'

'As you can imagine, this is all devastating for me to take in. I need to talk, Gideon, to get it off my chest which might help me. If I internalise all my thoughts, they'll magnify and get all out of proportion.'

'Go on then, I'm listening. I'll be your psychiatrist. Do you want to lie on the settee?'

Grace felt irate. 'I don't need a psychiatrist! This isn't a laughing matter. I need a sympathetic ear. I'd do this for you.'

Surrendering, Gideon raised his hands. 'Tell me, then.'

'Try as I might, and believe me, I've tried, I do not think there is any way in this world that Mum would have harmed Thadeus. Nor would she have moved the drugs from my bag.'

Gideon picked at some mud under his fingernails. He liked his hands to be perfectly groomed. It created a good impression when he met people.

'Well, that's easy to answer and I'm surprised you need me to tell you. In a nutshell, your mother, like many others with mental health problems before her, when she was feeling well, decided that she was better and no longer needed the medication. So she stopped taking it. Subsequently she deteriorated and her behaviour did so also. Be kind to her, Grace, she didn't realise what she was doing.'

'Yes, yes, I know all about that. But what really intrigues me is that she didn't stop taking her medication, did she? Because you were going round every day to supervise it.'

'You know – that thought's occurred to me too. Very weird. I never stayed very long as I had work to get to. Maybe she hid the tablets in her mouth and spat them out later. More likely though, I bet they weren't working. She had had lots of unwanted side effects. I'd have a quiet word with Phillip if I were you. He's

241

made a big mistake prescribing those. You ought to think of making an official complaint. Make sure he never does the same again. We all have to learn from our mistakes.'

Grace shifted uncomfortably in her chair. 'Actually, I have spoken to Phillip,' she announced.

'Good. Put it in writing too. Ask for your mum's care to be transferred to another consultant. One who knows what he's doing.'

Gideon switched on the television. He had had enough of this conversation. He was bored.

Incensed, Grace bounced up, grabbed the remote control and tossed it to the far side of the room, having first snapped off the television.

'Don't ignore me!' she shouted. 'I have spoken to Phillip and I know that my mother was not getting the correct treatment. Not because he made any mistakes but because somebody swapped her tablets for sweets. So little wonder she became ill. I think you did that.'

'Grace, darling, calm down. Oh my goodness, I think this is all getting too much for you. You sound delusional. You're clearly more severely ill than I first thought. I shall come with you to the hospital in the morning and get one of my colleagues to see you. Not Phillip naturally, that would never do. Now, I'm going to get you a little something to calm you down. It'll help you sleep as well...'

'What? Aspradirol? Like you gave me the night she took the overdose?'

Gideon looked shocked. 'What funny ideas you're having. Where did that come from? This is all very, very worrying. I'll just get my briefcase.'

Grace was shaking from head to toe as he left the room,

wondering what was going to happen next. He was not gone long. He burst back in. The door slammed against the wall.

'Where is it? My briefcase. Where is it?' He was shouting now.

'Where you always put it, I guess,' Grace stuttered.

'Well it's not there. It's got to be somewhere...'

He looked increasingly frantic as he looked behind chairs, under the table and by the bookcase. Cushions arced through the air, ripped magazines followed them as he hunted in a frenzied way.

'Is this what you're looking for?' asked an unruffled Harry, entering from the kitchen, his finger hooked around the handle of the briefcase. He dangled it tauntingly in front of Gideon who lunged forward to retrieve his possession.

Harry was too quick for him. 'I don't think so, my friend.'

'Give that to me. It's mine,' Gideon hissed between his teeth.

'Whatever's wrong? You're getting very heated about a simple little thing like a brief case.'

'There are important papers in there. They must not be lost. It's my research.'

'Good job you can trust me, then. Do you know Grace, I think it might be an idea to have a look inside.'

'No!' Gideon charged at Harry, who, taking a rapid step back, tossed the briefcase to Grace.

Gideon's face was suffused with venom. His fists were clenched; his chest rose and fell with laboured breaths. He desperately tried to regain control.

'Sorry! Got a bit over excited there!' he laughed artificially. 'I always was rather over protective about my research. Don't want anyone stealing it! It's potentially ground breaking.'

'Your research is quite safe, I promise,' Harry reassured him.

'Then give it me back, darling. Good game but let's act like adults now, eh?'

'Not until I've finished. Sit down, Gideon, and shut up.'

Harry gave him a helping hand and Gideon fell back into a chair. Harry stood close, on guard. He nodded to Grace, who, sitting on the floor cross-legged, snapped open the locks and let the lid fall open. Slowly and deliberately, she took out all the contents one by one.

'Papers, some letters, a fountain pen – oh that's the one I gave you. I'm glad to see you've been using it. An empty chocolate bar wrapper. Your wallet, two tickets for the theatre and no, I don't want to go, three journals, yesterday's newspaper and, oh! Harry, that's it! There's nothing else!'

'Look in the side compartments,' he urged, silently starting to panic.

Grace fumbled with the fastenings and then let out a jubilant cry.

'Harry, look at this! Mum's tablets, some curious yellow ones...' she put one in her mouth and crunched on it, '...mmmmm, yummy, chocolate and orange... and wait a minute, there's more. Well, who'd have believed it? Aspradirol!'

'Well, that is a coincidence,' Harry commented, his voice heavy with sarcasm. 'Anything you'd like to tell us, Gideon?'

Chapter Thirty-Seven

*L*ate evening on the intensive care unit. The lights were bright and while Sylvia stayed the same, a hive of activity surrounded the next bed to hers. A few hours earlier, after a splendid time at a party, one unfortunate young man, Mick Lewis, together with his girlfriend, Bea Miller, had unwisely accepted a lift home from a mutual friend, aware that he was well over the legal limit for alcohol but hoping that, as the distance was short, no problems would arise, in particular his being stopped by the police and breathalysed. His job depended on his clean driving licence. Theirs was a journey that was never to be forgotten, the worst decision they could have made. Rather than follow the road around the bend, the car had skidded, rolled over and hit a tree. The driver, with total amnesia for the ride, had clambered out of the window and staggered away, a graze above his left eyebrow and a bruised ego, unaware that one of his friends was dead and the other had multiple injuries.

A fractured tibia and fibula, ends of bone burst through the skin, a severe head injury, flailed ribs and a pneumothorax, the damaged body lay quietly, obliviously accepting the expert care he was receiving. Mick's parents were by his side, open mouthed by the complexity of all that was going on and bemused by the snatches of conversation that they picked up. Was his spleen ruptured? More to the point, what was his spleen and where was it and what did doctors do about it if it was ruptured? It was totally bewildering for them and they stared around, trying to make some sense of what was happening, occasionally glancing at Sylvia, hoping to be inspired by someone on the road to recovery.

Though her appearance had not altered one iota, save for the absence of jaundice, Sylvia had, biochemically, had a much better day. When considered on paper, or on the computer, the numerical details of her body's internal workings looked excellently promising. Finally her blood sugars were looking good and her renal function was creeping steadily in the right direction. The catheter bag, which for days had held only minute amounts of urine, now was bursting. She had lost a phenomenal amount of weight, with which, no doubt, she would be delighted, ultimately... all being well.

So preoccupied were the nursing staff with the new admission that, initially, no one was on the lookout for the slight change in Sylvia's ecg. Nothing sinister. An extra beat – an ectopic – every now and then. A common enough occurrence, even among the fit and well.

Joe, on the late shift, thought he saw one of the abnormalities as he was setting up an intravenous line, caught it out of the corner of his eye. Inserting the needle needed all his concentration – the veins were dreadful to puncture and when he did have time to check again, it all looked fine. He mentioned it to the senior registrar, Amanda Morgan, who nodded and advised keeping a watch.

The next half hour passed in a whirl. After intense assessment, it was decided that Mick was bleeding out, that his spleen was definitely shattered and surgery was required pronto. As he was prepped for theatre, his parents urged to sign consent forms, phone calls made, notes updated, all the attention was focussed on the tragic young man who still had no idea that he had lost his girlfriend. He was finally being wheeled out of the ward when Amanda picked up on the warning signs from Sylvia's monitors.

'Over here, now!' she called. 'She's going to arrest!'

Douglas sat up with a jolt. Something had happened, he knew it.

He and Charnley had spent a quiet evening. Supper with Jim and Margie – they really were good friends. Cheese soufflé, green salad then tinned peaches and ice cream with raspberry sauce. Very enjoyable and so kind of them to keep on asking him over. He really ought to repay their kindness and take them out for a meal. He made a mental note to do so; one day. God willing, Sylvia would be there too.

Despite their amiable company, he had taken his leave soon after they had finished, claiming that it had been another long day and he was ready to turn in. Margie had presented him with a loaf of freshly baked bread, a tin of homemade buns and a bag of – believe it or not – home-baked dog biscuits. He knew, and knew that they did too, that what he really wanted was some reflective time on his own, nursing his glass of whisky, going over the day's events.

He and Charnley had opened the front door, picked up the post and a handful of junk mail and turned up the central heating. There was no sign of the winter freeze letting up as yet and the tabloid press were enjoying a field day, promising more Siberian weather to come. Charnley had shaken his little body, padded into the kitchen for a long drink and then taken up his rightful place on his master's knee. Douglas had poured a rather more generous measure than usual. He saw it as a tiny celebration, that Sylvia was improving and maybe soon would be breathing on her own. Never a big drinker during the day, or indeed with food, this was his special moment and each drop of golden liquid coasted down his gullet lusciously.

They had watched the news, mostly bad. Then the weather forecast, equally grim unless you happened to be a polar bear, he commented to Charnley, or a penguin. He had laughed at snatches of a chat show, the host of which happened to be one of Sylvia's favourites and then, after not much of a fight, had allowed his eyes to close so he could think. He had fallen asleep instantly, only to dream of his beloved wife, in happier days when she was animated and optimistic and their sexual desire for each other was insatiable. Such bliss.

Why he woke, he had no idea. He just knew that something was wrong.

Before he had time to reach for the telephone, it was ringing. He knew before anyone spoke that it was the hospital and that he had lost the love of his life.

Chapter Thirty-Eight

'*H*ello?' Harry answered his mobile, not taking his eyes off Gideon. 'Yes…mmm…oh, no…mmm. I'll tell her, of course I will.'

'What is it?' demanded Grace.

'Come in the kitchen, I need to speak to you.' His voice was worryingly serious. Grace tried her best to read the message in his eyes. 'You,' he indicated to Gideon, 'don't move. I'll be back in a moment.'

'Me? I'm not going anywhere,' Gideon replied. 'Take all the time you need, but lob me a beer first would you, before you get embroiled in whatever it is you have to say.'

Dutifully replenished with drink, Gideon sat casually, one leg over the chair arm, tapping his foot in time to some tune that was playing in his head, awaiting their return. He strained his ears but was unable to make out what was said. At least this gave him some breathing space. He had to think rapidly before they came back and concoct an excuse for those drugs in his bag. The murmurings in the kitchen reached a crescendo, culminating in an animalistic howl from Grace. Gideon raised his eyebrows and had another gulp.

It was Harry who reappeared first, leading Grace, head bowed low, shoulders heaving up and down, the kitchen towel covering her face. Carefully, Harry guided her to the settee and sat down next to her. He cleared his throat and patted Grace's knee. Beneath the towel, she nodded.

'I'm afraid we've had some very bad news. Sadly Sylvia died a short while ago.'

Grace wept anew. Part of her wanted Gideon to come and console her, to make it all better but most of her wanted him as far away as possible. At least with Harry next to her she felt safe.

'Well, that's terrible news,' began Gideon. 'Not totally unexpected in view of the way she abused her body. But... she's out of her misery. Let's try to look positively at this.'

'Do you have one atom of kindness in your soul?' Harry growled at him.

Gideon drained his bottle of beer, belched and wiped his mouth. 'Harry, my dear, in this case, quite definitely not.' He got to his feet. 'As far as I am concerned this is a particularly satisfactory outcome so I'm going to pack a bag and go. I'll collect the rest of my bits and pieces at the weekend. If you'd be so kind as to pack them up for me, Grace...'

Harry interrupted. 'I'm delighted to hear that you're leaving but I think the very least Grace deserves is an explanation. She's got to cope with her loss, her grief, help her father. Please, before you go, help her understand. Sylvia had nothing to do with any of this, did she? She was a totally innocent party to the disruption you caused. A convenient scapegoat. But why?'

Gideon roared with laughter. 'For someone who looks such a complete twat, Harry – by the way who does cut your hair? – you're quite bright. An uncommon feature in general practitioners I find. Maybe you're the exception that proves the rule.'

He thought for a while, enjoying watching Grace's distress.

'OK, I can't see that it would hurt to tell you a few things. There's nothing you can prove and it will always be your word against mine, so I'm not worried in the slightest. I hope you can hear me under that towel, Grace, and for Goodness' sake don't do any drying up with it now it's got your snot all over it...

'I came to Harrogate on purpose because I wanted to meet Grace. You were so naive, MY dear, you played right into my hands from the word go. Fluttering your eyelashes at me, coming across all coy and shy. Remember that first cup of coffee I brought you? How it tasted funny after fruit, you said? A little added something, I think. Shame it wasn't tasteless but the effect was pretty good, wasn't it?'

'I thought I had food poisoning,' Grace spluttered, aghast. 'You said you'd had it too...oh, I get it, you were making that up.'

'Correct. Ten out of ten. Scratching your car was easy, so was letting your tyre down. You welcomed me into your life without a murmur and I could not believe my luck when I discovered that your mother had an illness that was so open to manipulation.'

'So you did stop her drugs.'

'Of course. The effects were dramatic, weren't they? Quite over and beyond what I'd hoped for. In a way she played right into my hands. Credit where it's due, she knew that I didn't really have any true feelings for you. Say what you like, mother's instinct and all that...'

'This is incredible,' cried Harry.

'And I made the phone calls. They were fun. You should have heard your little frightened voice on the other end, Grace, trying to sound stern and brave. It was all I could do not to burst out laughing. Yes, I broke your best glasses and the kitchen window. The glasses – they were nice, mind you. I did like them, but… they had to go because you loved them.'

'I don't understand any of this,' Harry said, turning to Grace, 'do you?'

'No,' was her simple reply.

'That letter of complaint upset you didn't it? It was trivial but I knew you'd worry. You with your wish to be perfect all the time and have all your patients love you. That was an actor that I'd arranged to come. Clever, huh? I've really had such fun.'

'You took her engagement ring, I know that much,' Harry interrupted.

'What?' Grace was astounded. 'How?'

'I took your coat by mistake when you shooed us all away from the party. The ring was in the pocket. I hoped it'd got there by mistake and you'd find it and give it back to Grace but you didn't.'

Gideon applauded slowly.

'Very good, Sherlock. A very good imitation, wasn't it? Obviously not real. I mean who would want something that showy and gaudy on their finger? I could see you didn't really like it, Grace, but, as usual, you hadn't the guts to say so, you just pretended all was perfect in your perfect little world.'

'I…I don't know what to say,' Grace blurted. 'Did you take the drugs from my bag?'

'Ah, yes. Yes I did. That was a bit of a gamble, I admit. I had no idea how long it would be before you might need them. You might never have noticed but Madame Fate was on my side, rather as she has been all along, you might say and lo and behold, off you went on that house call only to find you'd no pain killers.'

Gideon got up and stretched.

'This is thirsty work,' he admitted and wandered off, only to come back with three bottles of beer. He offered two to Harry and Grace and pulled a face when they refused. 'Suit yourselves.'

The three of them sat in silence, Gideon smirking, Harry and Grace lost for words.

A terrible feeling came over Harry. 'Did you kill Thadeus?'

'Who?' Gideon was momentarily confused.

'My cat,' Harry reminded him. 'Don't pretend you don't know who I'm talking about.'

'Ah, the cat that came to stay. I abhor cats. Can't bear their supercilious expressions, the creepy way they coil around you and that purring noise they make.'

'I'll take that as another admission then,' Harry said, sadly.

'Actually, I didn't. Much as I was disgusted when I saw him sitting there, blinking at me, eyeing me up and down with contempt, I didn't kill him. I did kick him across the kitchen when he tried rubbing against my legs but no, his demise was nothing to do with me. I cannot deny that it was a very conveniently timed event that usefully contributed to Grace's anguish. So bizarrely I find myself indebted to a creature that I loathed.'

'Thank goodness for one small mercy.' Grace hugged Harry's arm. He was able to feel her shaking. On second thoughts it might have been him shaking. Losing Thadeus ranked pretty high in his list of awful life events and whilst it tugged at his heartstrings to think of his adorable pet killed by poison, it was a small consolation to know that Gideon was not responsible.

'Sad about your dad, wasn't it Grace? Fracturing his neck of femur. How brittle are the bones of the elderly. More luck to me, I'd say. I was aiming for a few bruises, taking him off the road for a few days, or weeks if I was really blessed. Giving me an easier access to Sylvia. But a fracture, needing surgery and then the bonus of a pulmonary embolism... bull's eye!'

Grace started to speak.

'And before you ask, no I didn't tell him to stop his anticoagulants. As if I'd do a thing like that! I'm very fond of your dad, you know.'

'I find that very hard to believe.'

'Oh, I am, I am. He has done nothing to upset me. He's a good bloke, one of the old school. I enjoyed hearing him talk about his orthopaedic exploits.'

'Did you give Sylvia the aspradirol?' Harry tried to sound confident but felt his courage trickling away the longer he sat there.

'Isn't this the bit where I confess and then you reveal that you've got a tiny tape recorder concealed on your person and have captured all my words for ever? Let me see. What type of hideous tie have you got on today, lurking under that growth on your chin? My word, snakes. Reminds me of a joke. Why did the boa constrictor sniff? Any answers? Because the adder 'ad 'er handkerchief! Probably a microphone hidden in one of their tails, or is that just where you spilled your dinner?'

'For God's sake Gideon. Tell us.'

'Now how could you think such a thing? Of course I didn't give her the aspradirol. It might have been there in my briefcase, as you've seen. A patient returned it to me. If Sylvia chose to take them when I was out of the room, then that's wholly her business.'

'You are evil,' Harry concluded. 'Why would you do any of this? Why Grace? Why her parents?'

Gideon ignored him.

'And now Sylvia, dear Sylvia is dead. God rest her soul. My work here is done, so I'm going. Grace, for me, it has been a pleasure. I hope it has been hell for you and I hope that continues for the rest of your life.'

Chapter Thirty-Nine

'It is with regret that we announce the sudden death of Dr Gideon Miles Bartholomew Barlow, MD FRCP (Hons), aged thirty-nine years old. He was discovered deceased two days ago at the hospital. Suspicions were aroused when his office door was noticed to be locked and security staff had to break in. Dr Barlow was found to have taken his own life by injecting a lethal cocktail of anaesthetic drugs into his arm.

'Dr Barlow was born in Winchester, Hampshire and spent his early years living there with his family. The son of William Henry Barlow, the respected pathologist, and Emily Barlow, he attended the local school until the death of his father. He then spent his teenage years at boarding school after his mother remarried Nigel Hardcastle, local landowner and breeder of racehorses. In honour of his father, Dr Barlow refused to change his name.

'A prestigious career followed as he graduated with honours from Cambridge University and then completed his postgraduate training at various centres of excellence including in Edinburgh, London and New Zealand. He was a leading light in the management of multiple sclerosis and was on the verge of a major breakthrough in the drug management of Parkinson's disease, the same illness that claimed his father's life.

'He came to Harrogate only recently but in that short time revolutionised the neurology department. A physician of excellence and diligence, he was much respected by his colleagues and patients alike. His death comes as a huge shock to all who knew him. Sadly he was pre-deceased by his family. His closest friends described him as never having recovered from the death of his mother, five years ago, from a heart attack and indeed on the desk in front of him, he had begun a note that read,

'"My darling mother, I will always love you. Revenge is a dish…"

'A memorial service for his life will be held in the hospital chapel on…'

Grace was reading the local paper.

And all of a sudden, she understood. She was transported back to Mrs Emily Hardcastle's green sitting room, she saw the string of pearls around her neck, her blue lips, the fear in her eyes and the photograph on the floor of the handsome young man, who was unmistakably Gideon.

Chapter Forty

J aney burst out laughing and Andrew joined her.

'Excuse me, do we know you?' Andrew asked with difficulty.

'Ha, ha, hugely amusing,' replied Harry. 'Grace is back today isn't she?'

'Yes, for the morning, then she's going to pick her mother up from hospital. She's finally coming home.'

'Excellent. It's been a long haul.'

On cue, Grace entered the room. She looked restored, her cheeks plumper, her hair recently trimmed and highlighted, a pair of navy tailored trousers showing her figure off nicely and a lilac cashmere v-necked jumper.

'Morning, everyone!'

'Good to have you back,' Andrew greeted her.

'You look fab,' Janey agreed, giving her a big hug and taking the opportunity to whisper in her ear, 'look at Harry!'

Grace turned. Her mouth dropped open. Was that man in the corner boiling the kettle really Harry? What had happened to the wild hair and the birds' nest beard? Where was the animal tie? Instead she saw a handsome, clean-shaven man, with professionally cut blond hair. He was smartly dressed in dark trousers, polished shoes, yellow checked shirt, open at the neck. The only incongruous part of his transformation was the multiple Elastoplasts on both his hands. He caught her gaze and smiled at her.

'I thought it was time for a change,' he explained.

'Wow, Harry!' Grace was astounded. 'You look absolutely amazing. Doesn't he?' She referred to Andrew and Janey.

'Well, it's certainly a change,' chuckled Janey. 'And one for the better, if I may be so bold. Who's for a slice of date and walnut loaf? Buttered of course.'

Grace went over to Harry.

'I'll never, ever be able to thank you enough, Harry. If it hadn't been for you and your clever plans...'

'Don't be daft. You did most of it. You played a blinder pretending that your mother had died, especially as I'd had the call saying she was out of her coma. I think you've hidden acting talents.'

Grace shook her head.

'I don't think so. It had to be done but I know for sure that I never want to do it again.'

'Nor will you have to.'

'I couldn't have managed without you...'she repeated.

Harry turned to face her. 'It was team work.'

Grace smiled. 'Yes it was.'

'And,' Harry put his hands on her shoulders, 'I think we make a pretty good team, don't you?'

Ignoring Janey and Andrew smirking in the background, Harry amazed himself by kissing Grace on the lips, his joy knowing no bounds when she kissed him back.

'The best,' she whispered.

Suddenly embarrassed by their applauding colleagues, they

broke apart.

'Whatever's happened to your hands, Harry?' asked Grace, concerned.

'Ah, well, that's the new kittens. Roly Poly and Phyllis.'

'Oh, Harry, you've got two! How wonderful.'

'I was rather hoping you might like to have one of them, Grace,' he suggested.

'I'd love to! I can't wait to come and see them. Maybe later, when I've picked Mum up?'

'Wonderful. And some supper?'

'I can't think of anything I'd like better. Oh, by the way, I'd bought you a little something to say thank you but I'm not sure now if you'll like it.'

She handed over a small soft parcel. Harry ripped the paper off and revealed a silk tie, black with golden lions on it

'I thought it was rather appropriate,' Grace apologised.

'It's perfect.'

The End